James Cairns McMahon lives in Scotland. During a varied career he has been a bricklayer's labourer, milkman, tax inspector, accountant and businessman. Fitting writing around a hectic family life, he also enjoys bridge, football, padel and golf, attempting to improve the latter since he was eight.

This book is dedicated to my mum, dad and brother, Archie, who nurtured and encouraged my love of books and reading, and to Carluke Library where I spent so much time as a child.

James Cairns McMahon

PARALLAX

AUSTIN MACAULEY PUBLISHERS™

LONDON * CAMBRIDGE * NEW YORK * SHARJAH

A CIP catalogue record for this title is available from the British Library.

ISBN 9781528941617 (Paperback)
ISBN 9781528942065 (ePub e-book)

www.austinmacauley.com

First Published (2021)
Austin Macauley Publishers Ltd
25 Canada Square
Canary Wharf
London
E14 5LQ

I am indebted to my wife, Amanda, and my t

enthusiastic encouragement. I have been tryi

would have given up long ago but for their su

PARALLAX

(Definition)

The effect whereby the position of an object or body appears to change when viewed from different lines of sight.

Prologue
July 11th – 10:15pm

She had his undivided attention from the moment she turned to face him in the car, dropped the hood of her parka and thanked him for stopping. He tried not to let his interest show as she wedged her rucksack between her legs and confirmed that she was heading for Prestwick Airport, but it was obvious from the way he behaved in those first few seconds that he was attracted to her. He pulled back into the traffic when she had settled, explained that he lived close to the airport and asked if she would like to dry out at his home before he took her to the terminal. She was surprised by his suggestion but accepted quickly. It would be great to get out of her wet clothes. She was soaking and very cold.

She did most of the talking on the short journey to his house. Her agreement had been instinctive but as the road changed from dual carriageway to an unlit country lane, she began to question how sensible it was. Her apprehensiveness heightened when he stopped at a set of electric gates that were set into a stone wall and fronted a long driveway. She made a joke to relieve the tension she was feeling as he buzzed the gates open. He parked in a wide courtyard at the bottom of the drive and escorted her into the two-storey building through the back door. When she shrugged off her jacket in the kitchen and he could see the rest of her body, his scrutiny became even more pronounced. She sat on the floor to take off her sneakers and socks, giving him another chance to watch her. He couldn't find any words and seemed reduced to a nervous combination of staring and smiling. That made her feel more in control and much less anxious. She was accustomed to men reacting in that way and took advantage when it suited her. A hint that she would like to do more than just change what she was wearing got the response she wanted: the offer of a shower to warm up, which would also give her time to consider what to do next.

He took her out of the other side of the kitchen, along a corridor that led to a wooden-floored hall by the front door, then up to a large bedroom with an en suite. There were family photographs of him with an attractive woman and two teenage girls in the hallway and on the stairs – but his family weren't at home.

She thought about her options as she undressed. Whether she should play it out and make the most of the position she found herself in, or just get him to drop her off when she had freshened up. The key to that choice was how she felt about him because it was clear he was taken with her. Her earlier worry was gone. She could concentrate on what she did best.

He wasn't unattractive – in fact, he was good looking, in an old-fashioned sort of way – and suited the casual clothes he was wearing; a black, Nike polo shirt and dark chinos. *In his mid-forties*, she thought, and importantly for her decision, *well off*. The house was substantial, sitting in what she guessed were its own grounds, and expensively furnished. She'd had another plan for the rest of the night, but this was random, more exciting and the type of situation she enjoyed. She stepped into the cubicle, turned the temperature dial up and adjusted the volume until the water from the retro-style showerhead drummed over her. Her nipples hardened as she soaped her chest and luxuriated in the heat. She smiled as the water washed away the suds, made her decision and nodded to reaffirm her choice.

She lingered over drying herself and worked through how to make certain the next hour developed as she intended. When she was happy with the first stage of her game plan, she dug out a small toiletry bag from her rucksack and cleared the mirror above the washbasin with the end of the towel. She gave her teeth a quick clean and ran her tongue over them. She checked her smile in the mirror and tousled her short black hair, before caressing her lips with a rose-pink lipstick. A hint was all she needed to highlight her full mouth. She removed the top from a miniature bottle of Tom Ford Black Orchid, and dabbed her neck, cleavage and inner thighs, experiencing a familiar arousal as she breathed in the perfume.

She closed her eyes and shook her head, enjoying the sensations it created. What she had in mind would be erotic – and potentially lucrative. It was unfortunate that her phone was out of charge, but she would be able to work around that later if the night unfolded as she anticipated. She had no doubt that if things went well, she would add him to her list of benefactors.

There was a white robe hanging on the bathroom door, but the very short, electric blue dress sitting on top of a large pile of clothes on the bed looked better suited for what she had in mind. She held it against her and examined the label. An 8. Her size. She slipped into it. It was a bit tight around the chest but other than that, fitted well. There were no shoes in the room that she could see. Which was a pity. High heels would have completed the outfit. She sat on the side of the bed, looked at her image in the mirrored wardrobe doors and slid the side zips of the dress up to expose more of her thighs. She crossed her legs and examined them. *Lights, action – then camera*, she thought as she grinned at her reflection.

He was standing at the rear of the kitchen, cradling a glass of red wine when she came back downstairs. He put his glass on the table, shook his head but didn't speak as she walked over to him. She handed him her remaining damp clothes wrapped up in the bath towel. He bowed his head slightly, before taking them through to the laundry room and bundling them into the drier beside her parka and socks. He'd already put her Converse All Stars on top of the boiler.

By the time he returned, she had rescued his wine and was settled on the green leather settee at the side of the room. She signalled him to join her, finished what was left of his drink in one long swallow and pulled him down. When he was beside her, she manoeuvred his body onto the longer part of the L-shaped couch, spread herself over him and caressed his face. She forced his mouth open with her tongue, then moved her hands to his groin to gauge his excitement. He was hard, very hard. She smiled and pulled her head away as she fondled him, then kissed him again – much more deeply. When she was sure he was ready, when she was certain he was committed to making love, she moved apart again, unbuckled his trousers, and slid them and his boxer shorts down below his knees. He reached for her hips as she eased the dress up over her thighs and straddled his pelvis, pinning his upper body by pushing up his polo shirt and fixing the palms of her hands on his chest.

'Close your eyes,' she whispered as she dug her nails into his pectorals. 'You'll enjoy it more.'

He didn't flinch and obeyed her immediately. She had complete control of him, as she had hoped. She rocked her hips over him. He gasped and dug his fingers into her as she lifted her hands from his chest, teased his lips open, put the fingers of her right hand into his mouth and let him bite them. He was hers. She could tell he wouldn't pull away now. She moved his fingers between her thighs and pushed two of them inside her to let him know that she was ready. He rose towards her and she guided him in with her left hand. When he was perfectly centred, when he was buried in her, she took his hands and shaped them round her lower back, then over her breasts and up to her neck.

'Hold me. Tight.'

He did and started to thrust his pelvis hard against her. She could tell it would be quick from the way he was breathing and moving. She would have to hurry.

'Tighter! Squeeze me tighter!' she commanded and gripped his forearms to encourage him.

Again, he complied. The excitement of the constriction streamed through her. It was strong. Much fiercer than she had ever felt before. She wanted to enhance the feeling. She wanted it to immerse her and to achieve that she needed to excite him even more. She cupped her hands round his testicles and pulled them down. He reacted immediately and she leaned closer to him.

'Press! Harder!' She could barely say the words. His hands were powerful and were holding her throat very firmly. She felt him begin to climax and her body shuddered in rhythm with his. He gripped her even more forcefully. It was perfect – she was starting to come. She sensed his fingers spasming. She was vanishing.

'Cialo Chrystusa…'

Part 1

**"Detection is not only about the crime,
but also the restoration of order."**

P D James

Chapter 1
July 17th – 8:00pm

The *Always on my Mind* ringtone started as Scott came downstairs into the lounge. He crossed over to the coffee table and picked up his mobile. 'Hi Martin. How are you? How was the festival?'

'I'm fine… Well, I say that… But I'm not sure if I am really. There's something I need to talk to you about.'

'What?'

'I'll get to that. Best leave it to the end. How's Mary?'

Scott looked across to his wife and returned her smile, 'She's great. You know how pregnancy suits her. She's blossoming. Stretched out on the sofa as we speak. Waving hello and blowing you a kiss. Cup of tea and a box of Maltesers for company. She's trying to do the *Heat* crossword and finding it a bit of a challenge. Been stuck on "Spotted dog – 9 letters" for half an hour!'

Mary laughed and threw a Malteser at him, which he caught in his free hand, and pretended to eat as he walked over to her. He put it back in the box as he bent down and kissed her head.

He heard Martin suppress a giggle. 'Give her my love. And Donald? How's my godson getting on?'

Scott dropped into the single chair at the side of the settee. 'Just put him to bed. He's still fixated on *The Very Hungry Caterpillar*. I love reading to him, but I'll be glad when he gets tired of that story. No sign of it yet, though. I've been through it again. Twice! What a glutton that caterpillar is. And a very bad role model – it's a racing certainty for type 2 diabetes. Donald flaked out just before the end of the second banquet.'

'He's a great wee boy and he'll grow up all too soon. Give him a hug from me when he wakes up tomorrow morning.'

'I will – anyway what about you? How were Barcelona and the gig?'

There was a pause before Martin answered. 'That's the main reason I phoned. I need some advice.'

Scott could hear the concern in his best friend's voice, 'Ok? What can I do?'

'I was supposed to be meeting Kat there,' Martin said after another short gap. 'I stayed in Milan for a couple of days after the school closed and flew from there to Barcelona last Friday. Kat was coming in mid-morning Saturday. The plan was to have one night in Barcelona, then catch a train to Valencia on Sunday – the festival was in Benicassim, which is 50 miles north of there. I was going to hire a car in Valencia to drive up – we had booked a pre-erected tent. I had our camping gear with me – in that old ski bag I've had for years. I was late getting to the airport. I got involved in a session on Friday night with some guys I met in a bar down at the harbour. It started as a debate on independence for Catalonia – and whether Scotland would recognise it – then it ran on, as seshes do.'

'As yours do you mean.'

'OK – fair point,' Martin accepted. 'Anyway, I got to bed late and slept in on Saturday morning. I tried to phone Kat to let her know I was delayed but on my way. I couldn't get her. By the time I reached the terminal, the arrivals board showed that the flight had been in for more than an hour. There was no sign of her and no answer on her mobile when I rang it again, so I checked all the bars, cafés, shops. Nothing. I assumed she had got fed up waiting and gone on to the hotel. I went back, but she wasn't there. At that stage, I thought that maybe she'd taken the hump because I was so late and gone off somewhere else to make a point. But no show that afternoon either. Then I began to wonder if she had missed the flight. So, I phoned Ryanair to find out if she'd boarded at Prestwick. Useless bastards! Took forever to get through, to be put on hold for fifteen minutes, then told they couldn't release that information…'

Scott wasn't sure whether Martin had finished and waited for a few seconds before responding. 'What did you do after that?'

'Kept trying the phone and texting. But I got no response – it just went to voicemail as it did the night before. By this time, it was late afternoon. So, I rang the hotel she works at in Nairn and managed to speak to the owner. I know him from the time Dad and I stayed there. He said she left for Prestwick on Friday morning, which is exactly what she told me she was going to do. I carried on ringing her mobile but there was still no answer. So, I stayed the night in Barcelona, then went to Valencia as we originally planned, picked up the hire car and drove to the festival – I didn't know what else to do. I had our tickets, and I suppose, in some strange way I thought she might be waiting for me at the entrance. I didn't find her and I'm not sure I really expected to. But at least it felt like I was doing something, making an effort. I kept wondering if she would appear at some point. She didn't, though.'

'No contact at all?' Scott asked.

'No – I had the boarding passes for the flight home on my phone, but she didn't turn up for that either. On the afternoon we were due back, Kat had arranged to view a small hotel in Ayr that's up for sale. I was going with her to see it. I had rented a car from the airport. The plan was to visit the property, then drive her to Nairn, stay the night, and come back to Edinburgh the next day. When I got to Prestwick, I picked up the car then went to the viewing, hoping Kat would be there. But she wasn't. The owner and agent were, but not Katerina, and the meeting hadn't been cancelled. They'd heard nothing from her. I apologised, said it was a mix-up on dates and left as soon as I could. I rang Sunny Bay again this morning. She's not at work, and they haven't had any contact with her since she left. I'm really concerned. What should I do?'

Scott shifted in his seat and stretched out his legs. This was the first time Martin had asked for his help in a professional capacity. 'I only spent a couple of days on missing persons. That was during my probationary period. But it was enough time to know it's better to report a potential disappearance as early as possible. Get information into the system quickly. I'll do that for you tomorrow. Send me an e-mail with as much detail as you can about her, with pictures, plus what happened last weekend and the times you spoke or texted. I'll do some digging and ring you tomorrow night.'

There was a delay before Martin replied.

'Thanks Scott. I wasn't sure whether to involve you. I don't want to waste your time, but I couldn't think of what else to do. She's a bit of a wild child. That's a big part of the attraction. We've only been together for a few months, so I don't really know yet what's normal for her. But she's never behaved like this with me before. We've never been out of contact for more than a few days since we got together. I'm struggling with the whole thing. Maybe she's just taken off. Got fed up with me, or her job, and left.'

Scott wanted to reassure his pal and finish the call positively. 'Let's see what I can find out – it's too early to speculate. You did the right thing telling me. It's probably nothing to worry about. We'll know more tomorrow. I'll get on it first thing and phone you in the evening. Send me the details as soon as you can.'

'I will – thanks again. It means a lot knowing you'll look into it yourself. Speak tomorrow night. I'll catch up with Mary then as well. Bye.'

Mary tilted her head and looked across at Scott as he finished the call. 'I got bits of that. What's wrong? Is Katerina missing?'

'Yeah – she didn't turn up to meet Martin in Spain and he hasn't heard from her since.'

'What's the story?'

Scott got up, lifted Mary's feet, and slid down onto the settee, folding her legs over his thighs. 'She was flying to Barcelona last Saturday to meet him. They were going to the Benicassim music festival. Martin was late getting to the airport.' Scott shook his head. 'How many times have we heard that? He couldn't find her when he eventually got there. He waited, checked all the bars, etc. and tried to phone. No answer. He went back to the hotel they were booked into. No trace of her there either. She didn't turn up during the festival. Or for their return flight. And she missed an appointment she'd made in Ayr yesterday, to view a property she was interested in. She hasn't been back to the hotel she works at in Nairn or been in touch with them. So, he's concerned. Probably with some justification.'

Mary shifted on the couch and flexed her feet against Scott's left leg. 'Let's hope it's something and nothing – a lover's tiff. Not the first one in Martin's sex life. And it won't be the last. That's the likeliest explanation. I'm sure you'll sort it out tomorrow.' She pulled herself up using his arm.

He helped her get to her feet and nodded. 'You're right. There's probably a straightforward answer. She's upset with Martin for some reason. Gone off to teach him a lesson. Martin hasn't picked up on why she's annoyed, which isn't difficult to believe, given his track record with women. Could be that. But I'll get it logged into the missing persons' database tomorrow morning and see if anything comes up.'

Mary yawned and stroked his right arm. 'Talking about coming up. Do you fancy an early night?'

He grinned and bent down to stroke her growing bump. 'Great – be a nice change.'

She tugged his hair to pull his head up level with hers and kissed him on the lips. 'It will.'

Chapter 2
July 18th – 9:30am

Area Commander Jim Turner wandered into the squad room and waved to Scott through the full-length window which fronted his office. Then, as he did every morning on arrival, Turner ordered a cup of tea, selected a handful of biscuits from the communal tin and retreated to his room, which was directly across from Scott's. Scott knew it was sensible to let his boss settle, enjoy his tea and move on to a second cup – another 15 minutes yet – before disturbing him, so he picked up his iPad and reread the email that Martin had sent just before midnight.

Hi Scott,

Still no contact from Kat. All the information I can think of is set out below. Hope it's helpful and look forward to talking to you when you know more.

Katerina Wysklow

Age 26 – see attached passport details

Born/raised Gdansk, Poland

No brothers/sisters

Mum still alive – her dad died when she was 17. I don't have an address or phone number for her mum. Kat has a Degree in Economics from Warsaw Institute of Applied Science. She came to the UK three years ago and has worked in catering and hotels since then. Present job – waitress/manager at Sunny Bay Hotel, Nairn.

I met her in late April this year when I was up with my dad on a golf break – we were staying at the hotel. It was just the two of us. My brother was away at Columbia University on a two-month work exchange so couldn't join us.

Pictures of Kat attached. 5ft 8 inches – about 9 stone, I think. Short dark hair – green eyes – slim build. No tattoos or piercings.

She isn't on Facebook or any other social media that I know about – when I asked about that, she said she liked to keep her private life private and was pleased I felt the same.

Friends – don't know – never been introduced to any directly but she mentioned a girl cousin who was working in Newcastle at the Football Club. In the marketing department, I think.

I saw Kat infrequently because I was teaching in Italy. Those times were:

1) *when we met – Dad and I were at Sunny Bay – April 20th-22nd this year*
2) *at my dad's for a weekend – May 15th-16th*
3) *overnight in Inverness – June 11th-12th*

Phone – iPhone 6 no 07797112202

Hobbies – drinking/partying! Again, that's what she said, but claimed there wasn't much scope in Nairn for that!

She was saving up to buy a small B&B – somewhere in Scotland – and bring her mother over to help run it. That seemed to be her main focus from my time with her. It was certainly what she discussed most. She even pitched it to my dad!

Polish passport – she sent me the basics I needed to book the flight back.

We were supposed to meet up in Barcelona on Saturday the 12th, go on to Valencia the next day, then to the Benicassim Festival. She was coming in from Prestwick that day on the 6.30am Ryanair flight (FR451). She finished at the hotel on Friday morning.

I spoke to her on the phone that Friday when I was waiting to board my flight at Linate Airport in Milan. About 8 am, Italian time. She was in the middle of the breakfast shift so couldn't say much, but she told me she was leaving after that – hitching to Prestwick and that she had a lift for the first part of the journey to Fort William. I got a text at lunchtime (13:48) to tell me she was at FW. Took that as Fort William. That's the last contact I had – I did try to call her on the Friday night – twice – first from the bar I was in and then later when I got back to the hotel – there was no response.

Anything else you need, let me know and I'll try to get it.

Best, Martin x

Scott sat back in his chair. The personal information on Katerina was quite sparse, but she and Martin were a recent couple, working in different countries, so that wasn't surprising.

Scott could have written a novel about Mary, which was appropriate given she was establishing herself as an author, with two books already published. Her first, *The Craig*, explored the history of Ravenscraig – the iconic steelworks in Motherwell, whose three cooling towers and gasholder dominated the skyline of the town. The account was told through the lifelines of twenty of its workers, including her dad, who had started as an apprentice at 15 and risen to be Production Manager on one of the mills. It was an intensely personal book. Mary had been five when Ravenscraig shut but could still remember the red dust sunsets which spread over Craigneuk, where their family home and the steelworks were situated.

The book had debuted to critical and popular acclaim and led directly to her next commission. *The Yards* wove the tale of shipbuilding on the Clyde from its birth, through the glory years when 'Clyde built' was recognised worldwide as a synonym for engineering excellence, to the work-in at Upper Clyde Shipbuilders in 1971 – the death knell of the industry that was the symbol of Scotland's manufacturing and trading might.

The third part of the trilogy, *The Pits* had been hijacked by a request from her publishers to write the definitive story of the Scottish referendum and how it shaped the political landscape thereafter. A topical project designed to showcase her writing to a wider audience. Mary wasn't keen initially, but the publisher's advance was significant and translated into a deposit for a bigger house just outside Carluke. So, she eventually agreed.

Mary had grown up in a close-knit family with her four sisters, and legions of extended relatives. Scott was an only child, brought up in a council scheme in a loving, but quiet, family home in Kirkfieldbank. The brightest pupil in his primary and secondary schools in Lanark. A solitary and diligent boy whose first real exposure to the outside world was his time reading Law and Politics at Edinburgh University – where he met Martin, and through him, Mary. His four years in Edinburgh and his relationships with Mary and Martin changed him. He became more sociable, less insular in his view of the world and his place in it. He remained studious, to the amusement and pride of his new friends, and was rewarded with a good degree – good enough to consider academia. That might have been the choice of the boy who started at Edinburgh, but the man who graduated was driven to connect more directly with people – to become part of a wider community. Scott didn't want to retreat back into a closed system, but at 21 wasn't clear what it was he needed.

His choice, and he still wasn't fully sure how he had come to it, was to join the police force. It was the most impulsive thing he had ever done. His relationship with Mary and his subsequent adoption into her family was the most important change in his life, and he wanted that same feeling in his career – the sense of being part of something bigger. The police force gave him that. He made Sergeant after three years, was transferred from Motherwell to Hamilton Police Station and switched to CID to get experience in that branch. He elected to stay in CID on promotion to Inspector, which was unusual. Most graduates reverted to the uniformed side at that rank. It was by far the bigger part of the overall force, which meant more senior posts and better promotion prospects. His decision to stay in plain clothes was seen as another sign that he was a real policeman, not just a politically aware graduate, gaming the system and scaling the ranks.

In addition to the kudos he gained from his fellow officers for that choice, he picked up two gold stars. The first came from solving a case that would have been embarrassing politically for the town if the police hadn't got a result. Large parts of the manufacturing base of the Motherwell/Hamilton conurbation had been undermined by decades of decline. The decay started with the closure of the local pits, moved to Ravenscraig, then Anderson Boyes (the world's largest provider of mining equipment in the 1960s and 70s and the area's next largest employer), before it infected the whole of Lanarkshire. In an attempt to reverse the deindustrialisation, the Scottish Government, Strathclyde Council and a local entrepreneur had joined forces to endow the new University of the West of Scotland with a fund to back high-tech engineering start-ups. The second company in the programme, Logitech, was an attempt to push 3D printing into new areas in healthcare. But over £400,000 of the initial capital had gone missing during the pre-production phase. The police investigation into the disappearance passed through more hands than a parcel in a Derry pub as it plummeted down the command chain and clattered onto his desk. The case was too small for the Serious Fraud Office and needed to be sorted by Strathclyde Region in the run up to the merger of the eight police authorities into Police Scotland. A major public failure could have weakened Strathclyde's negotiating position at that critical time. So, the enquiry that everybody wanted solved, but nobody wanted to own, finished its earthwards corkscrew with Scott. It would be easy to blame the graduate if it weren't sorted quickly, and the perpetrator seen to be caught and punished (Scott James isn't as smart as he thinks!).

One of Scott's strengths was his lack of fear about police politics. Scott knew the enquiry was tainted but felt no sense of concern about his own position as he read the file and worked out how best to approach the theft. He chose a line that seemed logical to him but was regarded as revolutionary by his superiors. Get someone who did this for a living to review the papers – a professional. Mary's eldest sister, Elaine, was married to Alan Hunter, a senior manager in the forensic accounting unit of PWC Glasgow. Scott cleared it with his boss, then brought Alan in to examine the books, records and the accounting and banking package Logitech used. Alan committed a week of his team's time on a contingency basis: no solution, no payment. The investigative team turned up on the Monday morning to interrogate the account systems and cracked what had happened in the first 48 hours. Logitech's financial controller had found a flaw in the internet banking and accounting programme his company had installed. Alan explained to Scott that there was no automatic bank reconciliation of payments made online, which meant that money could be siphoned off through fictitious invoices with entries made in the nominal ledgers to balance the books and hide the outflow. Scott struggled with the technical explanation and jargon on the first run through, but when Alan highlighted specific examples of how the fraud had been carried out and took him along the money trail from start to finish on the artificial entries, he saw it. The chain was clear as soon as he was shown it using real numbers.

He interviewed the financial controller with Alan present – not strict protocol but it worked and led to a quick confession and an agreement to return what was left of the money, which turned out to be the majority of what had been taken. Logitech was so happy with the outcome that it agreed to pay PWC, relieving the police of any liability. Scott became a local hero, even though a large part of the glory was reflected back up the command chain as superiors emerged from cover to claim credit.

Solving the case spawned another benefit. Alan showed Scott a note he was sending nationally to all PWC audit and forensic staff, setting out how the fraud had occurred, explaining the gap in the bank reconciliation system and suggesting additional audit checks when dealing with online banking systems. Scott adapted that idea. He had always kept meticulous files to which he added a post case review section titled, "What can we learn?" Jim Turner championed the idea and put it up for adoption by the new single tier force – a procedure to ensure best practice across the country; a way to align all the old regions into one gold standard. It created a lot of favourable PR and was used as a practical demonstration by the force to show the public and the politicians that Police Scotland cared about improving how it handled enquiries. Most of Scott's inspector interview centred on the Logitech investigation and how it led to the new process. When his promotion came through, he was also rewarded with a new nickname – "Scottnote".

He looked at his watch. Turner would be on to his third biscuit. It was the perfect time to approach him. He picked up two printouts of Martin's email and walked through the squad room to Turner's door. As he was about to knock, Turner glanced up and waved him in.

'Hi Scott. Are you going tomorrow?'

Scott nodded and sat down directly across the table from Turner. 'And I'm taking Donald. His first game. Mary says it's cruel to start him supporting Motherwell at five. She's threatening to report me to Childline.'

Turner laughed and coughed out a small piece of biscuit onto his arm. He looked at it for a second, licked his right index finger, then used it to pick up the crumb and pop it back into his mouth. 'She's right. It's a savage initiation rite but that's what dads do to their firstborn. Both of ours did. And we need to pass it on.'

Scott smiled, then paused. 'Can I discuss something with you, sir?'

'Of course.'

Scott separated out one copy of Martin's email and handed it to Turner. 'I've mentioned Martin Young, my best pal before. His girlfriend has disappeared. He's pulled together what he knows in that note.'

Turner scanned the two pages then read them more slowly. 'OK. I can understand why he's worried. What do you want to do?'

'The first stage is to find out if she boarded the flight. Julia's due back in just before lunch so I can get her to check with Ryanair, then log it into MisPers – get it on the system. If Katerina did fly to Barcelona, she's probably gone missing in Spain. If she didn't, then most likely she's still in this country. Either way, she's nowhere to be found. I'd like to go up to the hotel where she works – take a PC from Nairn with me and talk to the owner. I want to be able to tell Martin I went personally and give him any relevant information directly. Would that be a problem?' Scott paused. 'Would I be seen as too involved because he's a friend? Devoting too much effort to something that might not even be a missing person?'

Turner spread back in his chair, interlocked his fingers, and pushed out his arms. 'Do you know the nicest thing about you, Scott?'

Scot shook his head.

Turner laughed. 'You're so unassuming. Totally different to all the detectives featured in tartan noir novels. Every one of those fictional cops has a bundle of personality defects – huge psychological demons they spend most of their time wrestling with. And they're perpetually at war with their bosses. It's a wonder any crime ever gets solved.' He opened his arms and turned his palms up. 'But look at you. Happily married. In fact, the most married man I know. A wee boy you adore. Another wain on the way. Sensible. Logical. Non-confrontational. And dependable! Christ's sake! You're too good to be true.' Turner paused. 'The biggest flaw I've been able to spot in three years working with you is that you support Motherwell. But I'm guilty of that as well, so we'll ignore it. Mind you, you're a crap five-a-side player but that's not a criminal offence yet, unlike your tackling. Which leaves playing bridge as the only item on your charge sheet.'

Scott was becoming increasingly embarrassed by the flow of compliments from his boss – he felt himself start to redden and dropped his head slightly to avoid direct eye contact.

Turner shook his head and pushed back his unruly, brown hair. 'OK – end of lecture. But for a clever man, you're a bit naive. At present, your star couldn't be brighter. Logitech solved. The post case review adopted nationally. A graduate inspector who chose to stay in CID. You could sleep with the Chief Constable's wife and get away with it.' Turner bit his lip. 'No! I'm wrong. That would be an unlawful act!'

Scott looked up. 'So, it's OK sir?'

'Yes. Talk to the local station. Get them onside. We're slow just now so go up when it suits you. It will be a couple of months yet before the ethnic cleansing of Glasgow CID is over and it's safe to let someone as normal as you go there. It would be unkind to send you just now. There's more blood splattered about the Glasgow squad rooms than in an episode of *Game of Thrones*. Enjoy the sabbatical while you can. Arrange it for next week if that works and do me a note when you have more information. One of your specials – spelling out if it's MisPers or potentially more serious? We can use that as a basis for our decision on what to do next…' Turner hesitated and looked at the notes. 'Just one thing – find out, if you can, whether she's gone home to Poland. It would look a bit silly expending a lot of effort if she's safely tucked up at her mum's in Gdansk.'

Scott nodded in appreciation. 'Thanks. I'll try and get a number for her mum from the hotel and check that out. If I do go, I might take Mary and Donald up for the run. Providing Mary's feeling like a six-hour round trip with our son.'

'How long into it is she now?'

'14 weeks.'

'Any problems?'

Scott shook his head. 'None – Mary's the same as her sisters when it comes to pregnancy. They're all Olympic gold medallists in that discipline. Right up to and including the birth. Swiss watch-like precision. To the second.'

Turner grinned. 'Good, give her my best.'

Chapter 3
July 18th – 8:30pm

Scott was five years into his apprenticeship as a dad, but he still found it hard to calibrate degrees of excitement in his son. He knew that perpetual motion was an impossible concept scientifically, but Donald was the closest thing Scott could imagine to a proof that physics was wrong. He was always on – a constant blur of arms, legs, a thin white body and ginger hair. Or as Mary's dad described him after a full day of being in sole charge of his grandson, "A wasp on speed". Donald ran, jumped, and fidgeted his way through every waking minute – talking and asking questions constantly.

He was never still. Even when sitting his legs jigged continually, but he was unusually animated that night. As wound up as he had been on Christmas Eve or the night before his fifth birthday. And as a consequence, it had taken Scott longer than normal to get him settled. The cause was Donald's excitement at the thought of going to his first Motherwell game. He had worn the Motherwell kit his Lanark pappy bought him for his birthday since breakfast and evidence of all his meals was caked over the top. It was a struggle to persuade him not to sleep in it. Scott finally achieved that by telling him that the strip needed to be clean for the match – Motherwell v Kilnock, as Donald described it – and that Mummy would wash and iron it so it was perfect for the game. Mummy! Aye, right!

Scott welled up as he kissed his son goodnight. Tomorrow would be special – the next stage in what Scott hoped would become Donald's addiction with Motherwell. A love for the club that Scott wanted to be as important and as long-lasting as his own. Scott's all-consuming passion for his team had begun when he was four-years old, in 1991. The year of Motherwell's cup win, when he was taken to Hampden for what was considered, by neutrals, to be the greatest Scottish Cup Final ever. Motherwell 4, Dundee United 3 after extra time. Scott could still vividly recall bits of that day. It was Blu-ray clear in his head. His dad in tears – one of the few occasions Scott could remember his father showing emotion. The Motherwell fans dancing around him in the south stand and lifting him up, as the players brought the cup over, so he had a better view. Incredibly precious memories.

He wiped his eyes as he recalled that afternoon and how it had been key in cementing his relationship with his father – giving them something they would always remember together. He kissed Donald goodnight, took the strip downstairs, slipped it into the washing machine and selected the short cycle programme. He heard Mary enter the toilet just along from the laundry room as he came back into the kitchen. He found the last can of Old Speckled Hen in the fridge, opened it, and took a long slug before he sat down. He had almost finished it by the time Mary emerged and joined him on the settee.

'Are you OK?' he asked.

Mary groaned and shifted her position. 'I enjoy pregnancy, but I don't remember peeing as much at this stage last time. I know the wee one is only the size of a lemon just now but it's a lemon that's bouncing on my bladder and it's starting to really annoy me. I just want this part to be over.'

Scott laughed and shook his head. 'I know it's really hard for you. I suppose it's like how I feel watching Motherwell when they're forced back into their own penalty area, trying to hang on to a lead in the dying minutes of a game.' As soon as he said it, he realised the comparison wasn't quite as precise or as helpful as he had hoped.

Mary took his left arm in both hands. 'I love you. You know that. And you're a good man. But any repetition of remarks like that and you will suffer.' She squeezed his arm tightly. 'Really suffer!'

He winced. 'I'm sorry. Really stupid analogy. Fir Park's much more painful!'

He got the punch he expected and deserved, then took Mary's hand and kissed it. 'Cup of tea?'

'Great – but I'll make it. I'll stick some toast on as well. Just fancy toast and some of my mum's blackcurrant jam. You should phone Martin. He'll be hanging on, worried that you haven't called yet, wondering why and thinking the worst. I'll talk to him when you're finished.'

Mary got up and started filling the kettle as he dialled. 'Hi Martin. Sorry I'm a little later than I planned but Donald is really hyper about going to his first game tomorrow and it took me a while to get him into bed and calmed down.'

Martin laughed. 'Don't worry. The wee soul. That's lovely. Well, lovely apart from the team you're dragging him to see. He's my godson and I should have some say about this. He should get the chance to support a proper football team. We should be taking him to Tynecastle. Not some provincial sandpit.'

Scott snorted. It was a recurring theme. 'GTF! On a point of detail, you might have missed because you've been in Italy – it's not a sandpit anymore. Best surface in Scotland now, which might explain why we lost as many games at home last season. We're not used to playing on a bowling green – we're better on a beach! Anyway, Donald's committed to Motherwell. It's part of his genetic inheritance. Like his dad and granddad. We're picking up my father on the way. It's a huge day for him as well. He's more excited than Donald. Christ – two kids to contend with. What more could I ask for on a Saturday afternoon?'

'Enjoy it, if it's possible to use that word in conjunction with Fir Park, and good luck. Buy Donald a pie. Tell him it's from Uncle Martin.'

'That's just what he needs on top of all the excitement.'

He heard Martin laugh again. 'It's a key part of our rich cultural heritage – a pie at the game is traditional. Best to introduce him to it now. But don't let Mary find out it was me that suggested it.'

Scott switched the mobile to his right hand before he answered and flexed his left elbow to relieve a bit of cramp. 'No chance – if I tell Donald it's from you, the first thing he'll say to Mary when he gets back will be "Uncle Martin told Dad to get me a pie". Donald's a high-fidelity digital recording when he feels he has something to report.'

'OK – a risk I have to take then.'

Martin went silent, and Scott knew he was waiting for his news. 'We've made some progress on Kat.'

Another pause. 'What?'

'The most important thing we've been able to confirm is that she never boarded the flight from Prestwick. Ryanair let us know that this afternoon. So, she's probably still in this country.'

'That's good. Isn't it? Anything else?'

Scott hesitated for a second, even though he had rehearsed what he would say. 'I had one of my team input her details into missing persons. No hit yet. Nothing from hospitals or accident reports, which is positive. It's still quite early in this type of situation, but if something comes up, it will be flagged for me right away. And I spoke briefly to the hotel owner, John Smedley. She's still not back

31

there and he's heard nothing from her. But I got a number for Kat's mum from him. It's just possible that she's over in Poland. I haven't rung yet. I've been thinking it might come better from you. Be less worrying if you called. Not the police?'

He heard Martin draw his breath in and then exhale. 'OK, I'll do that. Not exactly sure what I'll say. But… Text me the number. I'll phone now, see if I can get her. I'll call you back. Let you know what she says.'

'OK, thanks. If you reach her and Kat's not there, see if you can find out any information about the cousin who works at Newcastle United. We need to try and contact her as well. See if she knows anything.'

'I will.'

Scott killed the call, found the Polish number on his phone, and copied it to Martin as a text. He walked over to Mary. 'Did you get that?'

Mary handed him a cup of strong tea. 'Yes. You did the right thing asking Martin to phone. It'll be much less scary for Kat's mum than a call from the police, and he'll find out more.' She smiled. 'Sit and have your toast and tea.'

Scott had finished both before Martin rang back. 'How did it go?'

'I got her. Her English is fine, and she knew who I was. Kat's talked to her about me. They speak regularly, every couple of days. Kat had also told her about the festival and not to expect any calls when she was in Spain. Said it would be too expensive to ring. But her mum's heard nothing since the day Kat left the hotel. She doesn't know where she is. And she's worried.'

Scott paused for a second. 'OK, that's one possible explanation ruled out. I had arranged to go up to the hotel in Nairn on Monday, subject to whether we found anything out from Kat's mother. So, I'll definitely do that now. Interview the owner – see what extra information we can get from him.'

'Should I come with you? Would that help?'

Scott had expected Martin to make the offer and had worked through how to handle it. 'I've thought about that. It's better if I go on my own. Keep it to the police at this stage. I don't want to risk any crossover, any confusion by the owner about who is doing what and who's responsible for following up on what he tells us. I'll phone you on the way back, let you know what I find and discuss what we should do next.'

Martin sighed. 'OK, this is your gig. I'm desperate to help, do what I can, but I'll leave it to you. I didn't get much on the cousin other than a name – Petra Slishke. No number or where she is. Kat's mum promised to phone her sister to get more details. She'll text me when they've spoken to confirm where Petra is working and living with a contact number.'

'Thanks. That will be helpful – and try not to worry. You know I'll do everything I can to find out where Kat is.'

'I know you will, and I understand that it's more sensible for you to take this on rather than me. I just feel a bit powerless… Anyway, I need to come over and see you all. I've done my time with Mum and Dad. What would suit?'

'Mary wants a word – she'll sort out when. We can fix it up finally when we speak on Monday.'

'OK. Bye.'

Scott handed his mobile to Mary and listened to her reassure Martin that he had done the right thing contacting them and asking for Scott's help. She finished the call by emphasising how good Scott was at his job and that if anybody could find out what had happened, it was her husband.

He was slightly concerned by how fulsome her praise had been and grimaced when she finished the call and gave him his mobile back. 'No pressure then – Supercop Scott James to the rescue.'

Mary smiled and took his hand. 'Don't get all defensive with me – I know you better than anyone. I understand you're a bit uncomfortable with me telling Martin how competent you are at your job, but you are good, and Martin trusts you implicitly. You'll get to the bottom of this – as you always do with a problem. You'll analyse it like you would a hand at bridge. Split it up into its component parts and work away at them until something drops out. Then you'll use that to move on to the next piece, then the next, until you have the full picture… You'll find her!'

Part 2

**"One of the luckiest things that can happen to you in life is,
I think, to have a happy childhood."**

Agatha Christie

September 4th – 11:30am

I don't know if this will work. I don't know if there is anything, I can do which will help me. But I need to try. I need to find a solution. Something to stop me sliding further away from the life I have worked so hard to build. Something to stop me losing my wife and family.

The girls haven't picked up on how troubled I am; Arlene has. She was solicitous when she first noticed the change in my behaviour, asking me repeatedly, "Is anything wrong?" I tried, "Nothing. Honestly". But she persisted, so I cobbled together an explanation about money being the cause of my sudden anxiety. Although she didn't query it, I could tell that she didn't believe me. She's waiting, wondering how best to broach the subject again. Maybe suspecting another woman? Which is right, just not in the way she imagines.

I have always been a problem solver. I would say it's one of my strengths – to the extent that I pride myself on being able to sort out all sorts of difficulties. But not this time. Not this mess. I had no idea what to do about the chaos I have created until a week ago, when I was helping Anna revise for her first science test of the new term. An exam on Newton's laws of motion. As we chatted through the examples in her textbook, I had a moment of clarity and saw my dilemma in a different way. That was the start of my attempt to find a way to deal with the consequences of what I have done.

I waited until Arlene was ready for bed and told her I needed to stay up a little bit longer to sketch out my next piece of work for Sky. I had another beer and jotted down my thoughts on the back of the A4 sheet I had used with Anna. I felt I had to see my ideas written down to decide if they made any sort of sense – if they would lead anywhere.

I began with Newton's third law: "For every action, there is an equal and opposite reaction". And I examined how that applied to me. That was the easiest part to link to my plight because what happened could not have been more destructive. So, by definition, my reaction to the event is bound to be equally damaging. It is the recoil from what I did that is pushing me farther and farther from my family. That bit looked correct on paper, and more importantly, it felt right too. I was encouraged and moved on to the next piece.

Newton's first law: "A body will continue at rest or in uniform motion unless acted on by an outside force". Again, the relevance to my situation seemed straightforward. My current trajectory, or how I am acting at present, is taking me away from Arlene and the girls. I need to alter it by changing my conduct. That correction will not occur by itself. Unless I make an effort, I will continue along the same path, doing the same things, and will become increasingly isolated from them. Hoping the predicament, I have put us in will somehow resolve itself isn't an option. That also seemed sensible as I wrote it out and thought it through.

Which led me to the final segment; Newton's second law: "The degree of change is proportionate to the force applied, and the mass of the object to be moved". The weight of what I did is huge, so I have to do something equally major to produce a shift from where I am heading and allow me to reconnect with my family. I need to do something radical. A small adjustment to my behaviour will not work. Setting it out like the pieces of a logic puzzle felt strange, but positive. It gave me proof that I needed to act, but I was jammed up on how.

I would still be stuck if I hadn't tuned in, by chance, to the Radio 4 series *All in the Mind* two days later. I was driving home from Glasgow Airport and station-hopping when I heard the intro to the topic. It was an update of a programme on the London bombings, first broadcast in September 2008, "How the Survivors of 7/7 Bombings have Coped". I was interested and kept listening. Then, ten minutes into that edition, an answer – perhaps. A clinical psychologist was describing her work with victims and what she was doing to help them deal with their experiences. Which, to a layman, came down to encouraging them to relive that day in minute detail; from waking up, through the explosions to the rescue and hospital. Step by step, over and over in constant repetitions. Because doing that – covering what happened bit by bit – put it in the past. Anchored it to July 7th, 2005. Not the present day. That exercise turned the victims' trauma into history, took it out of real time… And according to the presenter, the process worked. The survivors were managing their daily lives much better.

I wondered if a similar approach could help me. I wasn't sure, because my situation is very different. I am the perpetrator, not a victim. I can't go for a professional consultation to ask for help. But, after a day thinking about it, I decided I had nothing to lose by trying to adopt that advice. Because what I *can* do is write it out and explain what took place as if I was having counselling sessions – try to get as close as I can to the real thing and hope that it will have the same effect.

So, I will confess to what happened on July 11th, honestly and in complete detail, and trust that recording the events will be as healing as a course of therapy and allow me to live with what I did. I committed to doing that the evening after I heard the programme.

I have been rehearsing what I need to say and where best to begin ever since – to the extent of talking to myself when I'm alone. I have opted to set out my account as a series of notes, using the Mont Blanc pen Arlene gave me three years ago on our fifteenth wedding anniversary. She chides me for not using it enough. But as I point out to her, I keep it for special occasions. For birthday, Christmas, and anniversary cards. For signing my new Sky Sports contract. Important events. Being unfaithful to Arlene qualifies. Letting down my girls qualifies. Killing someone qualifies.

September 4th – 1:00 pm

I have given myself all of today to log my first entry. The girls are away at a two-day school nature camp in Crail. Arlene left just after nine o'clock to drive up to get them and take them to see her mother on the way home. They will spend the afternoon together, then have tea at the Anstruther Fish Bar as a treat. I have until around 10:00 pm.

It has taken me more than two hours to produce three pages. But I've started, which feels much more important than the amount I have written. I have something to build on.

Should I start by explaining that I didn't mean it? That what occurred was an accident? That I didn't even see the death happen? But I felt it. I knew something was very wrong. I kept my eyes shut for a few hopeful seconds – like a child pretending the dread wasn't real, that it would go away if I didn't look. But the horror wasn't imaginary, it wouldn't disappear. The rules of childhood didn't apply.

Although I'm desperate to put what I did down in writing, it's too soon for that. The psychologist emphasised how vital it is to go through the events leading up to the trauma in a logical, ordered way and put the event in some sort of context. I will do that in general terms first with a snapshot of my background. Then I can move on to the day it took place and switch to a full description of the incident and my attempt to cover up the death.

That approach is the complete opposite of what I tried to do before I heard the broadcast. Until that moment, instead of accepting what I had done, I spent my time obsessing about the different choices I could have made which would have prevented it happening. And not just alternatives on that night – I went back over decisions I made weeks, months, years before, always looking for an out. But there were too many. They multiplied and intermingled. I couldn't simplify them, couldn't keep to a single line. I exhausted myself, trying to construct scenarios where the death didn't take place, and virtually no time analysing what actually happened that evening. I know I need to reverse that mindset if I am going to have any chance of achieving some sense of normality, and the baseline is to explain my life up to that night in a simple, short way.

The beginning. I was born in Haddington 49 years ago, the younger of two brothers. Dad was a tax inspector – retired for nearly twenty years now. Mum taught Maths but stopped when my brother Alan was born and only went back when I started secondary school. We moved to North Berwick when I was four. Mum and Dad still live in the same house. The girls sleep in my old room when we stay.

I had a happy childhood. A very happy childhood. My big brother Alan, who is four years older, didn't tease me too much and wasn't too cruel as we grew up. That's unfair. Alan wasn't bad to me, and we have become closer since we both married and settled down. He was just more popular and better than me at most things that were important then: school, football, making friends and getting girls. But not golf. My Lightsaber.

I can still remember the first time I swung a club. It's the most graphic memory I have of my early years. Dad was a golf fanatic – still is. Golf is his only hobby. Mum also plays but is a part-timer, compared to my father. I recall the day he brought home his new set of Jack Nicklaus irons and can still picture him drooling over them in the lounge, caressing each one in turn, until Mum threw him out to soak off the labels in the back garden. He gave me the 8 iron to admire, teed up a ball and encouraged me to take a swing at it. I put my left hand down the shaft, placed my right hand above it and hit the ball before Dad could adjust my grip or stance. I struck it well. Very well. The ball flew away in a perfect arc over the back fence and onto the road. That shot tattooed "Love/Golf" on my knuckles for the rest of my life. Dad decided I had raw talent and the next week, at seven years old, I was decanted to the local pro, David Huish, for lessons. That was the first branch on the path that led to the death. If I hadn't become a golfer, Katerina would still be alive. But at that initial fork nobody could have predicted how our lives would intersect so disastrously.

I was 12 when I decided I wanted to be a professional golfer (that choice accepted by Mum and Dad on the proviso that I would go to university first). My handicap was plus 2 at eighteen, when I started at Edinburgh University and I was the losing finalist in the British Amateur at twenty.

Although my favourite and best subject at secondary school was English, I made a career choice and did accounting and business management at Edinburgh

University. Safe, and a guaranteed job if I couldn't make it as a golfer. I didn't fully integrate into student life – didn't make many close friends other than members of the university golf team. Most weekends I was away playing in golf tournaments or back at home practising, not socialising in Edinburgh. I finished university with a good degree, albeit in a subject I found dull, and for the first time since I could remember, had a choice to make. My boyhood dream and the fact that I had no real love for business made that an easy decision. I didn't want to spend the rest of my life as an accountant without finding out if I was good enough to be a professional golfer, so I opted to try for the European Tour. Mum and Dad were reasonably well-off but not rich. They were supportive but I didn't want them to risk the majority of their savings on the gamble that I would be successful on the tour.

I decided to work for a couple of years to put together enough money of my own to have a run at it. I was lucky. I got an introduction through the captain of the university team to Brian Young, a member at the Royal Burgess Golf Club in Edinburgh. A wealthy, outgoing entrepreneur in his early thirties and a keen golfer. We got on from our first meeting and he employed me as a financial advisor in his business. The job consisted entirely of PR and entertaining, mainly playing golf with his clients, and allowed me ample time for practice. I enjoyed the whole experience and it went well. So well that Brian offered to sponsor me for a year on the tour if I got through qualifying school. The deal was a 50/50 split of anything I made after paying back the costs of competing, if my winnings didn't cover the expenses Brian picked up the tab. It was an offer I was delighted to accept and the reason I was able to pursue my teenage dream.

Brian Young. My first employer, but more importantly, my backer and friend. A man who stayed a friend when I was able to make it on my own without his financial help. Someone I have known for almost thirty years and perhaps the one person I can share some of this with when I get through the initial stages of my story.

September 4th – 4:00pm

The *All in the Mind* programme stressed how important it is for participants in counselling to voice their emotions as they go through their stories, and not just recite facts. My conversation is with myself, through this writing. If I am going to benefit from it, I need to include how I feel now as well as how I felt when it happened. I have to try and make this as close to a real consultation as possible.

So – I'm unsettled as I write this. But not to the same extent I have been in the two months since the death and not quite in the same way. I don't feel as overwhelmed by the mixture of guilt, denial and fear of being found out, as I have been since it happened. I am sure that I will always carry the shame of what I did. I never expect to lose that, but I think that I can deal with my guilt if I can get the rest of my emotions sorted. If I can bank down the terror of being exposed, and of my family finding out. The guilt is my penance – to cope with it I have to stop pretending the death didn't happen, stop inventing ways in which it might not have occurred. I have to take responsibility for my actions, and to do that I need to continue the story.

The middle. I got through qualifying school at my first attempt and joined the European Tour the following year. There is no point in going through a full reprise of my 22 years on the Pro Circuit. I kept my card all that time. And I made a good living in the latter years when the prizemoney rose exponentially. But I was a journeyman, not a star. Highlights – one win. The Portuguese Masters at San Lorenzo in 1998, the year the course opened. And second in the Standard Life Scottish Open at Loch Lomond 12 months later, when Colin Montgomerie won. But, much more importantly, where I met Arlene.

Which is why I need to spend time describing that week and how I felt, because it was the next major change in my life – the second fork in the journey that led to the death.

After three rounds at Loch Lomond, the only thing on my mind on the Saturday night was that I had a real chance to win the event and the opportunity to jump up a level into the top echelon of players. I shot a near flawless 68 on the Saturday to follow two good opening rounds. That put me in the final pair in the last round as joint leader. Monty was in the group in front. My form held up as the other challengers fell away and I was one behind Monty, and one shot ahead of my nearest competitor when I got to the 18th tee.

I felt calm as I watched Montgomerie launch his second shot to the last green. There was no rapturous applause, so I knew it wasn't close. I felt fine as I pegged my ball up – not nervous. I hit a good drive and found the right side of the fairway. I took my time getting up to it and then waited as Monty two-putted for a four. I had to be below the hole to give myself the best chance of the birdie I needed to force a play-off. I visualised the shot, took a deep breath and hit a great 6 iron – fifteen feet short leaving a right to left uphill putt. The pro putt. I remember the applause as I got to the green and then the complete silence as I stalked round the hole to line up my putt. I checked the scoreboard behind the green when I got to my ball. I can see it still. The names 'C Montgomerie – 15. I White – 14', then three players tied at 13 under. As I looked, I thought about the financial consequences of where I might finish. If I was too bold, and three-putted, it would drop me back into a four-way tie for second. That would cost around £30k. Second place on my own would push me back into the top 40 in the European money list. I shouldn't have done the calculation. I should have focused solely on holing my putt. But I was thinking defensively. I left it 12 inches short – right on line. The crowd groaned. I sank to my knees, playing the part of the unlucky, gallant loser, but I was acting. I had played safe.

I recall walking back to the locker room after the prize-giving, accepting the congratulations and condolences of my fellow pros, and realising that I knew a lot more about myself as a result of my decision and that it wasn't a defeat to recognise my limitations. I wouldn't lead a life of quiet desperation, I told myself. I would be brave in other ways. I was – with Arlene. The best choice I ever made. Which was a direct consequence of how I was feeling in the half hour or so after I finished my round.

Arlene was subsidising her Pharmacology course at Strathclyde University by doing part-time modelling and was working as a hostess in the main sponsor's suite. I can see her as I write this. Absolutely beautiful. Long, dark red hair, cute freckles and fantastic legs outlined in a mini kilt. I had noticed her the previous day and had probably stared at her, but we hadn't spoken. She was handing out full champagne flutes to a crowd around Monty when I entered, but she spotted me, broke away and walked over. Before I could say anything, she told me she had seen me looking at her and hoped I would move on from looking to speaking. She smiled as she spoke, then blushed. I fell completely.

My sex life up to that point was limited – I had only one serious relationship at university, with a Spanish girl who was doing a postgrad in English Literature. That faded out naturally, because of the time we spent apart. The tour was different, with no shortage of attractive women who were happy to spend time with the pros. But those experiences were transitory. Arlene was my first and only love.

We married two years later, a year after Arlene graduated. And a year after that, she gave up her post in the Pharmacology Department of Glasgow Royal Infirmary to travel with me to some of the more glamorous events on the circuit. She did that until Anna was born. The tour had largely emigrated from the UK by then to encompass the Middle and Far East, as well as Europe. The money rose in those years but that didn't fully compensate for the time away. My dislocation worsened when Cathy came along. I kept going for another eight years but with less and less enthusiasm. Then I was given a chance to change my life. I was offered the pro job at Irvine Gailes: a prestigious, new £10 million course in Ayrshire with ambitions to get on the Open Championship rota. I accepted, and we bought a farm outside Symington. We converted part of it into a 6-hole track – I had fantasised about owning a house with a golf course, when I turned pro and now, I had one. And I was a fulltime family man for the first time. I had everything I wanted. It should have been perfect. But it wasn't.

The End. I wasn't as happy with my new life as I thought I would be. I began to think my best days were behind me and I let that affect me. The truth was that I missed the excitement of competition. Not the grind of flying round three continents, but the buzz from teeing it up each week. The new role hadn't worked out as I envisaged and that was another negative. The aftershock from the financial crisis caused the membership to stall. The club's income didn't match what had been projected and that had a direct effect on what I earned. We had to dip into our capital to meet our living expenses for the first time since we got married. I have always been careful with the money I made, but a large chunk went on buying and converting the farm, and with much less income coming in, I began to calculate how long our savings would last. Arlene went back to work, part-time, to help our position.

The financial pressure was bad enough on its own, but I also made the mistake of stopping practising and ran down my training regime. I began to drink more and put on two stone. Arlene came out in sympathy with me. She and I were drifting and seemed to be stuck with our new companions; middle age spread and growing money worries. If our marriage was going to be affected by how I felt, it should have been at that point. But it wasn't – not then. We still loved and wanted to be with each other and stayed close as a couple. I am proud that we didn't unravel under that strain. We held together and dug in to make our new life function.

Sky Sports rescued us just before we started to come under real stress. They were short of personnel to cover the PGA Championship at Wentworth and needed another commentator to walk round with the players. I was asked to try out. A bit part, but one I really enjoyed and apparently that came across. The feedback was that I had been articulate, funny and had a different slant. I was offered a year's contract for far more money than I had imagined and put on a camera in the studio as well. They say television adds 14lbs. I was three stone overweight! The girls mentioned it – their embarrassment about how heavy I looked, mingled with pride at seeing their dad on television.

TV also put me back in more regular touch with the tour. Old friends encouraged me to think about going on the Senior circuit when I reached fifty. They preached its virtues: good fun because of the shorter courses, and real camaraderie. Plus, if I could re-establish my game, there was serious money to be made in the USA. I bought the beans. It was the catalyst I needed to get back into training, dieting, and practising again. I dropped 30lbs in three months. I had escaped normality – I was ready for the next adventure. Just not the one I tripped into. Not infidelity… Not death.

Have I done enough to explain my life up to that point and how I felt just before it happened? I think so. I was much happier about myself and my family life. I was about to get more exposure on Sky and was only nine months away from competing on the Senior Tour. I felt I was involved again – I felt enthused and was certain that nothing would disturb my new equilibrium. The best laid plans!

Now. I need to cover what happened in every detail I can remember. I have run a pro-am competition at Irvine Gailes since I took the job. I had 24 teams entered this year, the best field yet, including a lot of acquaintances from my early days in Scottish golf. Each team, made up of one pro and three amateurs, puts up £500, which means the prizes are meaningful for this type of event. £5k for the winning pro and a golf holiday in the Algarve for the amateurs in the top team. A number of sponsors return year after year, including Brian Young, who has put in a team to support the event from the start.

Friday, July 11th, the day before the event, began normally. I woke to my alarm, set as usual for 7.30am, showered and dressed. Then we had a family breakfast; one of the real pleasures I have come to appreciate since I left the tour. Anna and Cathy were up, even though it was the school holidays. They ate with Arlene and me and gave me a kiss and a hug when I set off to the course. I stopped at Kirkland's Newsagents in Symington village to pick up my copy of *The Times*, as I do every day I am at home. The overriding emotion I have when I recall the first part of the day is our closeness as a family through the easy routine of getting up, dressing and eating. Just that togetherness – it's the thing I want back more than anything else.

I can remember having to discipline myself to go through my new practice regime after I had done my initial chores at the club and not let it slip because of the pro-am the following day. I finished a session with a new TaylorMade driver I was considering changing to and had a bowl of soup and a sandwich for lunch. Then I went back into my Pro Shop to go through the last-minute checks, which are essential in ensuring the event runs smoothly. I was in the shop for a couple of hours and was ready to go back out on the range when Arlene phoned – and from that point I have almost total recall of events. Her mum had fallen and been taken by ambulance to A&E in the Victoria Hospital in Kirkcaldy. Arlene was just about to leave home with the kids to drive there. She was intending to stay the night at her mother's house and would let me know later whether she would make it back for the event dinner on Saturday. I told her not to worry about the function – her mum was much more important. I also suggested we swap cars – Arlene should take my Volvo SC90 – in case she had to bring her mum back – and leave her Audi with me. She agreed that made sense and turned up at Gailes about 30 minutes later to do the handover, which gave me the chance to say goodbye in person to the girls and tell them to be sure and make a fuss of their nan. I remember Arlene giving me a kiss, before sliding into my car and adjusting the mirrors and driver's seat. She put the window down to say goodbye, called "I love you. I'll phone tonight when I know more" and waved as they left the car park.

I decided there was no point going out to practise again so I grabbed a ham roll from the clubhouse kitchen before tracking down Dave Butler, the head greenkeeper. The final task that day was to walk the course to choose and mark the hole locations, which would be freshly cut the next morning for the competition. I had arranged to do it slightly later, but Dave was happy to bring the inspection forwards. The weather was fine when we started, but by the time we reached the par 3 11th – the signature hole – clouds were starting to obscure Ailsa Craig. Arran had disappeared by the 15th and it was raining lightly when we left the 18th green.

Dave went to order the beers, while I returned to the shop to change my shoes and check if there were any last-minute call-offs. Arlene phoned as I shut down my computer. She had good news. Her mother's leg was badly bruised but not broken. Mum was shaken by the fall but would be discharged at lunchtime on Saturday unless there were complications overnight. Arlene said she would stay until her brother got there from Dumfries the next day, but she would be back for the dinner.

I can remember the end of our conversation exactly. I said that was great and asked her to wear my favourite dress, the electric blue one I bought on our 10th anniversary as a "You're not getting old – you're still very sexy" present. I told her I had noticed it in a pile of clothes she had put aside for the church charity shop, rescued it and laid it on top. Arlene protested that she was too heavy to get away with it now, but I persisted. I can hear my words, "You're not – wear it. You know what it does for me!". We finished the call with me pleading and both of us laughing.

I locked up as I said goodbye to her and ran through the rain to the clubhouse. Dave and two of his staff were in the bar with Andrew, the younger of my assistants. A few members who were playing in the event joined us. One pint slipped into two, which is my limit – especially as I hadn't had a lot to eat. The rain had stopped by the time I walked back to Arlene's car, but the temperature had dropped dramatically. I felt cold. I remember I looked across to Arran as I buzzed the doors open. The sun was dipping behind the island, setting up the vivid pink and orange shades that characterise sunsets in Ayrshire. But just as I was about to get into the car, it was obscured by a huge black cloud – it created the sort of darkness from which Ming the Merciless might emerge. I slipped into the driver's seat, laughing at that image.

I felt hungry after the beers, so instead of taking the slip road onto the A78 dual carriageway, I turned towards Irvine town centre and Mamma's Fish and Chips shop. I was almost in the town when I changed my mind, telling myself that if I wanted to keep my weight under control, I had to forgo pie suppers. I slowed down. I was pleased with myself. I remember clearly how virtuous I felt. There was cold chicken in the fridge – leftovers from our roast the previous night – that would be much healthier for me.

I did a U-turn, and as I completed it, the cloud burst. It was torrential – almost hail. I stopped, put on the wipers and demisters, and turned on the radio. It was tuned to Radio Scotland and I caught the end of the Bryan Burnett show, "Get It On". Bryan picks a theme and listeners phone in with suggestions to match. He was introducing "Say Hello – Wave Goodbye" as the final choice; the theme that evening was opposites. I was singing the opening line, "Standing in the doorway of the Pink Flamingo crying in the rain" when I restarted the car. I had only driven about 100 yards when I saw a hitchhiker walking up to the Annick Road roundabout, totally drenched by the hailstorm and holding a sign with Prestwick Airport printed in white letters. I pulled up and beeped the horn. It was a woman.

Why did I stop? I know I felt sorry for them because of the heavy rain, and I had nobody at home to hurry back to, so I had time to be a good Samaritan. Was it those two reasons? Or the beer? Or because I was on a high, belting out a tune from my adolescence. I'm still not sure. Probably a combination of all these feelings. But the worst decision I've ever made. Because in less than an hour, she was dead. Dead with my hands around her throat.

Part 3

"There is not a crime, [...] which does not live by secrecy."

Joseph Pulitzer

Chapter 4
July 21ˢᵗ

Scott made the trip north to Nairn without Mary and Donald. Mary had already committed to a lunch with her agent at Rogano in Glasgow to discuss PR for the book and an offer from Alan Clements, Director of Content at STV, to front a new arts review programme. It was an appointment she had forgotten about when Scott first mentioned the possibility of the trip and only remembered when her agent emailed her late on Sunday afternoon. Mary attributed the memory lapse to pregnancy brain. Scott spent fifteen minutes on the phone with his mum on Sunday night, arranging for her to babysit Donald and drop Mary at Carluke Station, as Mary sat opposite him mouthing apologies, pointing to her tummy then making the sign of a gun at her right ear.

It was one manifestation of the different mental state Mary was in as an expectant mum. The others were just as worrying. Mary still saw herself as a rock chick and was proud of her love of indie music. She had been an avid listener to BBC Radio 6 until eight weeks into the pregnancy when she had been persuaded to listen to Radio 2 by her mum on the assurance that it played some good tunes. She gave it a try and found herself submerged in a warm, comforting bath of music that she had sung along to in her formative years with her sisters and mother in the kitchen when they were cooking or baking. The experience created hugely nostalgic feelings and Mary now spent more and more time turning over to the station. She took a break from writing each weekday to cosy up to the dulcet tones of Ken Bruce, introducing PopMaster at 10:30 am, and then texting Scott with her score on that day's two quizzes. It was a change in her that Scott was still getting used to, and one he teased her about on a regular basis.

He would have preferred his wife's and son's company, but traffic was light and the weather was good, so the run up the A9 was enjoyable. He spent the early part of the journey listening to Radio 4, then switched to BBC Radio Scotland to keep up to date with any traffic issues. But for most of that time, he daydreamed about Motherwell's victory in the opening game of the season and how animated Donald and his father had been at the match. A win, and in the sun! A high odds double at Fir Park. Donald was always excited – that was his default setting – but Scott smiled as he remembered how engaged his dad had been during the game, which culminated in him lifting Donald up to hug and kiss him when Louis Moult scored the third and decisive goal. Scott couldn't recall his father kissing him much as a child. Or telling him he loved him. But with Donald, his dad was completely different. Any emotional blockages swept away in a maelstrom of affection for his grandson. Scott wasn't jealous. He had grown up sure of his parents' love, even if they rarely voiced it. And he was delighted that they could show such affection to Donald, who reciprocated it in spades!

It was only when Scott stopped outside Aviemore for a comfort break and a cup of tea that he pulled himself back from wallowing in the aftermath of Saturday afternoon and fantasising about how great the rest of the season was going to be. He took his drink over to an empty table by the window and switched his focus to what he wanted to get from the visit. He had sketched out his approach to the meeting and how it might develop before he left work on Friday night. He reread his notes in the café and added some further points that he wanted to cover. When he was happy with his revised crib sheet, he went back to the counter and bought four strawberry tarts – an introductory offering for his fellow officers. All policemen loved a treat, and homemade cakes were an upper echelon one.

He arrived at the Nairn police building 90 minutes before his two o'clock interview at the hotel. It was a small station, and in danger of being folded into Inverness in the post-merger efficiency drive, which was in full spate within Police Scotland. Nairn had a compliment of one sergeant and two PCs. He shared a sandwich with them, then produced his box of goodies from the car for dessert. It had the desired effect. His hosts' interest was maintained as he went through the background to the disappearance, explained that Katerina was now posted on MisPers and outlined what he was hoping to get from the session with the hotel owner. Sergeant Cummings told him that Katerina wasn't "known" to the local force – a useful additional check to the PNC reviews his team had done on Friday, which had confirmed that Katerina had no record with the police. Scott was allocated PC Bob McKinnon as his assistant and liaison with Nairn.

McKinnon was a local man, 20 years in, but still enthusiastic, as far as Scott could tell from their brief conversation at the station and in the car.

McKinnon gave directions to the hotel, which was only three minutes from the station and situated 400 yards from Nairn's main attraction, the championship golf course, which featured regularly in the top 100 UK golf venues. They drove into Sunny Bay just before two o'clock. Scott took in the house as he slowed at the entrance – the three-storey red sandstone building looked well kept, as did the mature gardens and small pond at the bottom of the lawn. The hotel didn't do lunches on a Monday and the car park at the side of the building was empty, apart from a battered old Land Rover. John Smedley, the owner and manager, was waiting for them on the front steps. Smedley was a thin, angular individual, with a milky white, unhealthy-looking pallor – a bit like a cup of tea made by an American. He showed them into a large conservatory which jutted out from the front left-hand side of the hotel. The room was airy, filled with light and warm from the strong sunshine. It looked out on the gardens, then over a large park and cricket pitch, which ran down to the promenade and beach.

Scott waited until the tea service arrived before he went through what the police knew so far; a longer recital of the basic facts that he had given Smedley on the phone. He picked up his cup and sat back in his chair when he finished. 'So that's all the information we have at this stage. I assume since you haven't been in touch that you've heard nothing over the weekend?'

Smedley shook his head. 'Not a thing'. He looked warm, and in Scott's view, a bit uncomfortable in the tweed suit he was wearing. He paused, fidgeted in his seat and fiddled with his tie. 'It's worrying. Bit annoying as well, to be honest. She's a great waitress and general help. She's very bright. Nothing is too much trouble for her. Kat's really good with the guests, which is important given the sort of offer we have here. We pride ourselves on our personal service. She's chatty. Always has a word with them. She's extremely popular, and I've come to depend on her. The temporary help I've pulled in isn't anything near as good.'

Scott grimaced in sympathy, took a small sip of tea, and rested the cup on his knees. 'Can you give me some more background on her? When she started? Where she came from? The sort of stuff we covered briefly when we spoke.'

Smedley leaned forward. 'I've checked our records to confirm that my recollection was correct. She came here in mid-March and went on our books officially at the end of the month after a two-week trial. She'd been working at

Culloden House Hotel before then. Didn't like it there, she said. I can understand that. One of my ex-staff, Jeannie Seaton, is an assistant manager at Culloden. I keep in touch with her. She knew I was looking for someone for the season. Jeannie did the introductions. Recommended us to each other. Kat said she wanted to leave Culloden because it was too big, really impersonal and trading on past glories. No fun – unlike here, which is a constant barrel of laughs!' Smedley smiled briefly, sat back in his chair, and folded his arms. 'I liked her right away. Kat was fresh; really lively and outgoing when I interviewed her. She worked out very well. It's been a good fit.'

Scott could see that PC McKinnon was labouring with his notes. To allow him to catch up, Scott refilled his teacup and played with a biscuit. McKinnon finally stopped scribbling, looked up and nodded. Scott shifted forward to re-engage Smedley. 'What were Kat's main duties?'

Smedley clasped his hands and rested them against his chin. 'Everything, I suppose. Waitressing mainly, but she helped out anywhere I asked. Even the kitchen on occasions. She was more than passable on the basics and very keen to understand the economics of how the business worked – in fact, in the last few weeks, she started to help me with keeping the accounts. She was good at that – she was interested. She was a Kat of all trades!' He glanced down at the floor, then back to Scott. 'Don't know why I'm saying "was". Stupid.'

Scott wanted to keep him talking. 'It's natural. Don't worry. When did she meet Martin?'

Smedley nodded before he replied and looked more confident. 'I verified the dates from our booking register. It was April 20th to 22nd. Martin and his father were up for a golf break. His dad's birthday present, I think they said. They stayed Tuesday to Thursday. Played at Nairn, Dornoch and Castle Stewart. I did the bookings for them when they confirmed the accommodation. Kat was serving their table. She's always friendly.' Smedley paused for a second and glanced at his hands, before continuing. 'They got on well. I could tell from the banter during the meal. When she finished for the night, she joined them for a drink. I don't encourage that sort of thing generally, in fact I had to speak to Kat about it before, but Martin's dad asked very politely if it would be OK. I agreed and she went upstairs to change. I was doing the last of the setting up for breakfast when she came back down. Safe to say they liked her new outfit. I left them to it. It's an honesty bar at that time. Guests fill in slips for each round. They were the only ones still up.' He raised his eyes! 'I don't imagine Kat spent the rest of the night in her own room. That was the start.'

There was a nuance Scott wanted to explore but he felt it was better to let the interview develop naturally and come back to it. 'Do you know how often she saw Martin after that?'

'Only a couple of times, I think,' Smedley said, after a pause. 'We've been full all season, so she's had limited time off. She went down mid-May to stay with him at his dad's from what I remember her saying, and they had one night together in Inverness. I know that because I booked it for them. Pal of mine's B&B.'

Scott nodded. The information tied in with Martin's note. He looked across to make sure McKinnon was keeping up before he continued, 'Thanks. That's helpful. Can we move on to what happened two weeks ago? How much time had Kat booked off?'

'Six days – Friday to Wednesday. She was due back on Wednesday night to start breakfast service on Thursday morning. She's been such a good help that I let her have an extended break and use most of her free days until the end of the season in one batch. My daughter-in-law came in to cover but she couldn't stay beyond last Thursday, so I'm struggling a bit now.'

Scott knew how important it was to empathise with Smedley – keep him onside and talking freely. 'I'm sorry about that. When did Kat leave that Friday morning?'

'After service finished – about 10:30 am, I guess. She'd organised a lift with a couple who were going to Fort William. She was intending to hitchhike from there.'

Scott rubbed the side of his face and leaned closer to Smedley. That information was important in finding out what might have happened to her. He wanted to get Smedley's view. 'Why hitchhike? Take the risk of not getting a lift? Of being late? Missing her flight?'

Smedley sighed softly and pursed his lips. 'I asked the same questions. She said it would be more exciting. That using public transport was "ordinary". That was the word she used. Plus, she had the lift to Fort William. That was a major part of the journey in her eyes. She said that if she got stuck, she could always get the train to Glasgow from there and that she had plenty of time. The flight wasn't until Saturday morning.' Smedley hesitated then cleared his throat, 'I think there were other reasons as well.'

'What?'

'Kat was careful with money and I think hitching was part of that. She was…is saving up to bring her mother to the UK and start a business together. A café or small bed and breakfast. She was very popular with guests, as I said. Got bigger tips than any waitress I've ever employed. We operate a tronc. Kat felt we shouldn't. She was very single-minded on that subject. Wanted to keep her own tips. Not put them into the pool. It was a source of friction I hadn't resolved, but I was going to give her the majority of the money in the tronc at the end of the summer. She deserved it.'

Scott nodded. 'That's one. You said reasons.'

Smedley looked slightly embarrassed and stuttered over the start of his response, 'Men find her very attractive. She was well aware of the effect she had on them. Enjoyed it. She told me she wouldn't have a problem getting a lift from male drivers.'

Scott checked again to make sure McKinnon was capturing all the information Smedley was providing. 'Who gave her the lift to Fort William?'

Smedley reached inside his jacket pocket and produced a slip of paper. 'Thought you would want this.' He passed it to Scott. 'Bill and Marion Curtis. Really nice English couple in their early 70s. They come up and stay here every year on their Scottish tours. When Martin rang to ask about Kat and told me she hadn't turned up, I called them. They dropped her off on the south side of Fort William. At the guest house where they were staying. Linnhe View, which is on the main road out of the town. The A82. They left her about 1:30 pm, they said.'

Scott took the note, shifted in the chair and rested his right hand on the coffee table. It was critical not to show any irritation, but it would have been useful if Smedley had told him about the Curtises on Friday. The two-day delay in speaking to them wasn't helpful in picking up the next stage of Katerina's journey. Scott could have chased down that part of the trip over the weekend. He tapped the glass top of the table with his thumb and index finger. 'And since then you've heard nothing?'

'Not a thing.'

'Did she have any close friends in the town? Anyone she socialised with?'

Smedley shook his head. 'No one I know about. Nairn isn't that lively a town, and Kat worked every shift she could get, including virtually all the nights, so not much scope for going out.'

'What was she wearing when she left?'

'Let me think.' He closed his eyes for a few seconds. 'Dark jeans, a multi-coloured shirt, trainers, and she was carrying her black parka, a blue rucksack and a sign for Prestwick Airport.'

'OK. That's helpful. Can we have a look at her room?'

Smedley nodded and got up. 'Follow me. It's a bit pokey. A converted attic. I haven't touched anything.'

They walked behind him up two flights of steep, narrow stairs into a very small room on the right-hand side of the top landing. There was barely enough space for the three of them. Scott had to bend to avoid banging his head on the sloping ceiling, which ran down from left to right to a solitary window that looked out to the back of the car park.

Scott did a quick scan of Kat's accommodation. The bed was made and the room was tidy. There were no clothes lying around. Four books and an iPad were balanced on the tiny bedside table. He opened the door of the only wardrobe. It was neatly laid out and contained a small ensemble of clothes, all of which looked to be relatively new. Mid to upper price range, he guessed, then checked the labels: Biba, Karen Millen and Ted Baker. Five pairs of shoes on the floor. All high heels, with a pair of long boots folded over them. Underwear on the shelves; neatly stacked and fresh looking. Scott closed the door and pulled open the drawer on the side table. It was chock-a-block. The only cluttered part of the room. He emptied the contents onto the bed and sifted through them. Pay slips, bank and credit card statements and a pocket Michelin Guide.

He looked over to Smedley, 'As you said, nothing obviously wrong at first glance. We'll keep the iPad and papers. Leave you a receipt. See if there's anything in that which gives us an indication of where she might be, or what's happened. We'll also take a sample for a DNA match. Just in case we need that at a later stage. I don't mean to sound unduly alarmist, but it's better to do it now whilst we're here.'

Scott reached back into the cupboard and found the hairbrush he had noticed earlier. He checked it closely. It held a number of dark hairs, and importantly, a few with roots.

'Would you bag that please, PC McKinnon? And the papers and iPad separately.'

As McKinnon began his tasks, Scott motioned Smedley out of the room and back down the stairs. 'Just one thing,' he said, when they reached the bottom. 'You said Kat was friendly with the guests. Normally friendly or a bit more?'

Smedley frowned and moved his right hand to his mouth, 'I don't want to say anything bad about her'.

Scott nodded. 'I understand – but it all adds to the picture I'm trying to build. Might not be relevant, but the more we know, the better the chance we have of working out where she might be.'

Smedley twisted his mouth and fingered his chin, 'OK. She was very friendly… If you know what I mean. I saw her going into a guest's room a week or so after she started. She'd been chatting with him earlier at dinner. Single guy. Mid 50s, I guess, so 30 years older than her. I tackled her about it next morning after breakfast. She said it was just a late-night drink. The guy wanted her to have a nightcap with him in his room. When I pressed her about it – and maybe I was imagining this – I felt as if she was coming onto me. It was subtle. But if I'm honest, I don't think I was wrong about it. I backed right off about the night before. Perhaps that's why she did it, to put me on the defensive.' Smedley coughed a couple of times and cleared his throat, 'She liked the attention she got from men. She was very good at talking to them, flattering them.'

Smedley stopped as the sound of feet coming down the stairs got louder. McKinnon emerged holding up three evidence bags. 'Got it all, sir.'

Scott forced a smile, 'Great.'

He turned back to Smedley, 'Thank you for your assistance, Mr Smedley. If you hear anything, let me know immediately. I'll keep you up to date as well.'

Smedley half smiled as Scott shook his hand. 'I hope you find her. I hope she's safe.'

Scott spent half an hour at the station house when he dropped McKinnon back, having another cup of tea and taking the Duty Sergeant through the interview, but it was more politics and being seen to give the local force its place than hoping to advance the case. He finished by giving Julia McDonald's email to McKinnon and asked him to send Julia the contact details for the Curtis family. It was after four o'clock when he returned to his car. He took off his suit jacket, laid it on the back seat and removed his phone. He scrolled down to Martin's number on his favourites, slid into the driver's seat, checked the hands-free mode and dialled. Martin answered on the second ring.

'Hi Scott.'

'Hi Martin, I'm just leaving Nairn. I spent a couple of hours at the hotel with John Smedley. It…'

Martin jumped in before he had finished, 'What did you find? Is there any clue about where Kat might be?'

Scott waited before answering. He had little to add to what they had discussed on Friday but was keen to sound upbeat. He thought about his words, 'Not directly, no. But her room looked normal – nothing to suggest anything untoward has happened. So that's good. Plus, Smedley was very open and eager to please; he gave me some more information about Kat's lift to Fort William. I'll have that followed up tomorrow – again, it's useful.'

'Is that all?'

'No. According to Smedley, she was hitchhiking to Fort William to save money. We'll talk to the couple who gave her the lift. See what else they can tell us. And there were a lot of documents in her bedside cabinet – bank and credit card statements. I've taken them to review. I'll start that tomorrow as well. We've also found her iPad. That should be helpful if we can access it. Do you know the pin code she used to protect it?'

'No – the only time I saw her with it was when we stayed with my folks. But I know she used 2004 on her phone. I remember her telling me that she had changed it to the day and month we met. Which I thought was sweet. She might have the same one for her computer.'

'I'll check that when I get home – call you if it doesn't work to see what else you can think of. I'm sorry there isn't a huge amount to report now, but we'll know more when we go through the papers and if we get into her iPad.'

There was a delay before Martin replied, 'I feel really strange about the whole thing. Sort of displaced almost – partly involved but partly not. As if I should be able to help more but can't.'

'That's normal. You've done everything you can at this stage. I know it sounds trite but try not to worry. Listen – you need to come over and see us as soon as you can. Donald's desperate to tell you how great Motherwell are, and Mary wants to cross-examine you about your time in Italy and how the book's coming along.'

'OK, I can't disappoint Donald – and Mary giving me a hard time might make me feel more like myself. When suits?'

'I talked to Mary about that last night. We're going down to Bamburgh on Sunday for two weeks – our summer holiday. To the farm cottage her family takes each year. Come down for a couple of days. It would be great to spend some time together. It's only two hours from Edinburgh.'

'OK – that sounds like a plan. Something normal. If you can describe time with Mary's family as normal! That might make me feel better. I'll sort out the details later this week with you.'

'Good – It'll be great to see you and catch up. Mary and Donald will be delighted as well. I'll call you Wednesday or Thursday when I've had the chance to analyse the stuff we found in Kat's room. Bring you up to date.'

'Thanks Scott. Bye.'

'Bye.'

Scott was on the outskirts of Nairn by the time he finished the call to Martin. He wanted to talk to Julia McDonald and pulled into the first layby he came to on the Nairn/Inverness Road so he could dial her landline. She answered on the second ring.

'Hi sir. How did it go?'

'Fine, Julia – about what I expected. Nothing obvious to point to what's happened to Katerina, but we got a lot of background from Smedley and I found some bank and credit card statements in her room, plus her iPad. That should help us start to build a picture of her day-to-day life and give some idea of where she might be.'

'That's good.' There was a short pause. 'OK, sir. I've just got a note from a PC McKinnon – it has details of Bill and Marion Curtis – what's the story with them?'

'They were guests at the hotel and gave Katerina a lift from Nairn on the Friday morning. They dropped her at Fort William, according to what they told Smedley. Can you give them a ring – get the full SP about the journey? But only after you've done a PNC check on them.'

'Of course, sir. As you always tell me. Do it. Log the fact you've done it on the file. Make sure it's clear to everyone on the case that you've done it. Are you expecting to find anything?'

'No. They sound like an archetypal retired couple, not Fred and Rose West. But let's eliminate them at this stage if we can. One specific point to cover.'

'Sir?'

'The trip from Nairn to Fort William seems to have taken three hours. Sounds a bit long. Ask them about it.'

He heard McDonald laugh. 'Maybe he's just an "old codger" driver. No risks. Enjoys the scenery. Takes his time. I know a driver like that.'

Scott smiled. He had a reputation as the slowest, most careful driver in the station and there had been many occasions when he had heard colleagues say, 'Don't let MSDM James drive – we'd like to get there sometime this week.' Julia played it back to him regularly. 'Careful, DC McDonald, you could cause me to lose concentration and have a crash.'

'I doubt it, sir – sounds like you're parked.'

His final call before he resumed the journey was to Mary. He caught her halfway through the train journey from Glasgow Central to Carluke. The reception was poor, so she wasn't able to tell him about her lunch, other than it had been exciting and she would talk him through it once Donald was in bed. That was enough for Scott. He had just wanted to hear her voice and that she was well.

He said goodbye and pulled back into the traffic – the trip home would take more than three hours, possibly longer if traffic was heavy. He used most of the time to replay the interview with Smedley; over and over, trying to work out whether he was more than just a concerned employer. Smedley had been nervous for a large part of their meeting – fidgeting a lot and adjusting his clothing more than Scott thought was normal. But did that mean anything? Smedley had admitted that Katerina had come on to him. Did it go on from that? Were they a couple sexually? Scott spent some time considering that possibility but settled on the view that Smedley was unconnected to the disappearance. The logistics didn't fit. Assuming Katerina had travelled to Fort William with the Curtises, that put her three hours and 100 miles away from the hotel by early afternoon. Julia would confirm that directly. If Kat had vanished from Nairn, then Smedley would be worth a closer look – a much older man with a beautiful young woman working for him. A woman who had used her sexuality to play him, on his own admission. But at present, Smedley was a low priority in looking at the cause of Katerina's disappearance. Scott ran through the other work streams in his head. He would get Julia to coordinate the review of CCTV at Prestwick and the phone records and GPS location tracking. He would concentrate on the iPad and the financial statements. When he was satisfied, he had covered all the open aspects, he turned on Radio 4 to catch the *six o'clock news*, which was followed by one of his favourite panel games, *Just a Minute*. It was ending when he turned off Law Road into his drive.

His dad's car was still there, and he parked beside it. He had just picked up his briefcase when the front door flew open and Donald ricocheted into his arms.

'Daddee! You're home. I had a great time with Nan – come in and we'll tell you about it.'

Donald dropped down onto the driveway, took his father's hand, and pulled him into the kitchen where Scott's mum and Mary were sitting at the table. Scott kissed Mary as she turned her head up to him and put his hand on his mum's shoulder.

'Hi love. Hi Mum – how was your day with Donald?'

Scott's mum smiled and looked across at her grandson. 'Donald, you promised to let me see your new Motherwell strip before I leave. Away and put it on.'

Donald gave her a thumbs up and raced off up the stairs to his room.

'That's some boy you have there,' his mum intoned.

Scott smiled. 'I know. How exhausting was it?'

Scott's mum shook her head. 'On a scale from one to 10, with 10 representing a triathlon, it was 11. But I love him so much…you get through it. I just need a bit of a rest before I drive home.'

Scott sat down beside his wife and put his arm round her. 'Stay for your tea – we'd like that.'

Mary took his hand in hers, 'I've asked her. Sheena brought over a chicken hot pot to save me having to cook – which was very kind. Be good if she shared it.'

Sheena sighed. 'No, that's nice of you both, but I need to get home!' She looked at Scott. 'Your dad's phoned twice already – at 5:30 pm to ask when I would be back, then 10 minutes ago to ask if there's anything he could do to help get the tea ready. Your dad in the kitchen! That's something I need to prevent at all costs. I'll say goodbye to Donald when he comes down, then go and rescue "Home Alone"!' Scott laughed and was about to respond when Donald re-emerged, 'Nan, Nan, this is it – look at the back – Louis Moult – the best player in the world – I'm him.'

Sheena got up and hugged him. 'You are a darling, you are. Nan has to go now 'cause Grandpa needs his tea but Dad will play football with you in the garden.' Which Scott did, as soon as he said goodbye to his mum and changed out of his suit. They played until Mary shouted them in for their meal. Donald talked his parents through everything he and his nan had done during the day as they ate. Scott and Mary smiled continually as Donald went through his adventures. No wonder Sheena was exhausted.

It was 8:30 pm before he and Mary had the chance to sit on their own with a drink – a glass of Riesling for Scott and a Diet Irn Bru for Mary. He clinked his glass against hers and smiled, 'Alone at last! I'm dying to hear. Tell me about it!'

Mary returned his smile, 'It was really good – Frances was extremely supportive as usual.' She stopped. 'How can I summarise a two-and-a-half-hour discussion? OK, the book first. The publishers are getting a bit antsy, wondering whether we might have lost some of the momentum since Indy 1, and not sure whether the hubbub around the Brexit vote will compensate for that. They want it finished in the next eight weeks, which I've promised to do.'

Scott put his drink on the floor and squeezed her hand, 'Can you do that?'

Mary nodded, 'I think so – being given that final deadline will help me shape how I complete it and what the epilogue will look like. I'll manage.'

'You always do.'

'And the other news is that they've agreed to change the title.'

'To what?'

'Neverdum – The Quest for the Holy Grail of Scottish Independence'.

Scott laughed, 'Great, I never thought they would go for that.'

'Neither did I, and I have you to congratulate for it. It was your idea.'

Scott bowed with a flourish, 'Thank you, thank you, I thank you.'

Mary nudged him, 'Will you want joint authorship now?'

'No, I think the fact that I contributed 10 words out of 150,000 might make that a bit unbalanced. What about the arts programme?'

Mary snuggled into him. 'Good news again. They definitely want me. It would go out fortnightly, except during the Edinburgh Festival, where it would air Monday, Wednesday and Friday for three weeks. Ideally, they would like to start it later this year but want my thoughts on how soon I could manage to do that given I'm…' she stood up and pointed to her belly, '… due in January.'

Scott laughed and shook his head as Mary collapsed back on the seat. 'That does sound keen.'

'I know. I've said definitely not before I give birth. Frances will go back to them and get their thoughts. The even better news is that I'd have joint editorial control of the content with my producer and…' Mary turned to him, 'Guess how much they're offering per show?'

Scott sat back and took a sip of his wine, 'That's hard – I've no idea – £1000 an episode?'

Mary shook her head and raised her right hand.

'Ok – £2000?'

Mary raised her hand higher again.

'God, £3000?!'

'Not quite – their first suggestion is £2500. Frances and I talked about that and she's going back to ask for £4000!'

'No!'

'Yes, let's go for it. Think of the change that sort of money could make to us.'

Scott breathed in. It wasn't lottery winnings, but with his salary and Mary's writing income, another £8000 a month would put them into a totally different financial league. They had always agreed that money would not be the main driver in any decisions they made, but this was an extension of Mary's profession and seemed natural. 'If you say yes, it will mean a big shift in our lives and not just the money side. Do you want to do it?'

Mary nodded, 'I think so. It feels like the next step for me. But it might not happen – or, even worse, I try it and it doesn't work.'

'Don't be daft,' Scott said, as he laid down his empty glass. 'If you do it and they give you control of the content, you'll make it a success. No danger.'

Mary shifted closer to him. 'Ta, but that's enough about my day. How did you get on?'

Scott spent the next 15 minutes taking her through the interview, his thoughts about it and what he was planning to do next. He enjoyed discussing cases with Mary – she was always interested and made a good sounding board. He kissed her when he finished, 'So that's it – apart maybe from testing Martin's idea on what the code might be for Kat's iPad.'

'OK – go and get it then – I know you want to.'

He smiled, got up and went to retrieve his briefcase from which he extracted the tablet and switched it on. He tried 2004. It failed. Two more attempts. He looked at Mary for help. 'Reverse it,' she suggested.

'OK,' Scott said, and typed in 4002. It worked – he was in. But his next decision was harder. Whether to go any further or wait, as protocol stated firmly, and pass it to the specialist IT team to extract the information. He was tempted to at least access Kat's recent emails, especially as he was on holiday from Friday, but his discipline held, and he switched the iPad off and put it away.

'I shouldn't examine it myself,' he explained, as Mary laughed and shook her head. 'Standard instructions on all computers or smart phones we retrieve. But if there's going to be a delay with IT support, I might have to rethink tomorrow.'

Chapter 5

July 22nd

Scott gave the iPad to the technical team the next morning, along with the PIN protection number and explained the background and his personal involvement. IT Support was one of the major logjams in police work. Long delays in getting basic data extracted and processed were normal. But Scott had an answer – he hoped. He left the machine with Peter Rigby, the head of the four-man Lanarkshire section of the national resource. Peter played in Scott's five-a-side team and was a friend. Scott didn't tell him to bump it up the list, but he did ask for a favour and stressed how good it would be to have something back before he went on holiday so he could action any follow up before he disappeared. Peter promised to do his best and let Scott have a first cut by Friday morning latest.

When he finished the handover, Scott popped out to the Within Reach Café on Quarry Street in the old shopping centre and a one-minute walk from the police station. Although it did excellent coffee and home baking, Scott knew that it was struggling to survive the competition with the national chains which dominated the town. Scott always used it and encouraged his team to do the same on their coffee runs. It was empty when he got there, which wasn't unusual, and he was served right away. He bought two Americanos to take back to the station.

Scott nodded to Julia when he entered the squad room and indicated that she should follow him into his room. He lifted the two coffees out of the Within Reach bag and put them on his desk as she sat down and rested her notebook beside them.

Julia smiled broadly, 'A wee treat sir? Thank you. Any special occasion?'

'No Julia – just fancied one each as part of our catchup.'

Julia reached forward, took the lid from one of the coffees and took a sip. 'As good as it always is – really nice.'

Scott duplicated her actions and nodded after he had taken a sip. 'Yeah, it's great but there was no one in the café – at this time in the morning, it should be busy. I don't know how long it will survive.' He put his cup down and looked directly at her, 'So, bring me up to date.'

Julia had another, longer mouthful before answering. 'First, the Curtises. No criminal record – as we both assumed. They are mid-70s, retired 10 years or so now. He was an actuary – so he's bright. He put his phone on speaker so I could talk to them both. They said Katerina was very friendly with them at the hotel. They chatted and told her they were going to Fort William on the Friday. She explained she was hitchhiking to Prestwick Airport the same day. They offered her a lift – which she accepted.'

'Which ties in exactly with what we've been told so far.'

'As does the rest, sir – they left about 10:30 am. The reason they took three hours wasn't his driving – they stopped for a cup of tea and a scone midway at Invergarry, then for a comfort break, as Mr Curtis admitted, at Spean Bridge! Appropriate, eh Scott!!!'

He laughed and signalled for her to continue.

'They got to Fort William about 1:30 pm and parked at Linnhe View – the B&B they were booked into. They were going back into town to get lunch and asked if Kat wanted to join them. She said thanks but she would push on – the last they saw was her walking along the A82, going south.'

'How was she in the car, did she say much?'

'They said she was friendly, quite chatty. She talked about the trip, the music festival and meeting her boyfriend – who she said was an English teacher working in Italy.'

'So, all of that ties in with what Smedley told us. Anything else? Did she make or take any calls?'

Julia looked at her notebook, 'Just one that they remembered. She made it. It was quite short, but they think she finished it by saying, "See you soon". They can't be certain – but it was "See you..." something. That was about fifteen minutes before they got to Fort William, they thought. The service on that stretch of road is very patchy, they said. She had tried before but couldn't get a stable signal. It was just after the second pit stop, so we should be able to use that timeframe to pinpoint the call when we get the phone details.'

'And she was wearing?'

'Jeans, dark parka, carrying a blue rucksack and a small sign for the airport.'

Scott drained the remains of his coffee and sat back, 'That fits exactly with Smedley's statement. Anything else?'

'No, sir.'

'So, do you think can we eliminate them as well as Smedley?'

'At this stage, yes. We need to find the next part of Kat's journey. If we can't do that, if we can't get anything after Fort William, then we can circle back, but I don't see them as suspects.'

'I agree. So, the phone company for her mobile triangulation and calls plus the CCTV from Prestwick.'

'I'm on both, sir.'

'Good. Her iPad is with IT and we have the pin. I've also got some basic financial information.' Scott reached into his briefcase and brought out the evidence bags. He handed the one with the hairbrush to McDonald. 'DNA profile. I'm not expecting anything, but we need to be thorough.'

Julia nodded. Scott put the other documents on his desk, 'Let's do a catch up when I've had a chance to examine them. Oh, and set up a group email for you, me, Turner and McKinnon so we get copied on everything automatically.'

Julia raised her eyebrows, 'Already done, sir. Surprised you felt you had to mention it.'

Scott smiled and waved her out of his room.

He spent the rest of the morning going through the bank information and the credit card statements he had taken from Kat's room. Both sets covered the six months from January to June. There were lump sums credited to the bank account, between the 26th and 28th each month – almost certainly her pay, which would be from Culloden House until March, then from Sunny Bay. An average of around £1200 per month, which equated to roughly 50 hours a week at the minimum wage of £6.50 per hour less tax. He found two payslips which confirmed his calculations. As well as those regular amounts, there were other occasional cash deposits. Two smaller amounts of £650 and £400 in March and May and two larger sums: £1850 in April and £1400 in June.

The most unusual feature of the statements was the absence of any cash withdrawals. There were none in the six-month period he examined. There were payments to a Visa account by direct debit each month but no cash payments out. By crosschecking, he established that Katerina had cleared the full amount of her Visa statement each month from her current account. The purchases on Visa looked like normal, everyday expenditure, averaging £250 per month; and as far as he could tell, mainly makeup and clothes.

His initial review raised two key questions, which he inserted into his case notes.

1. What was the source of the cash payments into her account? His first guess was accumulated tips, but John Smedley had said that Sunny Bay operated a tronc. That money wouldn't be paid out until the end of the season. The earlier one in March could have been tips from Culloden House, paid to her when she left.

2. How did she live? Her food and accommodation were met by the hotel but how did she fund the rest of her day-to-day expenditures?

And there was over £35k in the account. Kat was saving all of her salary, plus putting in extra cash as lump sums. She was clearly disciplined when it came to her finances but there had to be an additional cache of money, she was able to access. Was Martin helping her? Scott made a file note to ask him next time they spoke. It wasn't something he had considered before but he needed to find an explanation for the strange patterns the bank statement threw out.

He emailed Julia and asked her to follow up on the Visa card and bank account and establish if either had been used since Kat's disappearance. He ran through his notes again and then sent his review summary and the to-do list to the group email Julia had put in place. He had a stroll round the squad room to check if anything urgent had come in or if Julia had anything fresh to report.

As all was quiet, he left the station. He had no sense of guilt about finishing early. Things were very slow, apart from the work flowing from Kat's disappearance, and he had promised Mary that he would pick up Donald from his best friend's house in Wilton Crescent, which was at the southern end of Carluke and a mile from their home. Scott got there just after 4:00 pm and spent ten minutes extracting Donald from the pirate campaign he was waging. He was just strapping him into the child seat when his phone rang. The station. He backed out of the rear of the car to take the call.

'Hi Scott – Peter.'

'Hi Peter. I'm just picking my son up from his pal's. Can I phone you back?'

'Sorry, didn't know you were with family. I tried you at the station and they said you had gone. But I thought you'd like to know we've got a first cut of the computer data for you.'

Scott smiled at Donald and mimed to indicate they would be leaving as soon as he finished his call, 'That's quick.'

'We aim to please. Most of the other stuff we have on at present isn't time critical. This could be and I know it's important to you. Personal. That's why I called rather than send an email. There's some pretty unusual stuff on the iPad. I suspect you'll want as much time as possible to think about how to handle what we've found before you go on holiday.'

'What do you mean? What sort of things?' Scott said quickly.

'Not really something for the phone, especially if you've got your son with you. Can you come in?'

Scott had taken the rest of the day off, but Mary would understand, 'OK. I'll drop Donald home and drive back. I'll be about 45 minutes.'

'Perfect. You can take me for a pint after to say thanks. You might need a drink.' Rigby terminated the call before Scott could respond.

Scott pocketed his mobile. What was that about? He leaned into the car to kiss Donald. 'Home now. We need to tell Mum what happened on the pirate ship when we get back.'

Donald nodded vigorously, then turned his attention to how much of his left nostril he could excavate with his right index finger. Scott pulled out a hanky, 'OK, big blow for Dad! See how much we can get out.' A lot. Scott laughed as he buckled his seatbelt and deposited the hankie on the passenger seat.

It took a bit longer than he anticipated to do the handover. Mary was dozing when he got home and took a little while to come round, and Donald insisted Scott stayed to hear the pirate tale again. He phoned Julia to confirm that she was still at the station before he left, and even though the traffic was light, it was after five o'clock when he got back to his office. Rigby was sitting in Scott's chair, working at an iPad on the desk. He stood up when Scott entered the room and shook his head as he acknowledged him, 'This might be difficult.'

'Why?'

Rigby swung the iPad round so it faced Scott then hesitated, 'Some of the stuff on here is sexual in nature.'

'What do you mean?'

Rigby bit his lower lip and paused before he answered, 'Better if I show you first, then explain some of the background.'

Scott nodded his acceptance and looked over to the squad room, 'OK. I'll get Julia in. She's coordinating all the different aspects of this.'

Rigby opened out his hands, 'Are you sure? It's fairly explicit.'

Scott hesitated for a few seconds to think about it again. Julia McDonald was a key part of his team. A very capable DC who was a year away from her sergeant's exams. If the information on the iPad was as bad as Rigby was suggesting, it would be better if they saw it together. Less embarrassing than him seeing it first, then having to explain to Julia on his own. It was correct to involve her from the start. He opened the door to the squad room and caught her eye.

He waved her over. Julia knew Peter and nodded hello as she came into Scott's office. 'Peter's got something to show us from Kat's iPad,' Scott said as an introduction. 'But apparently it's adults only.'

Julia made a show of looking herself up and down, 'I think I qualify.'

Rigby entered the pass code and selected photos from the icons, 'So far, I've found nothing that shouts out from a really quick scan of the main sections, emails, diary, etc. No suggestion of a meeting on the day she disappeared or any email traffic. I'll do a separate report on that. But...' He paused. 'The photo section is very different. She was recording on that, or on her iPhone and uploading. But it's what she was recording.' He hesitated again. 'Videos and images of herself having sex. Four different sessions that I can find. All X-rated. In some of them we can see who she is with. Are you ready?'

Scott looked at Julia, 'Are you OK?'

She nodded, and Rigby touched the play icon on a recording dated April 26th. It looked to have been taken from the back seat of a car and showed Kat and an older man sharing the front passenger seat. Kat was naked from the waist up. There was a lot of noise which increased as she climbed on top of him. Some of the conversation was garbled, but in the audible parts Kat was asking the man – who was only partially in focus – what he would like her to do. Urging him to be honest, she would respond. Standing between his legs, their heads touching, Kat braced her back against the car roof and wriggled out of her jeans, before settling herself down on him. The man's voice got very loud at that point, almost shouting. The action became even more frantic before the sequence finished. It was just under five minutes long.

Rigby coughed, as if to punctuate the episode. He then clicked on a second video of a similar scene, but in a different car. Then he showed two bouts of Kat making love in bedrooms. The first was frenetic. The next was less hurried and almost looked posed – as if the man knew it was being recorded and had gone along with that, or indeed, was the director of the episode. That sequence ended

73

with lingering closeups showing every part of Kat's body – the final frame focusing on her vagina – which she spread open as the film ended.

Rigby moved to the side of Scott's desk. 'Four sessions over the last six months. The final one in June.'

Julia breathed out and shook her head, 'Christ. The only way she could have exposed more of herself would have been to swallow the camera!'

Scott sat down in his chair and put the palms of his hands over his forehead. He hadn't met Katerina yet. But he felt he just had – in a most intimate way. What would he say to Martin?

Rigby accessed the computer again, 'Another interesting bit is the notes section. Which seems to be linked to the videos. There's a brief description of what is probably the men – but only their initials, not full names. Some of the dates match up with the videos. It's heavily abbreviated but it reads like a TripAdvisor report; a critique of them. I think she was rating them. Two headings. W – SP. Then what looks like a combined score out of ten. Nothing else unusual that I can see on an initial run through of the emails, but I had no time to trail through any of the indexes or sub files. I haven't tried to access the hard drive yet either and I might not be successful given that it's Apple. But for the iPad it looks like WYSIWYG. I'll send you details of the videos and the notes section. I wanted to show you first, though.'

Scott exhaled loudly. 'Thanks Peter. We'll go through it again in more detail when we get your notes. I know I owe you a pint and I could do with one after that, but my pass is stamped. Back immediately – no pub!'

Julia grinned. 'Nice to see you're honest about being housetrained, sir.'

Scott indicated that Julia should stay and managed to smile at her as Rigby left the room. 'No point in pretending. I just do as I'm told.' He caught Rigby's arm outside the door. 'I know how "copies" of this sort of stuff tend to turn up in the station. But I'd be grateful if they didn't this time.'

Rigby nodded. 'They won't – I promise.'

Julia shook her head as Scott re-entered. 'Christ, what a mess.'

'I know, it adds a whole new dimension to what we're looking at.'

Julia sat forwards. 'Could that explain the bank position? The deposits and the lack of cash withdrawals? The men were her other source of income?'

'Exactly what I was thinking.' Scott exhaled loudly. 'Any progress on the phone location and CCTV?'

'Both promised tomorrow.'

'OK – let's call time tonight – pick it back up again in the morning when we've had a chance to think through what we've just seen.'

Chapter 6
July 23rd

Scott's plan to spend the two days before he went on holiday keeping up the momentum on Katerina's disappearance was altered by a domestic. Violence in the Central Belt usually spiked on July 12th, then dropped back fairly quickly to normal levels. That pattern had been followed in the week after the Orange Walk, until drink and an argument about food triggered an outlier on the evening of the 22nd – an assault with a kettle. The uniformed branch dealt with the initial call from a neighbour reporting the disturbance and made sure the victim was taken to hospital, before arresting her partner. It was the sort of incident that might have been ignored in a previous era but was now much higher on the priority list for Police Scotland. Scott was on call and spent most of Wednesday taking statements and interviewing the husband, who had sobered up after a night in the cells. He asked for a lawyer but when his rights were spelled out and Scott explained that he couldn't demand one at that stage, he accepted the position with a "fair enough", and accounted for his behaviour in two short sentences, 'Of course, I fucking thumped her. Ma tea was cauld.'

The paperwork and follow-up spilled into Thursday morning, by which time Scott had to cope with the standard recantation by the wife, 'I don't want to get Wullie into trouble 'cause he'll batter me again.'

It was mid-afternoon before Scott could get back to collating the new information on Katerina and trying to mould it into a better understanding of what might have happened to her. Scott knew that some officers at his grade found this type of exercise mundane – almost beneath them – and tended to delegate it to their team. He didn't. To Scott, it was the detail that defined all enquiries – information, and particularly its interpretation and interrogation was the key to building the best model of what had happened. Scott approached his investigations in the same way as bridge problems – establish as many facts as

76

possible before reaching a conclusion. The more facts, the less guesses were needed.

He had the shape of the case in his head when he got home that evening. He and Mary always discussed their work and used each other to test ideas they were considering. Mostly, it was Mary using Scott as a counter party. Every time she had a new idea about a book or how to structure parts of the narrative, she would talk about it to Scott first and get his initial thoughts before she committed to her angle. That had been particularly important to her when she agreed to take on the Independence Referendum as the subject of her third book. She and Scott debated the main lines to follow and what slant she should take. They chatted and sparred most nights about the tone Mary should adopt and how to treat the personalities involved. Scott's requests for help were more limited, but Mary had been very useful in letting him verbalise his thoughts on how to tackle the Logitech enquiry and had been instrumental in suggesting that he should use her eldest sister's husband to do the key forensic work – the work which broke the fraud.

Scott had wanted to talk to Mary about Katerina immediately after he first watched the videos, but Donald had stayed up longer than usual that Tuesday night and Mary had been exhausted and gone to bed when Donald did. Mary's mum was over for tea on the Wednesday, so again Scott had no opportunity to discuss what the search on the iPad had revealed. It was Thursday night before he and Mary sat down on their own and he told her. He asked what Mary felt the videos said about Kat, and more importantly, how he should handle the repercussions – especially the effect it could have on Martin. Mary's snap diagnosis from Scott's description of the recordings was that Kat was exhibiting narcissistic signs, that she might fit the profile of someone who needed to be admired, of someone who wanted to be the lead in the sexual drama. It was only as they talked through the scenes that Scott realised that most of the coverage showed Kat, not the men. Scott hadn't focused on that aspect until he discussed it with Mary, but he could see that Mary's analysis made sense. Until then, he had been solely interested in identifying the men she was with and wondering how to break it to Martin. He hadn't thought about what Kat's part in the action told him about the type of person she was. They eventually agreed it was best to leave telling Martin until they saw him at Bamburgh during their holiday. It was something that should be done face-to-face.

By Friday lunchtime, Scott had been through every aspect of the enquiry in depth again and updated his case file. It was one of the jobs he most enjoyed. Pulling together the facts to understand as much as possible about the investigation and drawing conclusions from what was known made him feel that he was in control of the enquiry and feeling in control was important to him. He sat back when he had finished and paged to the last section of his report.

What We Know About the Day Katerina (K) Was Last Seen

1) K left Sunny Bay Hotel at approximately 10:30 am on Friday July 11th.
2) She planned to hitchhike to Prestwick Airport (PA) to catch a Ryanair flight FR451 to Barcelona on Saturday July 12th at 6:30 am.
3) She checked in for the flight on Wednesday July 9th at 4:45 pm (an email confirmation from Ryanair on her iPad).
4) She didn't board the flight (confirmed by Ryanair).
5) CCTV from PA has no sighting of her. It has been reviewed from 1 pm July 11th to 8 am July 12th. Assumption – K never made it to the airport, or more specifically, she never made it to the main car park or inside the terminal buildings. CCTV only covers internal parts of the building and Car Park no 1.
6) K was given a lift from Sunny Bay by an elderly couple from Somerset who visit the hotel annually. The Curtises have no criminal record. According to them, they took her from the hotel and dropped her at about 1:30 pm, just south of Fort William on the A82 at the Linnhe View B&B. A separate note of a call between Julia and Mr/Mrs Curtis is in Appendix A. Kat was apparently lively and courteous during the journey and nothing she said or did gave any cause for concern or suggested she was doing anything other than heading for PA. She was wearing dark jeans, a coloured shirt, and was carrying a blue rucksack and a black parka but nothing else, other than the hitchhiking sign.
7) Phone location – appendix B. This confirms the initial pattern outlined by the witnesses for the morning and early afternoon – Nairn until approximately 10:30 am, then the trip to Fort William – it moves from there at two o'clock – following the A82 – there is a stop at Bridge of Orchy at 3:15 pm. Then on to Crianlarich for 4:30 pm. It stays in Crianlarich for two hours, then GPS tracks her on the A85 until her last

location, just north east of Paisley at 8:19 pm. No trace from then. That is consistent with her still heading for PA at that time (providing she had her phone and it wasn't in anyone else's possession).

8) Phone records for that day. Seven calls and five SMS texts. Two foreign calls to her mother's number, leaves five other calls and five texts. Three numbers are involved. One we know. Martin Young. One call received at 8:30 am and one text sent at 1:45 pm. The other two numbers need further follow up; one shows the subscriber as A Parsons, address: 1 Barons Court Road, Solihull, W Midlands. There was one call to that number at 2:30 pm. The other phone is registered to a company – Continental Shelf 3179, with an address at 119 Melville St, Edinburgh. Three calls to and from, and four SMS from 2:45 pm, until last one at 6:30 pm. Further information to be obtained on the company. All subscriber information to be crosschecked with the Sunny Bay guest register (see E below).

9) K's iPad shows evidence of multiple sexual encounters. So far, we are not able to identify any of the men, but we know that different individuals were involved in the sessions. The notes section seems to have reviews on six men identified by initials. One is MY so could be / is Martin Young.

10) K's bank account holds over £35k. No evidence of any cash withdrawals in last six months. HMRC details show her salary as the only source of income. Is payment from the men on the videos another income stream? If so, what does that mean in terms of follow-up enquiries?

11) No use of her phone, bank or credit cards since July 11th – she is completely off the grid from that date.

12) K had a business meeting set up for the afternoon of Wednesday 16th in Ayr but didn't show.

Next Steps for Discussion – To Review Resources and Time/Budget (G – below)

A. Search her room at the hotel again – Have we missed anything?

B. Interview staff at Culloden House for more background on her time working there.

C. Obtain her phone records for the last three months and analyse.

D. Identify all people she phoned/texted in the week up to Friday as a first cut off, as well as those on the day.

E. Analyse Sunny Bay guest register to check whether any initials match the iPad notes section.

F. Consider an appeal to the public – *Have you seen this woman?*

G. What resources should we allocate to the case? What is appropriate?

H. Chase up details of her cousin in Newcastle (M Young).

What Has Happened? Where Is She? Possibilities

She has gone away without telling Martin or her employers at the hotel. But: None of her clothes are missing, other than what she took on Friday, as far as we can tell. There have been no phone calls from her mobile and no use of her bank or credit cards since the Friday she disappeared. No new job has been notified to HMRC. Leaving aside why she would do that, the evidence is against that explanation.

Something happened to her en route to PA. She has come to harm. But: There is no trace of her in hospital, nor any mortuary reports of anyone fitting her description. Nothing has shown up from MisPers. So, it is probably more complex than an accident.

Is this still a missing person? Or something worse?

Scott ran off four copies of the report and dropped one each on the desks of Jim Turner, Julia McDonald and PC Colin Morris, who had been added to the team working on the disappearance. All of them were out. Scott checked his watch. He had an hour before the briefing – more than enough time to pop out and get the items on the shopping list Mary had given him. The most important was factor 50 sunscreen for Donald. All Scott's family had some trace of red in their hair; his hair was sandy (in his own estimation), but in certain light, it could look a little more ginger – a fact Mary used on occasions to tease him. But in Donald, red was in its full glory. Donald had burst from his mum's womb like a matchstick, burnt red hair fully covering the top of his head. At five, Donald was the full stereotype of the genus – red hair, skinny, white and freckles. Beautiful, but requiring gallons of cream to protect him. Donald's theme tune would always be "I've got sunscreen on a cloudy day".

Scott had another important reason for going out. To get a treat for the afternoon meeting. It had taken him a little while at the start of his police career to understand how vital biscuits, cakes and other comestibles were to working shifts. How much they were seen as an exciting counterpoint to normal routine. Everybody loved a treat – regardless of rank, sex or time of day or night.

His introduction to a central part of the ritual had come at the end of his first month, when he produced his payslip to Sergeant Williams – his immediate boss at the time – and told him he hadn't worked all the overtime he had been credited with. Williams had smiled and explained that it would be far too complicated to revise the calculation after it had been paid. It would be much easier if Scot gave him the extra £15 in cash and Williams would use it to augment the biscuit tin for that month. Scott had complied happily.

The next month, Scott's hours were high again. He went to see Williams, who smiled and suggested… Williams had joined the police force long before O Levels and Highers were obligatory entrance requirements. Although not academically gifted, he had gained a deep understanding of one of the key laws of the Police Universe – time was relative – overtime doubly so. In those days, the biscuit barrel was full of brands that were extinct elsewhere, but which continued a precarious existence in Motherwell; Penguins, Mint YoYos, Abernethys.

Now, in Hamilton, the biscuit box featured more modern selections; KitKat, Tunnock's Caramel Wafers and the biscuit which was just the right size to pop in a oner, Jaffa Cakes. But today, Scott needed something more extravagant. He was going on leave – which was a special occasion (as was coming back from holiday, as was Motherwell winning, as was…). Scott called in at the Co-op on Campbell Street on his way back to the station and went straight to the bakery section. It didn't take long to make his choice – fruit slices…iced fruit slices – the densest and most unhealthy cake on display. The top of the periodic table of treats – the uranium of cakes.

The offering was greeted with universal approval when he produced the box with teas at the start of the briefing session. There was a full five minutes of head nodding, finger licking and murmuring of appreciation which ended when Turner put down his cup and ran his hand over his mouth, 'Good choice Scott, very good choice. I love the sensation of teeth dissolving you get with an iced slice.' Turner paused and looked round the group, 'OK, let's go through your report.'

Scott took the team through the general outlines of his report, then passed over to Julia, who covered the specific areas of investigation and led them through the timeline from when Martin had first contacted Scott, to the latest information they had. Scott took over for the final part of the session and emphasised the actions and follow up he expected over the two weeks of his holiday. They spent the last 10 minutes dealing with questions on that and what might have happened to Katerina. Julia undertook to add the new thoughts to the case log.

The meeting drew to a natural conclusion around 3:30 pm. The others left but Turner asked Scott to stay and stood up when just the two of them remained in the room. He stretched his arms above his head, yawned, rolled his shoulders and sat back down. 'Good report, Scott. Up to your usual high standards – asks all the right questions.'

'Thanks.'

'But there is one thing we can't let happen.'

Scott knew what was coming and steadied himself, 'Sir?'

'We don't want to be het.'

There it was – Turner's favourite phrase – being "het" was Turner's policing nightmare – his personal version of Hell.

'Do you think there's a chance of that, sir?' Scott replied softly.

'Unlikely, but possible. We've done the right thing so far; taking it seriously, devoting resources to it. Unlike that poor woman from London found on Gogarburn Golf Course two weeks ago. Been missing for three months. Her family reported her disappearance the first night, said it was completely out of character and the MET did nothing. Completely in character. Lazy arrogant bastards! Which is why they have the IPCC right up their arses. That's not going to happen here. We've done everything by the book – and more.' Turner stopped and gnawed his bottom lip.

'Sir?'

'The only issue, and it's still just a potential one at present, is your closeness to Martin Young. That's the second way we could get tigged.'

'Should I stand down, sir?'

'No, I'm not saying you should hand the enquiry over – not just now. But I am going to set up a meeting with DCI Alan Johnston when you get back. I've talked about him before. Alan was my sergeant when I joined Strathclyde. Taught me everything that's good about how I do the job and got me through to sergeant when he made inspector. He heads one of the major investigation teams in Glasgow.'

'I've heard about him from other people as well – he's seen as one of the good guys. I'd be happy to get his advice about what to do next. I've never worked anything like this before. Having him guide me would be helpful.'

Turner smiled. 'Great – I was hoping you would feel like that. I'll send him a copy of the report and set it up. I'll also ask him for his thoughts on where we are so far and for his view on what level of commitment we need going forward. I don't want to get caught out, but we don't have the budget for a large, long-lasting enquiry. Alan can advise us.'

'Thanks, sir.'

'There's another interesting little fact for you to think about when you're away.'

'Interesting, sir?'

'Yes – I had a call from ACC Alan Kinney just before our meeting'

'Assistant Chief Constable Kinney, in charge of the Crime Campus?'

'The very same – as I'm sure they chant in Gartcosh – "There's only one Alan Kinney – one Alan Kinney".'

'Sir?'

'Yes. Sorry, got a bit carried away. Don't want to prejudice your view. He called to do some digging on your career so far. How bright are you? What sort of character? And how Logitech was actually solved? Was it really you who did it? He had pulled your file. Said that as well as your Degree, you had good Highers, Highers that indicated numeracy.'

Scott shifted in his chair, 'Well I got a B in maths, if that's what he means, but I haven't really used it since.'

'Must be. Anyway, he wants to meet you when you're back. To offer you a job at the campus. You would be Police Scotland's liaison with GCHQ on cybercrime, and related areas, as he described them.'

'GCHQ? Cybercrime?' Scott shook his head a number of times. This was completely unexpected. He was expecting to move into Glasgow CID – into a traditional police role in the city. In fact, as he absorbed the news about the request, he realised he was conditioned to thinking that would be his next posting.

'Yes. Surprising for me as well!' Turner said. 'Anyway, think about it – bit of a change from domestic violence in Blantyre.'

Scott smiled, 'It is, sir – I'll do some reading up on the whole area and talk it through with Mary when we're away.'

Turner smiled, 'Just one more thing.'

'Sir?'

'Julia MacDonald.'

Scott nodded, 'She'll make it through her sergeant's exam. I've offered to help her, but I doubt she'll need much.'

'I agree, but that's not the point just now.'

'Sir?'

'The way she dresses, Scott – the way she dresses,' Turner repeated, his voice rising.

'The way she dresses?'

'Fuck sake Scott – this isn't a buy one, get one free repetition sale – you must have noticed – don't pretend you haven't!'

Scott paused and though about his answer. Turner was getting agitated and he didn't want to aggravate that. 'Yes, she does dress in a way that emphasises her figure.'

Turner laughed out loud. 'So well put. She does – she looked good in uniform and that's a difficult gig – but since she switched to CID…' he shook his head. 'Unbelievable for a policewoman – but the problem is that her skirts are getting shorter every week – in another month, they'll barely cover her arse. Somebody needs to speak to her about it.'

Scott rubbed his head. 'By somebody, I take it you mean me?'

'Indeed, I do, Scott, indeed I do.'

'What do you want me to say?'

Turner smiled. 'I'm happy to leave that to you, Scott. Don't want to cramp your style. It would have been much simpler years ago. We – you – would have said something along the lines of "Cover yourself up, lass, we can't get any work done because the men in the squad are spending half their shift in the toilets thinking about you". But we can't say that now, can we?'

'No we can't, sir.'

'Anyway, I'll leave it with you.'

'I'll think of something.'

Turner rose again. 'Good, now go home – that's enough excitement for one day. Give Mary my best.'

Scott got up as well. 'Thank you, sir. I will.'

Part 4

"We sometimes encounter people, even perfect strangers, who interest us at first sight, before a word has been spoken."

Dostoyevsky

September 18th – 8:00 pm

This is the first chance I've had in the last two weeks to continue my confession. I'm in London for a nine o'clock meeting tomorrow at Sky Sports' Head Office. I told Arlene that I had to fly down today to make sure I got here on time – which is partially true. The late afternoon flight from Glasgow to Heathrow was quiet – I had no one sitting beside me, so I was able to take out my journal, read what I've written so far and reflect on it. What I've said is accurate, but I wonder if it's skewed. Too many facts and not enough of how I am feeling? The history of what I have done in golf is comprehensive – perhaps too fully covered. On reflection, I can see that I have emphasised that aspect and shied away from a more in-depth explanation of how I am coping. Am I playing safe by doing that? Probably. But a fortnight ago, when I started, that was what I found easiest to write about. Family and golf are my life, but I have let golf dominate the initial chapters.

Is that the best approach? The problem is I can only do it this way – in writing – I have no one to prompt or guide me on how I get the correct balance. Nobody to help shape my narrative and challenge the way I am describing what happened. I will keep going and try to spend more time on how I am surviving and how I felt that weekend. The other thing that struck me going through those first pages was how carefully I have chosen my words. I have always been precise in what I write. I can remember my sixth form English teacher discussing my deliberateness in essay construction – and suggesting I might learn and develop more by being a bit freer with my style. So far, I have been vigilant in what I have recorded, but I will attempt to bring more of my emotions into the story as I continue. I was thinking this through as we landed and on the taxi journey to Brentford.

I got to the Hilton Hotel in Syon Park just after six o'clock and reread my journal as I waited for room service. I have lost my appetite since the July 11th, and as a consequence, have dropped a stone in weight. I am starting to look gaunt, which is another aspect of my condition that Arlene has picked up on. I am trying to eat more but it is difficult – I have only managed half of the steak sandwich and chips I chose from the menu. Now that I've finished and put the tray outside the bedroom door, I have no more excuses to delay. I need to get my attention back on the story. I need to recount what I did, how I behaved and push on to the most difficult bit of my account – and how it contrasted with my life at that point. I believed we were through the worst of our difficulties – we had a new start and an exciting future.

The best laid plans. Derailed by a series of wrong decisions – the main one being to stop and offer a lift to a hitchhiker at the Annick roundabout in Irvine. The hitchhiker was a girl. Her clothes were saturated, particularly her jeans. She was tall and wearing a black parka with the hood up. She opened the passenger door, slid into the seat, then turned to me, dropped her hood, and said, 'Thank you, this is kind.' She had a very slight accent, which I thought sounded Eastern European.

I was stunned by how she looked. Reliving that moment makes it real again. I can see her, in minute detail. She was incredibly beautiful; large green eyes framed by cropped dark hair, Slavonic cheeks and lips. A full mouth, no lipstick. Rain was sliding gently down her cheeks until she brushed it away with her left hand. I can recall her so clearly as I write this. I have that picture imprinted in my mind. After a slight pause, she leaned down to rearrange her rucksack, then introduced herself as Katerina and told me she was flying to Barcelona at 6:30 am the following morning from Prestwick to go to a music festival. I switched off the radio as she sorted herself out. I knew I was staring at her but couldn't help myself. She twisted around more in her seat. I could sense she was appraising me. We sat for a few seconds like that, but it felt timeless, as if we were in some strange form of suspended animation. Then a car tooted from behind. I came back to my senses; I shook my head and drove off. It was during that brief interlude that I made another impulsive decision and created a new branch in my lifeline – a diversion that led directly to her death.

As we pulled away, I explained that I lived on the way to the airport and asked if she would like to come back to the house to dry her clothes. I would drop her at Prestwick later. Why did I offer to do that? Because she was soaking, looked cold and I felt sorry for her? Or because she was so beautiful? Thinking back and re-questioning myself, I'm not sure why I did it. Up till now, I have found it hard to accept that my reason was sexual – that I asked because I was attracted to her. She was arresting, unusual, exciting. Even acknowledging all of that, I have so far convinced myself that it was a genuine impulse to help that triggered my invite – not any desire for her. But with the benefit of time to consider those few seconds again, I have to face up to the truth. If my passenger had been a man, or a less attractive woman, I wouldn't have made that offer. It was her appearance that influenced my decision. It is important I concede and record that.

She didn't respond immediately. I worried that she might tag me as some sort of weirdo. I felt embarrassed as I became aware of her scrutinising me. I kept facing the road, trying not to glance across at her. For a moment, I hoped she would say no – it would be less awkward and I could then just drop her at the airport.

We were off the roundabout, through the next one and nearly on the A78 before she answered. She leaned towards me, rested her right hand on my left leg, and said, 'That would be good'. I was excited by her touch, the way she looked and spoke. I admit that. I wanted to glance over at her but stopped myself. I was delighted she had accepted my invitation and my reservations about being seen as an oddball or a sexual predator, lifted.

She told me a little about herself on the way to the farm. She was Polish and had been in Scotland for three years. Her grammar was very good, and her accent was only just noticeable. She explained that she was working as a manager in a hotel in Nairn and had hitchhiked from there. I struggled to find sensible responses to what she said, apart from blurting out that I had played golf at Nairn in the Scottish Amateur and it was a great course. She did most of the talking, then went quiet as we turned onto Ailsa Road, the narrow country lane that leads to the farm. When we reached the electric gates at the entrance to the drive, she laughed and broke the silence. I remember her words, 'Downton Abbey?'

I could tell she was impressed. I wanted her to be. I was starting to experience the odd sensation that I was on a date. I parked between the outbuildings and the garage at the side of the house. I took her in through the back door and along the corridor, off which lie the boiler and laundry rooms. It isn't the route that shows the house at its best, but I was trying to avoid her wet trainers marking the carpets or the wooden floor at the front door.

She followed me in as I switched on the kitchen lights, then dropped her rucksack, shrugged off her sodden parka and let it slide onto the tiled floor. For the second time, I was captivated by how she looked – by her body; it's almost comic book proportions – slim but full-breasted. The blue and dark red cheesecloth shirt she was wearing was damp. It clung to every contour of her figure. I was conscious of staring again, so I closed my eyes and shook my head to try and distract myself. We exchanged a few, stilted words, and then to cover my self-consciousness, I asked if she wanted to take a shower to warm up. I said I would put her wet clothes in the tumble drier while she was doing that. She smiled at me, touched my arm, and nodded. Said it would be wonderful to get out of her damp clothes and that I was a gentleman to offer her that chance. Then she bent down, fished out a mobile and charger from her rucksack and asked if I would plug it in while she showered. She explained that her phone had died on the trip down from Nairn and she needed to check if she had any missed calls.

I rested the charger and phone on the kitchen dresser, then plugged them in. She watched me as she pulled off her Converse sneakers and damp socks and left them beside her parka. I said, 'Follow me,' and showed her through the house then upstairs to the spare room with the en suite. She took her time on the short journey and I saw her check out our family photographs in the hallway.

The old clothes Arlene had picked out for the charity shop were on the bed in the spare room – the blue dress on top where I had left it. I saw Katerina glance at the bundle before she took her rucksack into the bathroom. I felt uncomfortable about that for some reason. I don't know why, but I wondered if I should take them away. Before I could decide, I heard what sounded like the rest of Katerina's clothes drop onto the bathroom floor. She hadn't closed the door fully. I remember thinking, *Has she done that deliberately?* before berating myself for even considering that she might. Even as I did, I could feel my body responding to her presence. I was starting to get sexually excited. I was getting hard. I wanted to get away, so I mumbled, 'I'll leave you to it,' and retreated to the kitchen.

I noticed her wet footprints on the tiles and dried them with kitchen roll – then I wandered around for a short while, not sure what to do. I poured a glass of red wine from the bottle Arlene and I had opened but recorked the night before, as part of our new regime – "Just because a bottle is open, doesn't mean we have to finish it". I felt I needed a drink. Which I realised was stupid as soon as I took the first mouthful. I had already downed two pints of lager, and I would be driving again later. It was pure displacement – I was in an uncertain state and needed to do something.

I was nursing my drink, deciding whether to tip the wine back into the bottle, when Katerina entered, carrying her discarded clothes in a bath towel – and wearing the blue dress. I hadn't heard her, which shows how distracted I was. She glided over to me, maintaining eye contact all the way and taking in my reaction. She smiled when she reached me, put her right hand on my shoulder, and said she hoped I didn't mind her borrowing the dress until her clothes were dry, as it was more feminine than a bathrobe. I couldn't speak. I had no idea what to say or how to act. I just stood there, taking in the sight of my favourite dress – partially unzipped – displayed on a beautiful young woman. I shook my head, took her clothes into the laundry room and bundled them into the drier. I did it slowly, trying to work out what was happening. Trying to deal with how excited I was. Trying to understand why Katerina was acting so provocatively. It didn't seem real somehow. Then I remember checking my thinking. Querying whether I was reading her actions correctly. Telling myself to calm down, that it might not be what it seems, and adjusting my trousers so that my erection wasn't obvious.

When I came back to the kitchen she was sitting on our L-shaped, leather settee with my wine glass in her right hand. She beckoned me over. I went – couldn't stop myself. She took my left hand, drank the rest of the wine in one gulp, put the glass on the floor and pulled me onto the couch. As soon as I sat down, she started to kiss me. She opened her mouth and used her tongue to open mine. I responded.

I recall that moment vividly – I could feel the heat in her mouth and the taste of red wine, mixed with the tang of toothpaste. This is important. Very important. What I did was wrong, but I didn't initiate it. She kissed me. I would not have made the first approach. I know it's the "A-big-boy-did-it-and-ran-away" defence, but it's the only one I have. The only one I can accept about myself is that she took advantage of me – of the situation we found ourselves in. She was the protagonist – not me.

Her mouth was all over my face and neck and she put her hands down onto my groin and stroked me. I let her. I didn't take her hands away – or try to push her off. After what felt like only a few seconds, I was conscious that she was unbuckling my belt and easing my trousers down. Could I have stopped it at that point? I honestly don't know. All I know is that I didn't want to. The zips on the dress were fully open. She must have done that while I was out in the laundry room. I could see all of her lower body – she was naked under the dress. I wanted to bury myself in her. I confess that. I wanted her. I accept that was all I cared about in the moment.

She pushed me back on the sofa, sat astride me, pulled my shirt up and dug her nails into my chest. Then she bent down and whispered,

'Close your eyes – you'll enjoy it more.'

I did what she asked. She pushed the fingers of one hand into my mouth and encouraged me to suck and bite them. At the same time, she pressed her groin against mine and glided over my cock. I was aware of her perfume and of the faint smell of coconut. She prised one of my hands from her waist and slid my fingers into her vagina – I can remember how wet she was. Then she used her other hand to guide me inside her. Once I was fully inside, our hips rocking in sync, she grabbed my wrists and pushed my hands slowly up over her legs, bum, up around her waist and breasts, making me feel all of her, encouraging me to explore her body, before placing my hands on her neck.

'Hold me! Tight!'

I obeyed again. She flexed her body against mine and repeated the motion, gyrating slowly but firmly, increasing the pressure with each movement.

I felt her angle down again. Then her mouth brushing my ear,

'Tighter. Press!'

I complied. I wanted to see her, to look at her body. I was very excited. It had all been so quick. I was on the cusp of ejaculating, but I kept my eyes closed, and managed to hold myself back.

She bit my right ear, then breathed into it,

'Squeeze. Press harder!'

I did. I felt her hands reach down to my testicles and pull them. I began to shudder, to come. A powerful orgasm. I lost track of where I was and gave in to sensation.

I felt her move with me for a few seconds, then suddenly flop forward. I didn't know what was happening but as I started to think again, I heard two words: 'Cialo Chrystusa.'

The last thing she ever said.

Or I think that's what she breathed. I could barely make it out at the time, but I've looked those words up since. They translate as "Body of Christ".

That was hard. Writing it out. Having to slow my mind down to the pace of my writing. Having to think about how I felt and find the right words to describe those emotions. Reliving it. It was like creating a 3D movie of her death and then playing it back in ultraslow motion. I have thought about little else since that night but noting down what happened is different. The urge to bypass detail, to not acknowledge my part in the tragedy, is less pronounced that I thought it would be. By committing it to paper, I seem able to be honest with myself about how I felt and what I did.

Her final two words were barely audible – more a sigh than an exclamation. I can remember how I felt as she slumped forward with my hands round her throat. I knew something terrible had happened but couldn't accept it. Wouldn't accept it. I tried to believe it was just part of her sexual game. I kept my hands round her neck to support her weight but didn't open my eyes immediately. I don't know why I did that, or for how long I remained frozen.

My first awareness of movement was feeling myself detumesce and slip out of her. That was involuntary. Passive – but it jolted me – caused a judder sufficient for me to stop pretending that I wasn't there. I opened my eyes and looked at her – and immediately came back into the real world. But it wasn't my world. Not one I recognised. Not a world I wanted to be part of. Katerina was totally inert. She looked dead. I remember trying to convince myself that she couldn't really be dead. It was impossible. But she looked dead. She felt dead.

I took my hands from her neck and extricated my body from under hers. I cradled her limp body and arranged her on the longer part of the settee, kneeling beside her. I learned basic first aid when I was on the tour and reverted to that. I opened her mouth to check her airway was clear. I tilted her head back to lengthen out her neck and looked down at her chest, willing it to rise and fall with her breath. I checked for a pulse in her neck and wrist. Nothing. I rocked back and forwards swearing very softly, as if worried I would upset her if I swore loudly. Eventually I started CPR. 30 chest compressions – two breaths. 30 chest compressions – two breaths… Nothing. I lifted her down onto the floor to get more resistance and went through the same routine. Again, and again till my arms and chest ached. No response, she looked entirely lifeless. I rested with my knees on the floor tiles and my head on the settee and tried to think what to do.

The closest A&E to the house is at Crosshouse Hospital on the outskirts of Kilmarnock. It's six miles away, mostly along country lanes, and 15 minutes by car. The immediate decision I had to make was whether I should phone an ambulance? But what would I say? That I was making love to a young woman I didn't know and she died! Which was the truth, but what would happen then? I was sure that the hospital would contact the police, who would want to interview me. That prospect was bad enough, but the follow-up would be much worse. How could I explain what I had done to my family? How could I tell Arlene?

Describe what happened to my girls? Face my parents and brother? I couldn't. There was no version of telling the truth that wasn't unimaginably terrible.

That was when I felt the first swell of real panic, not when I realised Katerina was dead but when I started to think about the consequences of her death. I actually considered redressing her, driving to the hospital with the body and telling the admission staff that she had collapsed in my car and not mentioning anything else. It's a perfect illustration of how muddled my head was at that point that it took me a few minutes to dismiss the idea as mad. I had been inside her; my semen was still inside her. My explanation would break down immediately. A second wave of dread hit as I rejected that plan. And it was then I decided. I wasn't going to report the death. At that point, I knew I was going to hide what had happened. I was going to try to make sure that no one ever found out. I was going to protect my family. Which I knew meant getting rid of the body and any evidence that Katerina had been in the house. I could almost feel the hysteria lift me off the ground because I was aware that I was making the position much worse if the death came to light later. It had been an accident but covering it up would look awful if I were discovered, and probably turn what I was contemplating into a criminal offence. I thought about that for a long time, kneeling on the floor tiles. I couldn't see an alternative. I was committed to concealment – even at that stage – because of the effect it would have on everyone close to me if I was honest and called the emergency services.

I was trying to cope with that thought, and what it meant I had to do, as I eventually got up from my knees. I recall that I adjusted my pants and trousers and tightened my belt as I stood over her body. For some reason that seemed important. I don't know why. But on whatever level, it did. I walked to the middle of the room and laid my forehead on the granite surface of the kitchen island. It was cold – soothing. I closed my eyes and told myself to breathe deeply. 'One step at a time,' I repeated, then, 'Make a plan. Work through it, piece by piece.'

I checked my watch. It was 11:00 pm. I had to be back at the course for 7:30 am the next morning. Any later might be commented on as unusual. I had to use the next eight and a half hours to make Katerina, and every trace of what had taken place, vanish and get the house in order for Arlene's return. I remember telling myself, 'You can do it,' repeating the words 'Make a plan.'

That was the only thing I could think about in the immediate aftermath of the accident; the need to make a plan, a plan that would work. That imperative was the only thing on my mind. I knew that unless I did, and managed to execute it properly, my life, the life I had worked so hard to achieve, would be over. Just like Katerina's. That comparison stopped me for a while. I stood still for what seemed like hours with that single idea in my head. But it could only have been minutes that I was locked in that position.

Could I have tried to revive her for longer? With hindsight I am astonished that I jumped so quickly to "She's dead – what do I need to do to remove any trace of her connection to me?". I knew I wouldn't cope if the truth came out. I did the family calculus. Arlene might have forgiven me – in time. She would have listened, after the initial shock and rage. Seen it as a mistake; no, a catastrophic mistake – but given me another chance. I am not a player – never have been. Even on the tour where casual sex was as readily available as practice balls, I was a one-woman man, faithful for all the time I was married and away from home. That sounds stupid after what I did! But it's true. And my mum and dad would have stood by me – as would Alan. They would all have been hugely embarrassed, but they would have been there for me.

So, I might have done the right thing and reported what happened, if it hadn't been for my kids. Anna is at the age where I have almost flipped from being her hero and flopped into uncool and Cathy's only a couple of years behind. But I know I have their total love and trust. That's what I am proudest of, my role as their dad. More than anything I achieved in my golf career. I wasn't prepared to risk how the fallout from being honest would affect my girls. That was the part of the equation I couldn't solve. So, I had to hide what I had done and avoid the consequences. I had no choice, I told myself. I had to protect Cathy and Anna. What I did in those moments was to convince myself that to protect the girls and my relationship with them. I had to protect myself – and protecting myself meant covering up the death. QED.

I feel strange, writing this down. I've thought about that night continually since Katerina died, but in a piecemeal way until I began this journal. I have relived episodes from that weekend – instalments triggered by remorse, or prompted by panic, that I was about to be found out. And then imagining the shame that would bring on my family. But no matter how the recollections start, I always end up at the same place, working through the chain of events that followed one after another that night. A cascade of circumstances which caused me to be responsible for Katerina's death. I can list them:

1. Arlene being away unexpectedly.
2. Not meeting Brian Young for dinner because he cancelled last minute.
3. Having two pints at the club (not one or three, which would have meant I left earlier or later).
4. Setting out for the chip shop in Irvine, instead of taking my normal route home.
5. Changing my mind about eating and turning around.
6. The music in the car and that particular song – *Say Hello, Wave Goodbye*.
7. The rain.
8. Stopping.
9. Asking Katerina back.
10. The blue dress.
11. The first open-mouthed kiss.

Any alteration to that sequence would have prevented what happened! I believe that. But trying to find alternatives didn't help. It was counterproductive. I got stuck in an endless loop of how different things would be "If only…". Arlene often picks up on that mood and asks the woman's killer question, "What are you thinking about?".

I tell her I am trying to visualise my new swing plane, that I am imagining my hand position at the top of my fuller turn. She doesn't believe me, but it sort of allows us to get through, even though we both know it's not the real story. I'm not sure how long that truce will last. Which is why I need to finish this. Why I need to keep writing. Why I need to go back to that moment. Replicate what I was thinking and what I did during that long night and put it in the past.

The most difficult bit was dealing with the shock of what I had done and the subsequent fear – the hardest part was finding a way to function. I really thought I wouldn't be able to get through it, even though I knew how vital it was to sort myself out. I only managed to perform by drawing a parallel with what I've done for most of the last 40 years; play tough golf courses without making catastrophic mistakes. When that analogy came to mind that night, I thought it was weird, even stupid, but then the comparison started to calm me: gave me the courage to do what was necessary. No, "courage" isn't the correct description. What I did wasn't courageous. It was tidying up. Being competent under stress. To do that, I had to key into something familiar. My golf career was built on getting round difficult courses without dropping shots. So, I used that as a crutch and told myself I was playing in the Open Championship at Troon – narrow, fast fairways with heavy rough on both sides and a high wind. A ferocious test and one where I couldn't afford any errors. I had to focus on keeping the ball in play. And it helped. It let me think more rationally. It gave some sort of template to measure what I was doing. Without that read across to golf I would have been unable to act.

I began with the most basic question I could think of – what linked us physically? The answers were obvious and damning. My semen was inside her. Traces of her and therefore her DNA were all over my clothes, body, and the dress. The dress became a huge issue in my mind. I fixated on it. What could I do about the dress? The first thing was to get it off her. I can still feel what it was like removing it from her inert body. Lifting her arms and easing it up. I was terrified it would tear as I guided it over her torso and head, even though all the zips were open. I managed that but it took a while and even after I had done that I was left with the question, *What do I do with it now? Get rid of it? Wash it?* I froze in my parallel world. I was stuck on the first tee. I couldn't take the club back and I didn't know how to swing. I felt as if I had forgotten everything I ever knew about the game.

So, I did what I always taught myself to do on the golf course if I couldn't see a shot. I told myself to walk away and not attempt it. I forced myself to stop thinking about the dress, instructed myself to get her into a bath and wash her instead of worrying about that single aspect. I decided I would clean her inside and out, wearing rubber gloves. That would at least be a start! I went into the bathroom on the ground floor and pulled off some toilet roll, which I stuffed inside her vagina to stop any fluid dripping out on the way to the bedroom. I felt horrible as I pushed it in. It was utterly dehumanising, and I got an even stronger smell of coconut as I touched her. But I did it – shoved the paper in as far as it would go, then slung her into a fireman's lift and carried her upstairs and through to our bedroom. I laid her out face up in the bath, fished out the bits of toilet paper and flushed them away. Then I put the plug in, poured shower gel over her and turned on both taps. Fully. I went back down to the kitchen as the bath filled, checking for any stains or drops on the carpets as I retraced my route. There were none that I could see. I found a pair of Marigolds that I could squeeze my hands into in the cabinet under the sink and went back up, doing a second examination of the floor on the way – again, it appeared clear. I took a deep breath and began cleaning her. That was probably the worst part of everything I did that night. As the water rose over her thighs, I put my rubberised fingers inside her. I had to stop the first time I attempted it and pull away as I felt my gorge rise. I just got my head into the pan in time and I threw up in the toilet bowl. Twice. I rinsed my mouth at the cold water tap in the sink but could taste beer and wine in my throat when I restarted cleaning her. I kept scooping until the white contrails in the water showed that I was having an effect. Then I did it again. I also scrubbed her body three times, turning her over on each cleaning. I concentrated on her neck once I finished evacuating her vagina as I was worried about my fingerprints on her throat, given how hard I had gripped her. When I was as satisfied as I could be that she was clean, I pulled out the plug and ran the water and residue away, using the showerhead to rinse her and the bath. I made a mental note to do that again when I had moved the body. Arlene would shower before she dressed for the event and would notice anything out of the ordinary in our bathroom.

I sat down on the toilet seat when I finished and checked my watch again. Midnight. I had seven hours to get the rest of the clean-up done. I told myself that was ample time and I had no need to rush. But I had to decide what to do with the body, and I had no idea how to dispose of it. I got stuck again so I made myself concentrate on other jobs which required less planning. I needed to get rid of her clothes, rucksack. Her phone! I suddenly remembered. I had put it on charge. I ran downstairs and found it where I had left it – on the dresser at the back of the kitchen but the switch on the socket wasn't on. Switching sockets off and taking out plugs is one of my father's idiosyncrasies – one I picked up from him. I'm not as bad as he is, but I do go round the house switching lights off – particularly in rooms the girls have vacated – and the kitchen is one of my regular check zones so sockets are normally in the "off" position. I hadn't noticed that when I plugged the charger in and connected it to the phone – I had been too excited by Katerina. I picked the phone up and examined it for what seemed like an age. It was lifeless. I closed my eyes for a few seconds and swore at myself for being so stupid. If it had been active, I would have left a huge arrow pointing at our house. Then I panicked again. Could the phone be traced even if it wasn't on? I didn't think so, but I wasn't sure. If her mobile could be tracked to the house, everything I was doing was completely useless, in fact, worse than that. My actions were making it look as if I had killed her deliberately. I thought about using my iPad to check how mobile phone GPS locations worked but stopped myself. That would leave a trace if the iPad was interrogated later. I had to assume I was OK. I had to continue on the basis that GPS would have shut down when the phone ran out of charge, as there was no power to connect to the network. But where was that? She had said that it had happened on the way down. Irvine, or further north? I shook my head. It was too late to consider any other options. I was committed to the cover-up. I just had to hope the phone couldn't be traced any nearer to the house than Irvine.

I told myself to get back to doing something – not worrying. I had to deal with her clothes and other kit. I considered gathering it, packing it back into her rucksack, then dumping the rucksack – but where? Our refuse bin? Far too risky. Away from the house? I thought about weighting it down with stones, then dumping it in the sea, but that meant going out and it might be found if I chose the wrong spot. I didn't know anything about the tides and their highs and lows at the beaches close by, so I decided to burn all of her possessions. I picked up the rucksack from the bathroom Kat had used and pushed the cosmetics on the side cabinet inside it. Then I went to the living room to light the wood-burning stove that we had installed as one of our first alterations when we bought the house. Paper, kindling and firelighters were all there at the side of the range. Arlene, like me, is very tidy, almost compulsively so and replenishes as she uses. Putting on the fire was a distraction from brooding over what to do with the body and dress. I went into the garage to bring in a batch of logs and stopped to look at an old golf bag carrier I had dumped there. Could I use it to move her? I reckoned she would fit inside it – just. I went back in, put some of the smaller logs into the initial blaze and sat by the fire as I thought it through. What if rigor mortis set in while Katerina was in the bag and I couldn't get her back out? But rigor mortis didn't come on for hours – did it? Moving her that way could end like a scene in a Coen Brothers' film. A body stuck in a golf bag carrier! I couldn't face that prospect.

I fed more wood into the fire and considered going through her belongings. Would that give me any information that would help me? What did I know? She was called Katerina. She was Polish and working in a Highland hotel. She was travelling to Barcelona on the 6:30 am flight from Prestwick. Was she meeting anyone at Prestwick? I hadn't asked! Someone in Barcelona? I recall thinking clearly, probably for the first time since she died; *Don't complicate the situation.* I was finding it hard enough to cope with the jobs I had already. Extra information, in all likelihood, would mean additional complexity, which I knew

I would find impossible to deal with at that point. Knowledge about Katerina was odds against helping me do what I had to in the next few hours.

I emptied her rucksack and threw her passport, boarding pass, and Euros onto the blaze. When I had finished with the smaller items, I put in her neatly folded clothes, socks and underwear. I tipped in the entire contents of the rucksack, item by item, apart from a small jar of coconut oil I found in a side pocket. And I was left with the bag. There was just enough space to slot it in above the logs. It was partly synthetic; a mixture of fabrics which started to melt rather than burn before I could retrieve it. I had made another mistake. I knew it would stain the iron bars in the grate and I would need to scrub them when the fire was out. It was another item on my list of things to do.

I went into the boiler room, picked up her Converse All Stars, then the laundry room and retrieved her jeans, shirt, underwear, socks and parka. Her parka was still damp, even after having been tumble-dried and too big to push into the stove whole, but I threw on the rest of the clothes and her sneakers. The bars were already likely to be contaminated so I was less concerned about any effect melting rubber might have. I went back into the garage and found a pair of large, heavy duty, industrial scissors to chop up the parka. It took me 10 minutes to dismember her jacket and push it in piece by piece. I made another mental note that I would have to clean the whole grate out in the morning – not just the bars – and replace the paper and wood. Burning the clothes and rucksack helped. It had a positive effect on me. I went back to my golfing model. I was ticking off the opening holes on my imaginary round and I was still in play. The heat from the fire was so intense that I moved away and started my next task. Retracing the route Katerina had taken from the garage to the upstairs bathroom and back to the kitchen, I scrutinised it for any trace of her. And the car. I had to clean Arlene's car!

I covered a J-cloth in Dettol and went out to the Audi. The outside security lights at the bottom of the drive came on and I also switched on all the external and internal lights in the car. I wiped the door handles inside and out, the passenger seat and the dashboard and found the Prestwick Airport sign. I took it in, broke the cardboard in two and put the pieces on the fire. We have our cars valeted every two weeks at the golf course. The next session was on Thursday – I remember asking myself if I should leave it till then or have it cleaned somewhere else before? I knew that was a stupid idea as soon as I thought about it. I wouldn't have time to take the car anywhere on the day of the event and deviating from the regular cleaning regime would seem strange to Arlene.

I wanted to keep doing things, so I retraced our original route into the house through the corridor and the kitchen. I tried to remember what Katerina had touched. I knew she had handled my wine glass and the settee. I rinsed the glass with Fairy liquid and put it in the dishwasher. The settee is leather, so I sponged it twice with a fresh cloth and disinfectant, dried it with a dishtowel, then did the same to the floor tiles around it. I chucked the towel and cloths into the fire when I finished. We had dozens of dishtowels – Arlene wouldn't miss a couple. Our cleaner comes every Tuesday. That would be a backup to my efforts. I got new cloths and more disinfectant, then went up the stairs again, checking the carpet compulsively. No marks that I could see on my third review. After that, I moved into the spare room and rubbed down the door handle, light switch, sink, toilet seat, showerhead and tiles in the en suite. Then I wiped them all a second time with another cloth. I found an empty shampoo bottle on the shower ledge, which I cleaned and put aside to take downstairs and dispose of in the kitchen rubbish bag. The shower gel beside it was half-full. If I dumped it, Arlene might notice. So, I wiped it down and put it back on the shelf. Finally, I ran the showerhead full blast around every inch of the cubicle. As I did, I spotted a tiny patch of black hair in the plughole. I was sweating as I plucked it out, wrapped it in toilet paper and flushed it away. It would have been easy to miss. I stood in the en suite for some time after that, trying to keep calm and telling myself, *So far, so good.* I had seen the hair. I hadn't overlooked it. I was still OK – I was still on plan.

I went downstairs to see how fierce the fire was and to try to decide what to do with the body. The fire was still blazing, so I went through to the kitchen to try to think and saw the blue dress lying on the grey tiles. I froze – I couldn't move and I don't know how long I stayed like that – it was a visual reminder of what had happened and what I still had to do to purify the house. And I was still clueless about what to do with the body.

My first and second impulses were to get Katerina away from the house, bury her somewhere. But where? I know the area well but not "body-burying" well. I considered the Eaglesham Moors, which is about 30 minutes away from Symington. *Was that far enough to break any link to me*? I had taken the girls mountain biking there on the trails at Whitelee Windfarm. But it was very exposed. I'd have to get the car well off the road so as not to be seen hauling a body out of the boot. What if the car got stuck in boggy ground? I didn't have time for a much longer drive.

Perhaps Fenwick – right at the start of the moor and a lot closer? The tree planting there in the last 30 years came very close to the road in some places. That would provide more cover. I could dump it there. But how could I find a good place to hide it in the dark? How long would it take to decompose? I couldn't check that tonight. A computer record of that sort of query at midnight would be hard to explain. I seemed to remember that bodies decompose more quickly in the open than when buried. But if I left it exposed, that made it more likely to be found. And if the woods were managed...

I ruled out the moors and considered another location – the land behind the beach at Croy. A 30-minute drive in the opposite direction. The road down from the main highway is very steep, with a number of hairpin bends, but nonetheless still possible to navigate in the dark. The attraction of that idea was the ground behind the concrete promenade, which runs parallel to the beach for about half a mile. That land backs onto the hill, which overlooks the hamlet of Croy. It comprises a 30-yard ribbon of gorse and bramble bushes and is virtually impenetrable. If I could get the body into the middle of that stretch, it would be invisible from the beach side and probably from the hill as well. But how would I get her that far in? I would have to wade in carrying the corpse. I would get cut to pieces. Which was the benefit of putting her there – the brambles would be a natural barrier. In addition to the concern about disfiguring myself, I started to question whether the esplanade might be a local spot for "courting couples". If it were, I would have to abort and bring the body home again. I knew I couldn't face a return trip with the body in the car.

I was starting to run with panic. I told myself that this was the key decision – told myself that if Katerina's body wasn't found, then it would be hard, maybe even impossible, to connect her to me. I lectured myself that I had to take the time to get that correct. This was the key hole in my round – I had to play it perfectly.

I've just realised it's 3:30 am. I'm frozen – the heating in the room must have gone off hours ago and my fingers are starting to cramp from writing. I don't want to stop at this point, but I need to. Suddenly I'm exhausted – I need to get some sleep before my meeting in five hours' time. I will have to continue the story when I get another chance.

Part 5

"There is nothing more deceptive than an obvious fact."

Sir Arthur Conan Doyle

Chapter 7

August 11th

The summer holiday at Bamburgh in Northumberland with Mary's family – her parents, four sisters, their husbands and the 12 kids – was now a regular event in Scott's calendar. It was the third time the group had hired the farm complex which sat just outside the town on the back road to Seahouses. The layout of six renovated cottages, forming a circle around a large common area that housed a recreation hall, created an ideal location to meet, play and relax. The setup was perfect for the kids, who ran in a pack around the houses and the adjacent fields and woods from breakfast until they were herded up for that day's activity; trips to the long, clean beaches at Bamburgh, the religious outpost at Holy Isle or to Annick Castle – used as a setting for Hogwarts in the Harry Potter movies. The outings were all kissed with warm, sunny weather that added to the general feeling of wellbeing, which settled on Scott, Mary, Donald and the rest of the clan.

During the day, the focus was making sure the children were entertained and happy. His cousins included Donald in their adventures from the moment he got there. That was particularly pleasing for Scott, who was keen for Donald to socialise in a wider group and get involved in family gatherings in a way Scott never had as a child. The other kids treated Donald as the "special one" because he was the youngest. Donald loved their attention and trailed after his cousins with all the devotion of a Labrador puppy, looking to be tickled. They protected and wrapped him into the family in the same way Mary's mum and dad had enveloped Scott into the McGee tribe. Scott loved Mary's family; a loud, supportive, emotional and very funny mix. They were a bonus prize to winning the jackpot with Mary.

Scott had met Mary through Martin, and Martin through a determination to use his time at university to break out of the pattern his school and home life had represented until then. Scott was a quiet, sensible boy, who through primary school in Kirkfieldbank to secondary school at Lanark Grammar, didn't stand out, other than academically. His dad was a driver with Strathclyde Council and his mum worked as a waitress in Silverbirch, a large garden centre in Crossford, the next village along the Clyde Valley. There wasn't much spare money in the household, and he grew up in their 1950s council house in a scheme on the outskirts of the town, appreciating how important "special treats" were. His main hobbies, apart from reading, were sports. He was a keen, just about OK footballer, a poor to middling golfer and a good runner. He had friends – mainly from the football team – but they weren't close, and his life was largely solitary through his early teens.

Scott had two serious girlfriends during his time at secondary school. The first, Eileen Hamilton, was two years below him in fourth year when they got together and very attractive as well as bright. He "picked her up" at a local disco. It had been a huge boost for his confidence and social standing, but Eileen dropped him after two months for an older boy with a car and a social life. On the rebound, he had been taken in hand by Ruth Mitchell, a girl in his year, who was much plainer and a lot more earnest. He hadn't been entirely comfortable as her boyfriend, particularly when they started to have sex – and it was sex, not making love – in a very organised and safe way. He didn't feel he had advanced too far down the long and mysterious path he knew he had to navigate in his odyssey to understand women when he left school. So, he was pleased to have an excuse to drift away from Ruth, who went off to study medicine at Aberdeen. He went to Edinburgh as an unattached and slightly callow boy.

He had programmed himself to change at university. He knew he needed to become more worldly. As part of that plan, he joined three societies to broaden his circle of friends; orienteering, bridge and skiing. Orienteering fitted neatly with his running skills. Bridge was a game he had read about and wanted to understand, but it was skiing that brought Martin and him together. Martin had been on skis since he was four. Scott hadn't ever seen a piste, apart from on *Ski Sunday*. But as roommates in a hostel in Val Thorens on the university Ski Club's outing in their first year, Scott and Martin found that they shared a sense of humour, an ability to drink huge amounts of beer without becoming aggressive and a love of country and western music. Those common traits were more than enough to bond that week, but it was the final day of the trip which sealed their friendship.

Scott had been deposited in a class with nine other beginners and was struggling with aspects of his tuition. His general fitness and sense of balance were major assets and he had cracked turning from right to left. But not the other way! It became a topic of conversation and fun in the pub with the other members of the ski club. So much so that Martin offered to ski with Scott on the final day and sort it out with one-on-one coaching. Which he did on the first run; the long blue from the bottom of Val Thorens to Les Menuiers. Scott was hesitant and a bit stiff at first, but something about watching Martin exaggerate the weight transfer, from the right-hand ski to the left, clicked. The mental picture and physical movement were stamped in his brain, and suddenly Scott could turn to the right! It was a Damascene conversion. After two successful turns in a row, Scott lifted his ski poles into the air, turned to see Martin applauding him and fell. But it was a good fall – a victory roll. Martin helped him up and they cruised into the town.

It was very busy, so they took the chairlift up over the houses and beginners' slopes to practise on the steeper pistes above the village. The chair sailed over a bar just before the lift finished, a bar that required a sharp turn right from the run to slide into its narrow entrance. Martin had suggested stopping for a drink to celebrate Scott's newly acquired skill and signalled they were going in with his pole as they came onto the first part of the run. Scott breathed in deeply, hit the turn and it worked. He felt as if he was on rails and punched the air again when they stopped, then detached his skis and clambered up to the decking outside the bar. It was a warm, clear morning and they stood for a minute, looking out at the views back down the slopes and across to the outer runs at Val Thorens. *Romeo and Juliet* was playing loudly in the background. They ordered beers and moved to the side of the bar. Martin saluted Scott with his bottle of lager, 'You're a skier now.'

It was a great moment, made perfect by the next song on the compilation. *Always on My Mind* – the Willie Nelson version. They began to sing it at the same time, laughed at the same time, then both exclaimed, "My favourite song!" at the same time and became best friends in that instant.

They shared digs the next year – a two bed flat Martin's dad owned on Sciennes Road, just across The Meadows from the university. They drank together, worked together and went out on dates together. Martin's father was a successful local businessman who had extensive interests in the city, including a tapas-style pub on Nicholson Street, so getting jobs there as waiters wasn't difficult. It was pocket money for Martin but for Scott, a much-needed sub to his limited income. It also became the next stage in his journey to a better understanding of female psychology. Many of the pub clientele were attractive women of a certain age, dining without men. It wasn't a pick-up bar – it was a bit too classy for that – but it was a place where women tended to go in couples or in groups. Martin was an Olympic-class flatterer of the customers. Never so outrageously over the top that it became embarrassing, but obvious enough to let the women know he found them attractive. Scott didn't have Martin's easy confidence but picked up enough pointers to become more than passable at making women feel admired. Flirting had two main benefits. The first and more regular was bigger tips. The second, less frequent – but at least once a week, was the attachment of a slip of paper to the tip, with the mobile number of the tipper. He and Martin went out on single dates with some of the women – Martin more so than Scott – but they also enjoyed foursomes, which, on occasion ended back at the flat. Their exploits became infamous among their year group, earning them the nickname, "The Milfy Bar Kids".

It was a phase that Scott still looked back on with some wonderment. It helped his sexual education immensely and led directly to him meeting Mary. During one long session with pals in the Student's Union, he and Martin were cross-examined about their latest joint date. The general consensus of the body of the Kirk was that Scott and Martin must have deep emotional flaws, which meant that they couldn't manage relationships with their fellow students and so had to settle for less demanding older women. Martin took up the challenge, and a few days later, started seeing an attractive second-year English student, Daisy Hunter. Three weeks into the relationship, the inevitable joint date was suggested. Martin's new girlfriend had a best pal described by Daisy as "very attractive, but feisty – and unattached at present".

Scott became the "fourth musketeer" in a meeting arranged for 7:30 pm on a Friday night in the Dagda bar. He went along because his best friend asked him to; not knowing it would be a date that would change his life. The pub was only a five-minute walk from Sciennes Road through the east side of The Meadows and he and Martin were there on time. Scott had been brought up as a mannerly boy and was taught that being late was impolite. They were installed in a corner booth with their opening pints when the girls appeared, "fashionably late", ten minutes after the appointed time. Scott had met Daisy at their flat, and waved hello to her as the women walked over to join them. Daisy kissed Martin enthusiastically. Scott tried to hide his appraisal of Mary as she was introduced. She shook hands with both the boys, exchanged a chaste kiss and sat down. Scott found it difficult not to gape at his date. Mary was tall and rangy, wearing Gore-Tex walking boots, a pair of red cords which looked as if they had been electroplated to her legs and a tight black top sporting the logo, "Arrange the following words into a well-known phrase or saying *Pope the fuck*". And no bra.

Scott couldn't help gazing. As he looked up, he was aware that Mary had caught him staring. He wasn't sure what to say but knew his opening line was critical to how the night went. He returned her look, screwed up his nose, and said, 'I think I've got it.'

Mary tilted her head to the side and looked at Daisy. 'Not bad. Not great but not bad. So, you get another chance. What do I drink?'

He responded without thinking, 'Deuchars IPA!'

'Again, not bad. OK, final question for now. What has Martin told you about me?'

He went with his instinct and told the truth, 'Attractive. Fiery. Doesn't suffer fools gladly. Exciting company.'

That produced a wider grin from Mary. 'That's semi-accurate. Did he mention that we're ardent feminists?'

Scott shook his head. 'Shame. I was just about to offer to buy you a drink, but I don't want to offend you.'

Mary tapped the table with her hands. 'Don't worry. When it comes to drinking, Daisy and I are happy to put our principles in abeyance. So, two pints of Deuchars and two vodkas and fresh cranberry would be very acceptable! As a start.' She got up, indicated to Martin that he should shift, and when he did, she planted herself beside Scott on the leather bench.

And it had continued in much the same vein that night – a strange mix of flirting and challenge, until at closing time, Mary put her hand on his left arm and positioned her face close to his. 'You want to go out with me, don't you?'

Scott nodded, not quite trusting himself to speak.

Mary smiled. 'OK. Last question, I promise. What's the most stupid thing in the world?'

He returned her smile. 'Easy. Scientology.'

She put her arm round the back of his head and drew him forward into a kiss. She winked when they broke apart. 'Good answer. You win tonight's star prize. A date with me.'

He grinned as he looked at Mary asleep on the sofa, Donald at her feet with his Lego set and remembered that night more than 10 years ago. They had changed, but he hoped not too much, and for the better. They were still in love, rarely argued but were more adult and responsible – much less daft! They had grown up and into each other and parenthood, and it felt comfortable. Unlike Martin, the Peter Pan of the trio, the one who behaved most like his university days and the one who had altered the least. Martin was the archetypal student. Always willing and able to circumvent reality and responsibility at the slightest opportunity. For Martin, a decision deferred was a decision made. He was the polar opposite of his older brother, Kevin, who had got a First at Glasgow, stayed in academia and was now Macmillan Professor of Constitutional Law at St Andrew's – one of the leading experts in Scotland on how a "Yes" vote in the Referendum would affect Scotland's relationship with the rest of the UK and the EU. Someone Mary had consulted extensively and whose advice she had used to develop a key legal theme in her latest book.

Martin had shrugged off his third-class degree in English Literature as unimportant in his life plan and chosen a different path after graduating – a path less travelled. He elected to teach English abroad. So far on his world tour, he had bagged Shanghai, Busan in South Korea, Hong Kong and Sondrio in the north of Italy. Martin's ETA that day, on the much less demanding trip to Bamburgh, was four o'clock but up to now, he had failed to find his destination. It was 5 pm and they were still waiting. Mary had dozed off half an hour before, and Donald was settled for once – his excitement at seeing his favourite uncle tempered by a cup of milky tea and a slice of his gran's triple chocolate cake. Scott could feel his own eyes start to close. It had been a fun, if exhausting, afternoon playing football on the beach – approximately eight-a-side. His in-laws dressed uniformly in Celtic hoops and most of the other adults in Henrik Larsson tops, which showed off their body shapes directly and not too flatteringly. Their children sported a more varied ensemble of tops worshipping Celtic heroes. Only Donald and Scott broke the dress code in their matching Louis Moult Motherwell home kits. The highlight of a closely fought game, other than the cans of cold cider brought out at convenient intervals, was Donald being set up to score the winner in extra time to lead his team to a 18-17 victory.

Scott's head was dropping when his phone rang. He shook himself. 'Hi Martin. Where are you?'

'Just turning into Milton Farm Lane. I can see a scattering of houses at the top of it. Is that where I'm heading?'

'Yes. Pull into the courtyard, you'll see my car at the end of the first cottage – we're in that one.'

'Great. See you in a minute.'

Scott rested his hand on Mary's shoulder. She stirred slowly and blinked her eyes. He bent down to kiss her head. 'That's Martin. At last.'

Donald was already at the back door and had it open, looking out. A white BMW 3 series pulled up at the side of Scott's Renault. Donald flew across to it and jumped into Martin's arms as he got out. 'Uncle Martin! Uncle Martin! I scored the winning goal at the football this afternoon – that's because I was Louis Moult – the best player in the world!'

Martin kissed Donald, then lifted him up onto his shoulders and walked across the yard to Scott and Mary, his face beaming as he embraced them both, and kissed Mary. 'What a boy! What parents! Makes me proud.' He bent down and put Donald back on the ground. 'I've got some presents in the car for you Donald. Let's go and find them.'

Mary's family emerged to join in the welcome – wave after wave of them – and the greeting segued into drinks in the communal area, where Martin gave Mary's family an abridged version of how they had all met and what he had been doing since university. Martin was a natural raconteur – like his father – and his stories spanned first drinks into dinner – a carryout from Pinnacle's Fish and Chip Emporium in Seahouses. Alan and Ian, Mary's sisters' husbands, were dispatched to pick up the meal and bring it back. Alan because he could count and Ian because he was the fastest driver.

The meal moved on to homemade desserts, then more drinks, with no real chance for Scott and Mary to talk to Martin, until nine o'clock, when Donald came over from the table he was sharing with his cousins, and climbed onto his father's lap. It was the sign he was finally exhausted and needed his bed. Scott cradled him in his arms and rose. 'Time to get the wee man to bed,' he said to the rest of the company. 'Say goodnight, son.'

Donald managed a half salute as Scott carried him around the family for farewell kisses. Mary and Martin got up as well, said their goodbyes and followed Scott out.

It only took a few minutes to put Donald to bed. He brushed his teeth, begged to be allowed to sleep in his Motherwell kit and fell asleep as soon as Martin and

Scott pulled the duvet over him. They kissed him goodnight and went downstairs to the open plan living room. Mary had already opened a bottle of Shiraz and poured two large glasses for the men and a soda water and lime for herself. She handed the wine over, 'You deserve it. Both of you. Coping with my family for that length of time – and entertaining them! They're a powerful group of people!'

'But great company,' Martin responded and held up his glass in a mock toast. 'You two look great – a living testimony to the power of marriage.' He shook his head. 'And Donald – what a boy. Makes me realise what I'm missing.' Scott let Mary get comfortable on the couch, then slipped in beside her. Martin sat down in the chair directly opposite.

'Do you know what this reminds me of?' he asked.

'No,' Mary said.

'The first time you cooked for Scott and me in the Sciennes Road flat. It was about a week after you moved in with Scott – we had been out for a few pints and came back to find the flat immaculately tidy and infused with the smell of food – beef stew and rhubarb crumble – fantastic! It was such a surprise to find that behind that ardent feminist façade, was a true homemaker – you must remember?'

Mary shook her head and smiled. 'I do – but what brought that back to mind now?'

Martin laughed. 'I think it was meeting your family tonight. It triggered the story you told us at the flat that night, when we tackled you about how you were such a good cook.'

Mary bit her lip and squeezed Scott's hand. 'Oh my God, I remember. I explained how my sisters used to come back to the house on a Sunday. The women, including my nan, would be in the kitchen cooking, baking and singing along to the radio. My dad took his sons-in-law to the pub, then came back to the house to watch the football. Jesus. I told you about the Sunday I lost it. I was probably 14 – and into women's liberation. I was already simmering with frustration about the women working and the men sitting on their arses when one of them, I can't remember who now – but it wasn't my dad, called through for more cans of beer. I lost it. I took in four cans and threw them down on the floor – had a long rant about how disgusting they all were, how chauvinistic and how unacceptable it was – then stormed off to my room.'

'My nan came up after 15 minutes – when I had gone from raging to feeling a bit silly and sat with me. She told me she understood how I felt but that my dad was a good man, a hardworking man who, when The Craig was closed, didn't give up. He went back on the tools to find work and keep us all – that meant being away from his family – on the rigs and sometimes in the Middle East, but he did it for us. My nan made me see it a bit differently – I cried, then I went down and gave Dad a kiss – told him I loved him – he cried as well and hugged me – then being Dad he said, "Now, get off your bum and bring your dad a can of Export".'

Scott raised his glass. 'I remember that now. I'm a very lucky man to have a wife like that. Cheers!'

Mary joined the toast. 'You are,' she laughed. 'And don't you forget it!'

Scott looked at Martin, 'Have you decided whether to go back to Sondrio?'

Martin took a slug of wine then put his glass on the floor. 'I don't know what I'm doing after the summer. Depends on so many things. But mainly where Katerina is. I can't decide until I know what's happened to her.'

Neither Scott nor Mary spoke.

'Sondrio was a mistake,' Martin continued. 'My dad's been trying to entice me into the business since I finished uni. He made the same pitch to Kevin, but Kev had his get-out-of-jail-free card ready – a First, a PhD then the youngest professor for 100 years at St Andrews. What have I got to show for my education – bumming around the world teaching English?'

'It hardly competes,' he sighed. 'I've enjoyed it, admittedly, but it's not long term. Which is why I chose Sondrio; it's quiet – you've been there Scott so you know just how sleepy. They take the pavements in at the weekend. Makes Motherwell on a wet Sunday morning look like Las Vegas. The perfect place to finish writing the great Scottish novel I've been going on about for years. Except, unlike you, Mary, I can't write!'

Mary shifted in her seat. 'No, you're not being fair to yourself, Martin. Daisy always said you had the most natural writing talent in her English class.'

Martin laughed. 'Ah, Daisy. The fair Daisy. Do you still keep in touch?'

Mary nodded. 'Yeah, we speak regularly on the phone. She's in London now, working as a senior copywriter at WPP. She always asks after you – still sees you as the one that got away.'

Martin exhaled slowly. 'Maybe… Anyway, I'm not going to make any commitment yet to go back to Italy. I need to find out about Kat.' He looked at Scott. 'Any progress?'

Scott got up and poured the remains of the bottle into their glasses to buy a little time, even though he knew he would have to confront the issues raised by the videos. He shook his head to try and clear it. They'd had two beers when Martin arrived, then white wine to compliment the fish suppers and finished with port chasers – Scott wasn't in practice for that sort of session and was feeling the effects. With anyone else, he would have made an excuse, been circumspect, but this was his best friend. He would be honest.

'Some,' he said, as he sat back down beside Mary, 'But it's still early stages. I'm sorry if I'm repeating myself but we can follow bits of her journey. She got a lift from Nairn to Fort William from an elderly couple, who were guests at the hotel and we can track her phone from there to Braehead on the outskirts of Glasgow, until it goes dead about 8:30 pm. We know she didn't board the flight to Barcelona, and we've looked at CCTV covering Prestwick Airport and its main car park. No sighting of her there, so the assumption is she never got to Prestwick. And she had made a number of calls and texts that Friday. Some we can link to you and her mum. We're following up on the rest and all the stuff we picked up at the hotel…' Scott tailed off.

'Is that it?' Martin asked.

Scott shrugged, but didn't answer.

Martin leaned forward, 'I know you, Scott. I know you so well. There's more. But you're worried about telling me. Don't be. I need to know.'

Scott looked at Mary, who took his hand and encouraged him to go on, 'What sort of relationship did you have with Kat?' he asked, after a pause.

Martin sat forward. 'What do you mean?'

'Well, was it an open one? Were you seeing other people?'

Martin laughed. 'You put it so politely. We never really discussed it. But I think we both assumed we could see others if we wanted to. I was still living off and on with Hannah in Sondrio. I don't know about Kat, whether she had anyone else. We hadn't got to that stage. It was a bit early to be exclusive, or at least I thought so.'

Scott breathed out. 'That makes it a little bit easier.'

'Makes what a bit easier?' Martin asked quickly.

Scott looked directly at him, 'OK, I'll level with you. We managed to access Kat's iPad. There are some very explicit videos on it. Four different men on film, having sex with Kat. And one was taken after you and Kat first met. On top of that, there are references to another two men in the notes section, which has what look like appraisals of six different individuals. One is MY – that's probably you.'

Martin finished his wine in one long swallow. 'Does that mean anything?' he said, his voice slightly slurred. He shook his head. 'Sorry, that was a daft question. What I meant was – does it have any bearing on her disappearance?'

Scott sat back on the settee – he felt very tired but didn't want to yawn. 'I don't know. But we need to follow it up and try to establish who the men are. Once we do that, the next stage will be to talk to them about her – see what that leads to. Plus, I've gone through Kat's bank statements and credit card bills. Two things stand out. One – she never drew cash from the account. And two – there are random amounts of cash paid in, sometimes quite large sums. I'd like to understand both sides – particularly the money being deposited.'

'Tips? Martin asked. 'Could it be tips saved up, then paid in in batches?'

Scott shook his head. 'I thought that initially but the tronc at Sunny Bay hasn't been distributed yet.'

'What else could it be? Not men paying her?' Martin said loudly.

'Don't know, but possible. Were you helping her?'

Martin reddened. 'I've never had to pay for sex,' he said quickly.

'I know that – sorry, that wasn't what I meant. No – I mean were you sending her money to help generally?'

'No Scott, I wasn't.' Martin slumped back in his chair. 'Christ, what a mess. Is there any other news?'

'Well, there's been no activity on her credit card or bank account since that Friday and she hasn't used her phone or got in contact with you, her mum or the hotel.'

Martin sighed noisily. 'That's not good, is it?'

Scott took his time before answering. He was exhausted and desperate to go to bed but needed to give one last honest answer, 'If I'm truthful, no. I'm keeping an eye open for any developments. If anything comes up, I'll let you know immediately. I'm checking with my team on a daily basis and I'm going to get specialist advice when I'm back at work. We'll do everything we can to track her down – I promise.'

Martin leaned forward. 'I've got a bit more info – Kat's mum texted the details of her cousin's phone number and where she's working and living – it came as I was driving down here – in the rush of meeting and dinner, I forgot to mention it.' Martin went to his jacket and took out his mobile phone, 'I'll send it now.'

Scott got up and patted his friend's shoulder. 'Thanks – that will help.'

Martin hugged him. 'Find her Scott, please find her.'

Part 6

"No amount of guilt can change the past
and no amount of worrying can change the future."

Umar Ibn Al-Khattaab

September 26th – 9:30 am

This is another opportunity to continue my story. The girls are at their drama classes in Glasgow – UK Theatre School in West Regent Street. Arlene drove them to town and is meeting one of her pals for an early pre-Christmas shopping expedition. She will pick the kids up at 4:30 pm, when they finish. The golf club will be quiet today as the weather is so bad. My assistants, Andrew and Sam, will cope without me, so I have most of the day to carry on my explanation of what happened, time to think back to what I did and set out the next part of the story in detail. I need to put myself back into the mindset I had that night – at the point, I decided not to report the death. The moment I chose to cover it up. I have to record what I did during the remainder of that Friday night and the next day – get that part down before my family comes back. It is crucial to my sanity to complete that section. It will not mark the beginning of the end of my journal, but it will cover the end of the beginning.

The overwhelming urge I had was to get the body as far away from the house as possible. I can feel that pressure again as I think back. Every time I focused on what to do with the body that night, the answer I came up with was to dispose of it somewhere else. But I knew it was dangerous to try and move her. Could I cope with driving a car with a dead body in the boot? And putting the body in the boot of Arlene's car would leave traces that might be difficult to remove, even if I wrapped it up in some sheets or risked using the golf bag carrier. I was stuck again – locked up by indecision.

Then, out of nowhere, it came to me. An answer. The grass mound on my golf course. I dump all the grass I cut from my 6-hole course in a pile at the mid-point of the fields. Next to the burn that flows through the farm. I could use that pile to hide the body – at least temporarily. It was counterintuitive. The disposal site was on our property, but it was a location under my control, and that meant that I wouldn't have to go out again. The grass mound was 20 ft square and at least 4 ft high; half a season's grass was collected there already. I could lift part of that heap, put her body at the bottom under a duvet of damp, warm grass. That would work, I told myself. I was so relieved that I had found a solution that I wanted to do it right away. But sense prevailed. I knew it would be stupid to try to move her onto the course in the dark. It would be much easier to take her out at first light, in a couple of hours. I could use the tractor to transfer her.

The grass stack isn't visible from the road or the farmhouse, it is only overlooked by adjacent farm fields, so it was unlikely that I would be seen. I felt relief as I reaffirmed my decision. I could stop worrying about being spotted as I tried to dump the body or being pulled over by a police car with Katerina in the boot. But I wanted to be sure that it wasn't completely mad, so I forced myself to analyse it again. If I became a suspect, and Katerina was somehow traced to the farm, the police would most likely search the house, outbuildings and possibly the fields. If they did, then the mound was an obvious place to examine. So, she might be found. And if she were, I would have lost any chance of being seen as innocent. No matter how I tried to explain what I had done and why, hiding the body would undermine any story I told. These were the main negatives I came up with. But burying her on the farm bought me time, meant I didn't have to go back out, and also that I didn't have to transport the body in Arlene's car, which was a huge plus. On balance, it seemed better than taking the body to a remote location.

I made the judgment call and went out to open the gates to the shed where the tractor is kept, and the five-bar gate to the paddock. Getting up and out was helpful. The physical activity made me feel I was doing something to help my situation. The nearest house to ours is over half a mile away, and I convinced myself that any noise I made was unlikely to be heard and the chance of being seen at five o'clock was minimal.

As I re-entered the house, I decided to deal with her mobile next. I put the phone and charger into a tea towel and took them to my workbench in the garage. I placed the towel on the hard wood top and crunched it with a lump hammer, time and again, until both my arms ached. I reduced them to a uniform, level mash. Then I went back inside to dump the pieces into a small plastic bag, which I buried at the bottom of our kitchen refuse bag. I would put the bag in our outside green bin when I had finished the clean-up. I went through to the lounge, put more logs on the fire to build it up again and chucked the tea towel on it. I looked at my watch. 2:30 am. I was still on schedule to get everything sorted by seven o'clock.

But what to do about the major problem I hadn't solved yet? The blue dress. I went back to the kitchen and picked it up. I held it. Smelt it repeatedly. Did it have traces of her perfume? Of our sex? I couldn't detect any odours, but it had to be impregnated with her scent. The label was dry clean only. What choices did I have?

I could burn it. But what story would I concoct about its disappearance? An alternative was to put it back in the pile unwashed but bury it deep down in the bundle. I could take the chance Arlene wouldn't look at it again before taking the clothes to the charity shop with the other discards. I decided that was too risky. Especially as I had spent most of my call with Arlene asking her to wear it to the event – and saying I had put it on top of the pile. No, it was worse than risky – it was insane. Doing that was guaranteed to raise questions. So, I elected to wash it on a gentle cycle, dry it in the boiler room then replace it in the spare room exactly where I had left it earlier that day. I calculated that I had just enough time to achieve that if I started immediately. I forced myself up and walked through to the laundry room, put it into the machine and chose the short programme at $30°$C. After starting the washing machine, I turned on the heating to fire the boiler and warm up the boiler room. The dress would be done in 20 minutes. I remember noting the time on my watch, then going upstairs to get a hanger for it and putting that in the boiler room in preparation.

I went into the living room when I finished. The fire was still burning fiercely; it was a couple of hours away from being cold enough to clean. As I sat there, I ran through a checklist in my head.

Kat's clothes and belongings – all burning or incinerated already, other than her cosmetics and wash bag – I had to decide what to do about them. I emptied the bag and threw it on the fire. Then I put the contents on, apart from the bottle of Tom Ford perfume and the jar of coconut oil. The new additions caused the blaze to intensify as they fed the flames. I would put the ashes from the fire out later and replenish the paper and kindling. I poured the perfume down the toilet bowl in the cloakroom, then scooped out the coconut oil with a sheet of toilet paper and disposed of it the same way – I plastered the pan with thick bleach and flushed it twice. I took the glass bottle and jar out to my workbench and went through the same process I had with the phone. It was easier to smash them up and I had soon reduced them to a smooth glass paste, which I collected in wet kitchen paper and put into the rubbish bin.

I completed my review as I paced between the living room, the kitchen, and the garage.

Car - Cleaned and would be valeted on Thursday.

House - Route through it retraced three times and wiped down. Our cleaner is in Tuesday.

Tractor - Garage door open, as well as the paddock gate.

Body - Move at first light. In just over an hour.

My clothes - I would strip after I moved the body – wash and dry my clothes and put them away before Arlene got back.

As I was ticking off the tasks, I remembered we had two Patricia Cornwall novels in the house which might have some information on decomposition. I got them from the bookshelf in our bedroom and skimmed through the first; not much information I could see on that cursory look. But the second had a four-page explanation of how bodies decay. That description confirmed that bodies do decompose faster in the open air than when buried, and that a warm, wet location is optimal for degradation to occur – a place where insects can get to the body easily. Two weeks would see the bulk of the flesh go in "perfect conditions". A buried body took much longer. But I was going to cover my body in grass – which would be warm, humid and penetrable. I found myself thinking "good choice" and almost being sick again when I realised what I was congratulating myself for.

When I got over gagging, I instructed myself to get back to my To Do list. I checked my watch. The dress was washed, and I took it out of the machine then hung it up to dry in the boiler room. It was 4:00 am by then – nearly first light. I told myself – do it now. Move the body now.

That was the hardest part. I traipsed upstairs to the spare bathroom and stood over her. I can remember how I felt as I stared at her. She looked so diminished. It was impossible to visualise her as the woman who had excited me, the girl who had made me want her so much sexually that I had committed adultery. I don't know how long I stayed like that but eventually I picked her up. She was still damp, even though the central heating was now pumping warm air through the house. I put her over my shoulder without too much difficulty and carried her out to the garage, being careful not to let any part of her body touch the walls or doors on the way. She was noticeably stiffer – not completely rigid but well on the way. If I had left it much longer, I would have had a problem bending her.

I propped her up on the tractor seat and climbed in beside her. The tractor started first time and I edged my way out into the back yard, keeping her in place with my left hand. I crept the tractor down to the paddock and only increased my speed a little when I got onto the course. I scanned the next-door fields in the pre-light. No one that I could see – not even animals. The sun was just starting to clear the early mist as we moved along the first fairway. It was going to be a lovely day – but not for her or me. It took under a minute to get to the burial ground. I checked the surroundings again. Empty, completely empty.

I parked, jumped down and rested her across my seat. I picked up the pitchfork I keep at the edge of the grass cuttings, then walked slowly into the centre of the mound. The grass was damp from the heavy rain the night before and strong smelling at that time of the day. A smell I had grown familiar with over the last 40 years. An odour I can almost taste now as I recall how I felt that morning. The canopy was cloying and so heavy that it wasn't easy to clear a decent-sized rectangle down to ground zero. I began to sweat as I swung the grass to one side. I paused when I had made a grave, roughly 6 ft by 3 ft, then went back to the tractor and lugged Katerina into the clearing.

I placed her on the floor, then paused and stood over the body. As I did, I saw her again in my mind – how she looked as she took off her parka and then in the kitchen, wearing Arlene's dress. Full of sexuality. Full of life. That life ended by me. I started to cry – no, it was far more than cry – I sobbed. I don't know how long I was like that, but I became aware of the sun warming my face. I'm not religious, so I didn't attempt a prayer, but I did bend down and whisper, 'I'm sorry.'

I turned her over, so she was lying face down. I don't know why but I couldn't throw the grass on her whilst she was on her back. Covering her took less time than digging out a grave and I did it without a break. When I had finished, I tested how secure the grass lid to her coffin was, even though I knew that from my earlier exertions it would hold its position. The whole structure was heavily weighted, and it would need a high wind, coupled with very dry conditions to expose her. When I next cut the fairways and greens, I would add more grass to the mound above her to provide extra ballast. And would continue to do so during the rest of the summer and autumn. As I stood at the side of her grave, I told myself that I had done all I could to hide the body that day and for the next few weeks. I could review my next move later, but for now I was done.

I convinced myself that Katerina would never be found if I kept to my plan and didn't panic. I told myself that I had made the correct choice.

I murmured "sorry" again before I got back on the tractor. I looked through 360 degrees as I drove towards the garage. There was no one in sight. I returned the tractor to its bay, hosed down the seat and wiped it with the towel I had brought out with me. I lectured myself that it was another hole played in par in my golfing comparison. I was down to the closing stretch. I was in good shape and mumbled to myself, 'Don't make a mistake. Keep in the zone,' as I locked up the outbuilding.

I left the towel in the laundry to put in with my clothes, then went to inspect the fire, which had finally died out and was cool enough to work with. As I expected, there were blue and white marks on the grate from the rucksack and trainers. It took five minutes of intense scrubbing with a Brillo Pad to remove them. I took the ashes outside in the pan, covered by a large bin bag to prevent any spillage in the house, but decided not to put them in the green, general refuse bin, which sits at the back of the garage. They were still warm and I was worried they might burn through their container so I took them to the far end of the paddock which runs alongside the first hole – the most exposed part of the farm – and dumped them there. I picked up the detritus of smaller plastic parts from the rucksack and trainers and metal zips from her clothes and shoes and put them into a Tesco's bag I had stuffed in my pocket. That was safer than leaving them in the field, where there was just a chance they might be spotted. The remaining ashes would disperse by the end of the day. They were starting to move already in the very slight breeze. Arlene wouldn't come out here when she got home – neither would the kids – and I could check that all of the residue had gone on Sunday. I gave the ashes a couple of kicks to help spread them and went back to dump the bag – again at the bottom of the bin. The green general refuse bins are collected every Thursday and would be emptied in five days. I made a mental note to check the bin for a final time when I had finished all the other tasks.

I took off my shoes and clothes in the laundry and wandered around the house in my underpants for a final review. Had I done everything? No! I realised that I hadn't replaced the papers and kindling at the fireplace. Getting fresh wood was easy, there was ample in the garage, but I realised that I had only the current version of *The Times* to put back in the paper rack. Would Arlene notice? I closed my eyes for a moment and breathed deeply. I should have used that paper to light the fire – not the old stuff – but it was too late now. I had to finish my other jobs.

We wouldn't be putting on a fire for months. It would be fine. I told myself I was worrying needlessly.

I pulled off my underwear, put my clothes on a short-cycle wash and then went into the boiler room to switch off the heating and check the blue dress. It was dry and looked OK when I picked it up, but as I inspected it more closely, I could see some bobbles on the back. Small, but noticeable. A mistake. I remember swearing – almost shouting the words, but again, there was nothing to do but put it back on top of the pile of clothes in the spare room and hope Arlene didn't spot the imperfections.

I cursed myself about that as I walked along to our room and slid into the shower. I have never spent so long scrubbing my body and hands. When I felt "clean", I moved the handle, too cold to punish myself some more. I held it there for as long as I could take. I changed into a set of golf clothes and picked out a suit, shirt, tie and shoes for the formal dinner. Could I eat breakfast? It was 6:00 am. I would be expected to join in the bacon roll and square sausage feast at the course, but I felt I needed something before that. I hadn't eaten since five o'clock on Friday afternoon, so I had two Weetabix with raisins and milk and a cup of tea. I put the bowl and cup into the dishwasher. Like normal. I was scared that Arlene might pick up on the difference if I didn't tidy up and left them out unwashed. My paranoia was in full flight – heightened by the issues with the dress.

I forced myself to sit down to think before I left. Katerina had said her flight was at 6:30 am. Was she travelling with anyone? Was anyone waiting for her in Barcelona? How soon would she be missed? I thought she said she was meeting her boyfriend there. What would he do when she didn't turn up? It could be days or weeks before any questions were asked about where she was. By then, the bins should have been emptied, the house cleaned, Arlene's car valeted and the blue dress would be at the charity shop. I distinctly remember feeling a bit better at that point, but almost immediately worrying about how soon the police would become involved and how suspicious her disappearance would seem. I told myself that I had to stop asking questions about that. I had done all I could. I had to face up to my golf day. My staff, my team… Then Arlene at night. The most difficult part. I had to cope with the choice that I had made, not second-guess my actions. I had to concentrate on getting through the next 18 hours. I tried to keep that thought at the front of my mind as I did a final check of the courtyard, bins and the rooms we had occupied before I set the alarm and got into Arlene's car.

I set out for the course feeling… What? Even now, it's hard to find the words to describe my mental state. Numbness because of the fear? Relief that, up to that point, I had managed to cope with what I had done? I can only revert to my golf analogy again; I had finished the first round, was back in the clubhouse and I hadn't ruined my card. So, I was still in contention. But even as I tried to comfort myself with that thought, I was hit by a twin wave of exhaustion and grief as I drove up to the gates at the top of the drive. I had to stop. I put my hands on the steering wheel and rested my head on them, took a moment and told myself I had to keep going. Persuaded myself that the worst was over. I remember banging my head gently onto my hands – then pulling away and repeating over and over that I had to keep the same routine – do nothing unusual. My first stop was at Kirkland newsagents in Symington to pick up my copy of *The Times* and chat about the weather. I behaved like Mr Normal. That was who I had to be that day. Nobody could be allowed an insight into how I was feeling beneath that outward projection of business as usual.

I managed to carry that off in the paper shop, but I was feeling very fragile when I arrived at the course. My assistant pros were already there, helping to carry the goody bags from the shop to the main lounge. I put on the motley and high-fived them. Both were skippering a team and were desperate to score better than me! It was a big day for all of us. I kept the banter going about whether they had any chance of beating me. I'm not naturally gregarious. I was quiet as a kid and a student – quite happy with my own company and thoughts. But Arlene and the girls have helped to draw me out. As has presenting on Sky. And thinking back, that's what I did that morning. I presented. I acted the role of the host pro. Untroubled. In charge. That was my character for the day.

I took a moment to compose myself after that initial exchange. I walked over to the first tee and forced myself to stare at the course and sea. The weather was beautiful and that helped to lift me. It was the complete opposite of the night before. Warm and sunny, with a hint of wind: a combination which would create perfect playing conditions and an easy discussion topic with everyone. A number of deep breaths helped to settle me, then I kept myself occupied with a last-minute inspection of the practice area. I bumped into Dave Butler, who confirmed the greens had just been cut and were in perfect shape. Every time I caught myself thinking about the previous night, I countered it by telling myself I was in a different world that morning. The dark nightmare was over. I tried to convince myself that the death hadn't really happened, that it had been a bad dream and that I was now awake, and these were the sunlit uplands.

The members' lounge was set up for breakfast registration, goody bag handouts and my briefing on the complex format we were playing. I was there at 9:30 am, when the first of the teams started to filter in. Meeting and greeting are vital to the success of the day. Making all the competitors feel important is a must do. I know all the pros and a lot of the amateurs. I refresh my memory of them when I get the entries. A number play each year and I generally remember enough on the day to get through a 60-second chat.

Brian Young, whom I have known longest, turned up early and I couldn't avoid spending time with him and his team. He was well and business was good, he told me. Neither of his boys were playing – they were both out of the country. Brian was his usual ebullient self – the consummate salesman. I just had to reflect that enthusiasm back to cope – which I managed. He apologised for cancelling our meal the night before – said he was exhausted after playing Barassie and wanted an early night. I had forgotten about that in my earlier description of what happened on Friday afternoon and evening. How could I have? I usually have dinner with Brian the night before the event. Sometimes with Arlene – sometimes with Brian's sons if they are playing in the competition. We had set up dinner at Piersland House. Brian had texted me to call off just after Arlene phoned to say her mum had been taken to the hospital. Is that relevant? I didn't think so then but… he phoned me yesterday and asked to meet me to discuss that weekend. What does he know? That will be very difficult, but I can't think about it now. I have to keep to the narrative of the day of my golf event. I need to respect the timelines and cover Brian's part of the story later.

I grabbed a bacon roll and managed to keep that and a cup of sweet tea down as I chatted to him. After all the teams had checked in, I gave the rules presentation and when questions were over, I took my team to the practice area. That was about 45 minutes before the shotgun start at 11:30 am. A limited period just before playing is not well suited to detailed coaching. The best thing to do is instil confidence – tell the team members that their swings look good. It is vital to emphasise the need to keep a regular tempo and not quicken. I also look at them to correct any obvious alignment issues. I did all of that and hit a few looseners myself. We all trooped to the putting green after my short tutorial. Putting is the most important part of the game. One that most amateurs don't practise enough. I spent what time we had left on their setups and tried to get them into a pendulum swing and rhythm. And it seemed to work. My team were on fire on the first nine holes. They used their handicaps sensibly, and more importantly, holed everything. We got to the turn eight under par net. I played steadily but was going through the motions during the first half. I still felt traumatised. Thankfully, the muscle memory of having played golf all my life took over and I came into my A game on the tenth. I managed to shut out the death and focus on the course. I played the back nine as well as I've ever done. Five under gross on my own. I lost myself in the mechanics of hitting the ball and the momentum of captaining a winning team. We finished with 65 Stableford points, which – in the scoring system I had created – was a walkover. I showered, dressed and went to the lounge for a celebratory pint with my team, all the while trying to keep my mind solely on what I needed to do to get through the event dinner.

Arlene had texted me to let me know she had arrived. She was already circulating when I got there – charming the men as she always does – but *not* wearing the blue dress. She was with Brian Young and his team as I came in. She spotted me, excused herself and walked over. She put her arms round me and gave me a kiss. I can recall the moment exactly.

I pulled her into me and hugged her. 'How's Mum?' I asked.

She clasped me in return. 'Fine – complaining that she can't get on with the housework.'

'That means she's on the mend.'

Arlene smiled as she drew back, 'I hear you won by a country mile!'

I bowed but didn't reply.

'Was that wise?' she continued, 'winning your own event so easily?'

Suddenly, and I don't know why, I felt better. Was it because I knew she was so worth protecting? Because the surroundings were so familiar? Because I was where I belonged? I remember laughing and saying, 'Class will out.'

She giggled, squeezed my arm, and returned to her duties as hostess. Having Arlene there made the night easier, and I coped with the speeches, prize-giving and the mass "booing" when we went up to collect our trophy from Arlene. One of my team, Ted Richards, a partner in an Ayrshire-based accountancy firm, asked if he could say a few words. He was very drunk, almost swaying as he got to his feet and held up his hands for quiet. I can recollect what he said word for word.

'Thank you. I'm not a great golfer. But today for me and my team, it all came right. I've never won a big competition before. I know some of you feel it isn't right for the local pro's team to lift the prize. For anybody who thinks that,' he paused for a few seconds, 'get it right, fucking up you!'

Which received a standing ovation. And I laughed, really laughed.

Arlene left after we had been through the charity auction at the end of the dinner. She gave me a lingering kiss which said, "Don't be too late". But I had to stay, work the tables, and get commitments for next year, even if they were drunken pledges. I didn't get a taxi until about 2:30 am and wasn't home much before three o'clock. I crept into the girls' rooms to look at them sleeping and then padded into our bedroom.

My bedside lamp was on, but muted. Arlene was asleep on top of the bed…wearing the blue dress and high heels! I still don't know how I coped. I must have stood frozen for minutes, but eventually I went to our en suite to clean my teeth and douse my face in cold water to stop myself being sick. I managed that – just – but I couldn't stop myself from inspecting the bath for signs of anything I had missed. I undressed and attempted to slip into the bed without disturbing Arlene. I failed. She stirred and became aware of me. Snuggling in, she breathed in my ear, 'Special treat for the winner.'

I felt paralysed as I realised what she had said – transfixed – terrified to move. I couldn't make love – I have never felt less like having sex. I pretended to be asleep and after a couple of attempts to rouse me, Arlene got up, stripped off the dress and crept into bed beside me.

I still felt exhausted when I woke on Sunday morning as I had only managed to doze for a few hours. Arlene and the kids were already up and assumed my tiredness was the result of my exertions on the course and drinking to excess at the event. I was treated to breakfast in bed. That was something Anna and Cathy did for me when I was on the tour. On my first morning back, they would make me scrambled egg on toast and bring it up to me on a tray with a mug of tea. It was all so ordinary. If I had been on my own there is no doubt that I would have confirmed the cliché of the criminal returning to the scene of the crime. I would have gone out to the grass cuttings to see if they were still intact. I would have poked and prodded them to make sure. Luckily, I wasn't alone. I had my family to keep me from stumbling into that misery. Instead, I showered, got dressed and was given the luxury of half an hour with the Sunday papers, undisturbed. I looked at the sports section in *The Times*. I turned the pages, looked at the words – didn't take in any of them.

The tradition on the day after the competition is for the players to meet again at the club for a carvery lunch. Virtually all the teams stay over after the event, which, given the volume of alcohol consumed, is sensible and means they come back for the midday meal. I was the host again, so we trooped down to Gailes as a family at midday on another bright warm day. I managed to eat something and got through the lunch, helped by residual chat about the result and my victory. I lobbied again about the following year, and after most of the teams had eaten and gone, we decided to go for a walk along the coastal path which runs parallel to the 7th to 14th holes. Having been brought up in North Berwick, I think the view from the second tee on the West Course is the finest links panorama in the world, but Gailes runs it close, particularly on a fine day when Arran and Ailsa Craig are visible.

The walk helped me stay collected, at first. I was enjoying listening to the girls chattering as Arlene held my hand. After a couple of holes, she restrained me and let the kids get a little further ahead so we could talk without them hearing. My internal dialogue, as we strolled along the walkway, told me that I had done the right thing. I had acted to safeguard my family. The death had been an accident and once it had happened there was nothing, I could do to make things better. I didn't think about Katerina's family or friends. I gave no consideration to what they would have to go through in the coming weeks. I was focused exclusively on my own situation and whether I had done everything I could to eliminate any link between her and me. That was my only concern that afternoon.

I was daydreaming, more accurately "nightmaring" about that when Arlene stopped. She pulled my head down to hers and giggled. I can still hear every word.

'I'd hoped the blue dress would have its usual effect on you last night. That's the first time you haven't risen to the occasion when I've worn it!'

I tried not to react, apart from attempting to smile as she pressed her body against me for a second and then drew back. 'I'm sorry. I was so wiped out from the event that I fell asleep as soon as my head hit the pillow.'

Arlene squeezed my hand, 'You're forgiven. I guess I'll keep it and give you another chance to show me what you're made of. But I'll need to get it cleaned properly. It's a bit uneven at the back. Bobbly. I hadn't noticed that before. Dry cleaning might rescue it. Hope so.'

It took every part of my mental strength not to react. To keep calm, to behave normally. I'm still not sure how I did it.

I've been stuck at this page for half an hour now, unable to write any more, and Arlene and the girls will be back soon. Did that innocent remark kickstart the next stage in my deterioration? If Arlene hadn't mentioned the dress, hadn't said those words, would I be closer to forgetting it? No! Not forgetting it – I'll never be able to do that. But would I be nearer to putting it in the past and being able to enjoy some sort of family life? I'm not sure. But I do know I got worse from that moment.

Part 7

"The world is full of obvious things which nobody ever observes."

Sir Arthur Conan Doyle

Chapter 8
August 15ᵗʰ

Martin stayed for the weekend and left after lunch on Monday. He and Scott talked about the sex videos and what could have happened to Katerina a number of times after Friday night – but with no new information available on the Saturday or Sunday the discussion covered the same ground. Scott felt frustrated that he was unable to add anything to what was already known about Kat's disappearance and had to fall back on the promise that his team knew how important this was to him and were on it even though he was on holiday.

Scott kept in touch with his colleagues by email each day either early in the morning before the family woke up or later at night when Donald was in bed. Up to the second Tuesday, there was little information flow, but when Scott gave himself permission to check his iPad that night, there were two follow-up notes which did advance the enquiry.

The first was an email from DCI Johnston which had been sent to the team at 4:50 pm that afternoon. In it, Johnston apologised for the delay in responding to Scott's note and explained that he had just returned from his own holiday. The main part of his reply was devoted to examining how to stimulate a public response to the disappearance. He suggested an appeal in the local press in any towns that could have been part of the route from Paisley to Prestwick as well as *The Glasgow Herald*. He favoured starting with the *Paisley Daily Express* and *The Gazette* – covering Johnstone and Renfrewshire, the *Irvine Times*, and moving south to the *Ayr Advertiser* and the *Troon & Prestwick Times*. Johnston's view was that as Katerina was extremely attractive, this would help sell the story. He was sure the papers would run with her picture and a request for help from the readers. He offered his press officer to help place the report and to try to get it covered as an item on the BBC's *Reporting Scotland*. Jim Turner had accepted on Scott's behalf and the email trail ended with Johnston, saying he would get it done for the weekend editions and that he was looking forward to linking up with Scott the following week. Scott copied back his thanks and that he also was keen to meet up.

The second email had been sent later, at just after 7 pm, by Julia McDonald. The note outlined what she had found out about Continental Shelf 3179 – the registered owner of the phone which Kat had been in touch with most on the Friday she vanished. CS3179 was a subsidiary of Crammond Holdings Ltd. CS3179 was noted as a small company at Companies House – required to file only abbreviated accounts with little detail in them. But Crammond Holdings was a multimillion-pound business, whose directors and shareholders were the Youngs – Brian and his wife Sue, and their sons, Kevin and Martin. Scott had to read the latter part of the note a couple of times before he could take it in fully and allow himself to follow through the implications. It was a major development, perhaps the most important since the enquiry began, and showed another significant connection between Katerina and Martin's family. The regular contact between that company phone and Kat's on the afternoon she disappeared was hugely significant and could be the key to establishing where Katerina was, or what had happened to her.

Scott's first thought was that Martin might have a second mobile – paid for by his dad's company – and that Kat's calls to that number were to Martin. But he dismissed the idea immediately. That explanation made no sense – Martin would have mentioned it and said that he had been in touch with Katerina on that phone the day she disappeared. So that couldn't be the answer; it didn't fit the fact pattern. It was much more likely that it was another member of the Young family who had use of a company phone and it was that person who had been in touch with Kat the day she vanished. The final part of the note supported that view. Julia had also checked the location information for the phones that had been in contact with Katerina that day. The CS3179 phone started the Friday in Balerno in Edinburgh, then moved to Ayrshire along the A70. It was pinpointed to Barassie in the afternoon, then Troon in the evening. GPS showed travel between Troon and Irvine on Saturday, then the phone was switched off until Sunday night, when it reappeared in Edinburgh, specifically, in the Balerno district in West Edinburgh and into Pentland Avenue. Scott knew Martin's mum and dad lived in that street in the same house Scott had stayed at when he and Martin were students. The phone must belong to Martin's dad, mother or brother. There was no other logical explanation for what they now understood of the call history that weekend. Scott knew that Martin's brother Kevin lived in St Andrews, so he could probably be ruled out – which left Martin's mum and dad. Of the two, Martin's dad was the more likely to be the phone's owner and to be involved with Katerina.

Scott was keen to reply to Julia's final questions about what she should do next with the new information but knew that it would be a mistake to do it immediately. He wanted to talk to Mary about it and work through the consequences of what Julia had unearthed. Which he did for almost half an hour in bed as Mary was tired and wanted an early night. They didn't reach any firm conclusions but came up with a number of possible explanations for the calls. They did agree that Martin needed to know about this new link to Katerina – but not right away.

Scott responded to the email the next morning – but only internally. He couldn't let Martin have this new information until he had cleared the lines with his team and boss. He sent a short note to Turner and Johnston, asking for advice on how to take the case forwards, given that the extra connection between Scott and the Young family was now impossible to ignore. Scott reported that he and Mary knew Martin's father Brian and brother Kevin. He listed the occasions he had met them as far as he could remember. In particular, the times he had stayed at Brian's home in Balerno, when he and Martin were students, and the occasion he and Mary were guests there on their return from doing voluntary work in Malawi, a few weeks before Scott joined the police force. He finished by asking whether, given those connections, he should stand down from the enquiry to avoid any real or perceived conflict of interests. He sent his email at 8:15 am and spent most of the rest of the day on a family picnic at an old watermill and bakery, 15 miles inland from Seahouses.

He couldn't help checking his iPad as soon as they got back. There was a response from Johnston saying that he had conferred with Turner, confirming that Scott had done the right thing by asking the question about whether he should continue to lead the enquiry but saying it was too early to reach a final decision and that he would talk to Scott about it when they met. The final part of the note was a request not to discuss what had been found with Martin, until Johnston and Scott had met.

Scott talked it through again with Mary that night when they were on their own. They managed to construct a non-threatening scenario about what had happened – Kat had been in touch with a member of Martin's family that day, probably his father – but the purpose was to discuss Martin. They came up with a number of possible reasons why that might have happened before they went to sleep, the most specific being that Kat was planning a birthday surprise for Martin, who was thirty in September, and was liaising with his family about it. The calls were part of that planning. But in the light of day, Scott knew that supposition needed to be tested. The unanswered question was whether he should be the officer doing it – or someone with no connection to the family.

Scott had always been very good at compartmentalising his job and home life, and that helped him prevent the new information and the dilemma it created, casting a shadow on the rest of the holiday. The fact that virtually every minute was packed with activities also stopped too much introspection. Scott received one more detailed email on the Friday of their second week. It was from Julia and contained a note of her conversation with Katerina's cousin. Julia had managed to contact her using the number Martin had passed on from Kat's mum. The cousin was concerned. She and Kat spoke regularly and had run through some marketing ideas for Kat's bed and breakfast concept just before Kat left for Spain. Katerina promised to get in touch to discuss them in more detail on her return but hadn't phoned. It was another tick in the "something serious has happened to Katerina" box.

The email reminded Scott of the other issue he had to address when he got back – how to deal with Julia. He wanted Mary's counsel and waited until Donald was sound asleep and Mary was settled on the sofa with her legs up on the matching chair.

He opened his can of beer and sat down beside her, 'I need some advice.'

'On Martin?'

'No, something else,' he paused.

Mary smiled. 'OK – what?'

'It's work.' He hesitated again. 'A bit of an issue with Julia McDonald.'

'That's a surprise – I thought you rated her.'

Scott shook his head. 'I do – it's not her ability – it's the way she dresses.'

Mary sat up. 'What about it?'

'Turner is concerned that she dresses too sexily – he feels it's a distraction for the rest of the team.'

'Too sexily,' Mary said slowly.

'In his view.' Scott took a gulp from his can.

'What is your view?'

'I don't notice,' Scott said quickly.

'Don't notice?'

'No, I don't see her as a woman – I see her as a colleague.'

'A sexy one?'

'No—'

'Come on, Scott, she's very attractive. That night out when I first met her – the incredibly clingy dress she was wearing – she's hot.'

Scott paused. This wasn't going the way he had hoped. 'OK, she's not ugly – but that's not the point.'

'I think it's part of it,' Mary laughed.

'Right – but what do I say to her?'

'So, you admit she's not ugly – do you think she's attractive?'

'Not compared to you.'

'What?' Mary said, outlining her stomach with both her hands. 'I'm much bigger than I was with Donald. By Christmas, the Japanese whaling fleet will be sighted sailing up the Clyde with their harpoons set to fire. I'll be Fat Nan the Boxer.'

Scott burst out laughing. 'Fat Nan the Boxer?'

Mary laughed with him. 'Something my gran used to say – don't know why that came back to me now.' She took a deep breath. 'OK, I'm better now. Rush of jealousy over but I'm not going to waste any time thinking about her or about this so-called dilemma. It's simple. Just tell her to stop dressing like a slut. Tell her to man up!'

Scott sat back. 'Wouldn't that be seen as sexist?'

'Scott, I'm an expanding pregnant woman who's being asked to think about your glamorous assistant – I don't give a flying... I don't care about the sisterhood. Just tell her to do it!'

'OK, I will.'

That short interlude was the only wrinkle in the remainder of their holiday. They left mid-afternoon on the Sunday with the rest of the family, all of them heeding Scott's advice that they shouldn't drive in the morning after an extremely raucous and drunken last night. The highlight had been charades – men versus women – and Scott's attempt to mime *Last Night a DJ Saved My Life* created a special memory for everyone who witnessed it.

He had booked the Monday off as a final day's leave to help his dad redecorate the spare room that the new baby would sleep in when it stayed with its grandparents, but the first part of the morning was kidnapped by the announcement that the Chief Constable of Police Scotland had been suspended. Scott heard about it on the eight o'clock Scottish news, and then had calls from most of his friends in the force, either speculating about the reason or asking if he knew anything. The general consensus was that the main accusation against the chief constable was of bullying – with what sounded like a subsidiary charge of being English levelled at him as well. Scott knew that police work was fuelled by tea, biscuits, cakes and gossip. And the greatest of these, gossip, was in full flight. He arrived back in the station on Tuesday morning and got the latest information on the suspension. It took half an hour to shake himself free and make space for a debrief from Julia on the investigation.

Julia was bursting to bring him up to date. She had deposited her notes and two cups of tea on his desk and was pacing his room.

He grinned at her. 'It must be good – on you go.'

She smiled back at him. 'I went back up to Nairn yesterday and managed to do three things.'

He nodded. 'What?'

'The first was a more extensive search of Kat's room – I found a small leather satchel in her wardrobe – it was behind some shoe boxes – out of sight unless you moved them.'

Scott sighed, 'That doesn't make me feel any better – I missed that first time.'

Julia stopped pacing and sat down. 'So, would I have done if I hadn't taken the boxes out.'

'Thanks.'

'Anyway, there was a bundle of papers in the satchel – forms from Companies House, a bank statement for June and some financial projections for a business called Home From Home. The company name is HFH Ltd – changed from Continental Shelf 5111 Ltd. The documents show two shareholders, Katerina – 990 shares out of the 1000 issued, the other 10 are owned by Crammond Holdings.' Julia sat back and opened up her file.

Scott drew the paperwork towards him, and skim read it. 'Brian Young's company?'

'Yes, and it's invested in Katerina's.'

'How much in the bank account?'

'£5000 – paid on June 28th by bank transfer – I'm on to the bank to get details of the payer, but I'll have a fiver it's Crammond.'

140

'So would I – well done, Julia – get it logged.'

'I will, sir.'

'You said three things?'

'Yes, I interviewed Smedley again. He had spoken to his ex-member of staff, Jeannie Seaton, and he did a bit more digging about Kat with her. Turns out there has been gossip at the Balmoral about her and one of the guests – a night together, it was suggested.'

'Good work – the plot thickens, to coin a cliché!'

'Yes, Scott. The game's afoot. Especially as I think I might have a link from the notes section to some of the men – the third shoe!'

'Go on?'

'Well, the initials MY appear in the notes on the April 23rd, the day after Martin Young left the hotel. The day after they got together. And BY appears two days after Kat was at the family home. Brian Young?'

Scott nodded, 'That's excellent work, Julia, get it all logged. I'm seeing DCI Johnston at lunchtime. I'll talk it through with him.'

His meeting with Johnston was arranged for 12 o'clock at Bellahouston Police Station. Scott arrived well before the designated time and was happy to wait, but Johnston came down to pick him up as soon as the desk sergeant rang through. Johnston was tall and skinny, with grey cropped hair – unnaturally thin for a long-serving police officer, where time in the job usually correlated directly to weight gain. He held out his hand, 'DI James? A pleasure to meet the man revolutionising policing in Scotland.'

Johnston was smiling. Scott could tell the joke wasn't meant maliciously. He grinned and gripped Johnston's hand. Not a Masonic shake, he was pleased to note. 'It's good to be appreciated, sir. Nice to meet you as well – but it's just Scott, sir.'

Johnston motioned towards the stairs behind the main desk. 'Likewise. Alan. Not Sir. Come away through. My room's at the end of the second floor.'

Scott followed Johnston up a broad stairway, then along a corridor into a large, sparsely furnished room with an outlook across Paisley Road West and Bellahouston Park. He halted at the main window. 'Great view.'

Johnston smiled. 'One of the perks of rank, well, one of the few I exploit. But I do love natural light when I'm working... Drink?'

'Tea would be great, thanks.'

'Milk? Sugar? How strong?

141

'Just milk. Strongish, please.'

Johnston gestured towards a soft, old-looking seat by the side of the only desk in the room and popped outside. He returned a few minutes later with a cup of coffee for himself, a mug of tea for Scott and produced a small plate of custard creams from the back of his desk.

'Jim speaks highly of you, Scott. He has done for a while. I've read your reports and I can see why. They're logical, solid – no flights of fancy. Just the facts and good questions.'

Scott could feel himself start to redden and lifted his right hand to his face. 'Thanks. Jim speaks even more highly of you, sir. Two constant themes. Best boss he ever had. Best detective he ever worked with.'

Johnston laughed loudly. 'And?'

'And?'

'And... What else did he say about me? Opinionated? Left-wing? Lazy? Could do more?'

Scott shook his head. 'None of the above, sir! He mentioned that you've had a number of chances at further promotion but never went for it. He said that you're happy with what you do and that you enjoy it. And that you have a full social life outside the force, so a good balance.'

Johnston drained his coffee, put down his cup and rubbed his forehead with his hand. 'He's right. I am happy. I'm left alone – as much as anyone can be in today's force – so I get on with it. I don't create waves anymore, like I did 20 years ago. I was an arrogant bastard then. A self-educated working-class boy, keen to point out how clever I was and contrast that with how little my bosses knew. I've grown up since then. I'm a better copper for that. More rounded. I get what I need done much more easily now,' Johnston laughed. 'A rebel with a cause!' He paused and gnawed his bottom lip. 'Anyway, your case.'

Scott leaned forward in his seat. 'Jim was sure you could help me try to work out what's happened. I have so many questions. Is Katerina just missing? Or harmed and missing? I'm not certain what to do next. Should I pass it on? Am I conflicted because of my friendship with Martin and my connections with his family? Should I continue the enquiry myself given the latest information – the link to Crammond? But if it is worst-case and this is a homicide, I've never worked one before. In fact, I've rarely worked a major incident.' Scott shrugged his shoulders and opened his hands. 'What should I do? What would you do in my place?'

Johnston mirrored Scott's movement and shifted towards him. 'I can see why Jim rates you. Honest. And want the best answer. I've been through the updated review Julia McDonald sent yesterday and this morning. A couple of times. She's done well – a couple of interesting suggestions about connecting dates. So, let's examine where we are. Let's think about what might have happened. Give me your gut feel.'

Scott inched back in the chair and hesitated before answering, 'I'm sorry but I don't have one. Gut isn't my style. I'm much more about facts, logic, questions. I tend to approach cases like playing a hand in bridge. What information do I have? How does that information shape what I do? Can I find out more facts before I make any key decisions? Is that a failing in this sort of case?'

Johnston smiled. 'No, it's good. Well, in my opinion it is. I'd go further. The most dangerous thing in policing is gut feel. Let me qualify that – the wrong sort of gut feel. There are two varieties. The first is valid. A perfect example is interviewing a suspect. Do you believe them? That's when instinct is helpful. How do you feel about what they are telling you? Millions of years of evolution have made us good at that. If you can tap into that sense, that's a positive.' Johnston paused. 'But the second kind is harmful – prejudging the issues before all the facts are established. More cases go wrong because of that than for any other reason. But coppers tend to default to that position, especially the longer serving ones. The failures come in two flavours: Vanilla, "nothing to see here – move on please", where enquiries never get started or are aborted too soon. And Chocolate, "let's cut through the bullshit – get to the guts", which means they tend to ignore any evidence that doesn't support their interpretation and give undue weight to any facts that do. There's a clever name for that type of behaviour but I can never remember it.'

Scott knew that Johnston hadn't forgotten. This was another subtle test, 'Is it cognitive bias?'

Johnston smiled. 'Yes. That's it. Thanks.'

There was a rap at the door and a short, thickset man barrelled into the room and took up the space between the chairs. The newcomer looked at Johnston, 'We have a distinguished guest, I understand.'

Johnston levered himself up from his chair. 'DI James. Meet my boss, DSI Mull.'

Scott also got up and shook hands with Mull. 'Pleased to meet you, sir. Are you joining us?'

Mull shook his head vigorously. 'No. Just in to say hello. I'd only get in the way. You've got the best detective in Scotland here. Don't want the worst one involved as well.'

Scott was disconcerted by Mull's statement and wasn't sure how to respond. He chose diplomacy, 'I'm sure you're not, sir. But I am certain DCI Johnston can teach me a lot.'

Mull smiled and rested his hands on the back of Johnston's chair. 'Good. I like to see that sort of cooperation. Learning from each other. Liked your note on post case reviews. That was clever. We need bright folk in the force, not numpties like me. We have to build up a squad of intelligent policemen to keep the bastard politicians at bay. We need people who can try and anticipate their next moves and block them from fucking us about – like cutting our funding, then blaming us for the rise in crime. Keep it up, DI James. Look in before you go.' Mull gave a strange half-salute and retreated from the room.

Johnston grimaced at James. 'Don't mind Mull. He's not the brightest copper in Scotland, and he accepts that, as you heard, but he's the most resilient guy I have ever met – incredibly dogged. Doesn't matter how shitty the situation is, he just gets on with it. Never complains. So, he's become a fly tip for all the toxic garbage in the town. The saying in Glasgow CID is "If it's mad, bad or dull, sent it to Mull". That's why he's so popular, why he's got to DSI. And he's loyal, never tries to take the credit, and best of all, lets his team get on with things. Which is more than fine with me.'

Scott laughed. 'He doesn't sound bad as a governor. Is he the guy who was involved in the Glasgow Central hostage siege years ago?'

Johnston returned the laugh. 'The very same. Do you know the story?'

Scott shook his head. 'Not really. Headlines only. It was well before I joined. What happened?'

Johnston stretched his arms and rolled his neck. 'Short version. We were both DIs at the time but not in the same division. Mull's team were halfway through their shift when it all kicked off. Which is to say they were in the Corn Exchange having a bonding session over more than a few beers when three idiots tried to hold up the RBS branch in Gordon Street. Shambles! A completely screwed up attempt at a bank robbery. They ended up running out with less than £2000, firing their shotguns in the air. Glasgow's version of "The Wild Bunch". They charged into Central Station, just as Mull's squad came out of the pub. He followed them as they ran onto Platform 1 – the London service. They thought

144

they would jump on and get a train out of Dodge. But British Rail was running it then, so of course the train wasn't ready. The bams ended up in one of the first-class carriages with about a dozen passengers who I guess were thinking "WTF". It was at that point Mull's particular talent came to the fore. He walked along the platform until he found them. Waved to the three of them through the window. Mimed "Can I come into the carriage?". They let him! Madder still, he explained that he was a senior officer in Glasgow Police. They still didn't shoot him. He told them it was better to have him as a hostage than civilians. And they agreed. Let the passengers go. Kept Mull.'

Scott whistled through his teeth. 'I didn't know most of that. Amazing.'

'Don't use that word too soon. It gets more bizarre. He starts chatting to them. Gets on really well. Discovers they're all teddy bears. From Govan. At that point, their fate was sealed.'

'Why?'

'Mull is a tenth Dan, true blue, aye ready Hun. His dad was the custody sergeant at Govan Nick. A legend in the force. Ex-army. More prisoners fell down the stairs at Govan Station than the rest of Glasgow put together. Not a man to mess with – a no-nonsense policeman. And Mull's father went to every Rangers home game. Started taking Mull when he was three. Parked him in with the disabled section at first, then he moved him up through the rest of the stadium. Everybody knew it was Police Sergeant Mull's boy, so he was treated like royalty. Which is appropriate at Ibrox. That started his lifelong obsession with the Huns. Knows more about them than any man alive. And he imparted that knowledge to the bams through two long days in the carriage, broken only by intermissions for Irn Bru, pie suppers and bacon rolls. Forty-eight hours of nonstop history; right up to the present day – as it was then. Dick Advocat, Torre Andre Flo, the 6-2 humping at Parkhead. Hitler would have surrendered facing that onslaught. And after two days, they did. Walked out and gave up. Brainwashed.'

'Truthfully?'

'Yes. The full story's not widely known, but that's what Mull did. Got the George Cross. And deserved it.'

'Can I say amazing now?'

'Yes. In my lighter moments I think Mull's talents are wasted in the police force. They should be deployed on a much larger stage.'

'How?'

'Take Syria as an example. Drop Mull into the territory still controlled by ISIS at the start of June. Give him six weeks. By July 12th, ISIS would be marching to a completely different tune. They would have formed flute bands, bought the bowler hats and white gloves, and put on the sashes. Instead of trying to establish the Caliphate and taking over the rest of the world, they would be squabbling over who was going to bang the Lambeg drum outside the chapel. Fundamental Islam versus Mull's love of Rangers. No contest!'

Scott laughed. 'I will look in on him. It'll be great to hear the story first-hand. Meanwhile, back in the real world... What should I do next about Katerina's disappearance?'

Johnston raised the fingers of his right hand. 'You'll have thought about all of them, but no harm in running through your next moves. So, in order: One – try and find out more about where she was last seen. On that we have some good news. The press story worked. A couple contacted Paisley Police station this morning – they're sure they gave her a lift from the town to Irvine. One of my team has spoken to them and they are available for an interview this afternoon. They work at a call centre in Hillingdon Estate. Do you want to do that after you finish here? On your way back?

'Thanks, sir, I do.'

'OK – I'll get them contacted and told to hang on until you get there. The next thing is to do more work on the men highlighted on her iPad, as a follow-up to your DC's review. See if we can identify any more of them. And if we can, interview them. Do that yourself if you have the time. Third and finally, the Youngs. I think you should talk to your friend – her boyfriend – again. Tell him exactly what we've found out about his family. See what his reaction is. After you check that he was in Barcelona that weekend and not back here in Scotland! Plus, you need to follow up on the new link between Katerina's company and Brian Young.'

Scott shrugged his shoulders. 'We've done the work on Martin already. But it's not in the notes yet as we only got confirmation this morning. I can't get the flight details from Milan to Barcelona, but Easyjet confirmed he flew back to Edinburgh on the 14th. We're waiting for the Border Control information to confirm that as well,' Scott said quietly. 'Martin's been trying to get me since I got back from holiday to see if there's any update – I've fobbed him off the last couple of days. This will come as a shock to him.'

Johnston nodded. 'You're a bright man, Scott. So, don't take this as an insult to your intelligence – but in cases like this, 90 percent of the time, it's the family or boyfriend or someone who knows her who is responsible.'

Scott shook his head. 'I know that, sir. I know I need to do a bit more on Martin's movements to fully confirm them – and I will – but I also know he's not capable of hurting anyone.'

'Gut feel?'

'If you like, but I've been friends with him for 12 years. I understand how that sounds – so I will follow up.'

Johnston raised his eyebrows. 'You need to anyway, but the calls from Katerina on the day she vanished to a phone ultimately paid for by Crammond Holdings make that even more important. Crammond Holdings is a company whose shareholders and Directors are Brian Young, his wife, Martin Young and Kevin Young – which your note identifies as your pal, his brother and their parents. The phone is in the same area that Katerina was heading to at the relevant time – and the cherry on the cake is DC McDonald's work linking the reviews on the notes section of her iPad to the dates we know she was with the Young family – an MY goes into the notes file on the April 23rd – the day after she's with Martin at the hotel and a BY on the May 17th – just after she stays at the family home.'

Scott sat back in his seat, shook his head and pulled his legs towards him. 'I know – it all seems to point in one direction, but I wanted to discuss it with you first. I was surprised when the information from Companies House picked out Martin's dad as the person behind the company that has the contract on that phone. What should I do about that? Given what we now know, should I even be involved in the case?'

Johnston leaned forward. 'I've thought long and hard about that and discussed it with Jim Turner. He's more cautious. In his view, you should pass it on. He thinks that's safer for you – and him. I'm more adventurous. The Young family need to be seen. Martin first, I think, then his dad. It's almost certainly Brian Young's phone that was involved on the day she disappeared. He needs to be interviewed, by you, if you think you can do it, because you have previous with him and his family. There's a good chance you'll be able to read him and his explanation better than anyone else. Would you feel uncomfortable doing that?'

Scott hesitated. 'Yes, if I'm honest. It's bad enough with Martin and I'm not sure how I would handle a meeting with his father. It would be very embarrassing if he's the BY in the notes section of Katerina's iPad, as seems likely.'

'It's very short odds, given the history of how Martin met Kat, the fact his dad was there, the notes section, the phone calls on the day and the company links. So, if you can, take the interview.'

'Thank you, sir. I promise I won't let my personal feelings interfere with investigating this properly. There might be an innocent explanation – perhaps the calls were about Martin – arranging something for him – a surprise party for his 30th or to discuss Katerina's business, Home From Home?'

'You hope they were. Don't you?'

Scott nodded but remained silent.

'Don't make assumptions. Take the interviews – get the facts.'

'Anything else?'

'Two things. I bet I know what Jim's main thought on this is.'

Scott laughed. 'You're right – he doesn't want to be "het".'

'That's Jim – he likes his enquiries served sunny-side up, and in this case, he's correct to be concerned – given your links to the family. It's vital that you take Jim with you on how you handle it and keep his confidence.'

'I will, sir, and the other?'

'Probably the most important. Don't give up on this. It's interesting. The bulk of the stuff we see day-to-day is mundane. Contrary to fiction, violent death is generally easy to figure out. It's usually straightforward. Especially in Glasgow. Most of the time it's someone who knows or is associated with the deceased in some way. Drink and a loss of temper in the pub, a battering in a house domestic or a shooting in some pathetic drug war. The killer isn't hard to identify and find. So gut feel isn't really put on trial. But occasionally, cases need more thought. The whole situation is more complex and needs proper, deeper analysis. This could be that one in ten. So, is it hit and run? Or, given there's no sign of her, hit and hide? Or meeting one of her "regulars" and going off with them? Or blackmail gone wrong? Or is it totally random? It's intriguing. All we know is that she's been missing for six weeks and the longer we hear nothing, the worse it looks. Even if it shifts towards homicide, stick with it. That won't be a problem. Territory is less contentious now we're all one big, happy, unified force. If it is tagged as a potential murder and given to Strathclyde to run as a major investigation, it will come to me and I'll make sure you ride shotgun.

That's what I think will happen and I'm going to speak to Mull about it. Be good to work together. Learn from each other.'

Scott beamed. 'No! You've got nothing to learn from me!'

Johnston smiled back. 'That's where you're wrong. You'll see what I mean as this develops. I'll make a decision what to do once you've seen the couple at Hillingdon.' Johnston got up and held out his hand which had a slip of paper, 'Here's the details on them. I've kept you long enough. It's time to face Mull. He's in the room directly above. See him, then do the interview. Enjoy the rest of your afternoon – we can talk again tomorrow.'

Scott left Johnston's room, then stopped at the foot of the stairs, read the note and phoned Julia McDonald.

'Hi, sir.'

'Hi, Julia. Are you up to speed on the sighting?'

'It's just been added to the case log – Richard and Sally Hood – work at Alltime call centre, 121 Long Way, Hillingdon. She's the day shift manager, he's the IT support.'

Scott consulted the paper. 'That's them – Johnston's team are arranging for me to interview them this afternoon – do you want to do that with me?'

'Does the pope shit in the woods? Is the bear a Catholic, sir?'

Scott laughed. 'OK, it's 2:30 pm now, I need to do a PR meet with Johnston's boss – say 30 minutes – then out to Hillingdon – 10 minutes – can you be there for 3:30 pm?'

'Leaving now, sir, see you there.'

Chapter 9

August 17th

By the time Scott arrived at Alltime's car park, Julia's car was sitting in the visitors' section. She got out when he had manoeuvred into a space and popped into the passenger seat of his Renault.

'Nice to see you, sir. Finally,' she added softly.

Scott laughed. 'That wouldn't be another comment on my driving, would it?'

'No! Of course not, sir,' she said, shaking her head.

'Good – I'm pleased about that. What do we know about the Hoods?'

'Glasgow didn't do any background checks this morning, but I knew you would want that done. Bill Nixon ran them through PNC as I was driving here and phoned to saying nothing came up.'

Scott nodded. 'OK. We've no reason to suspect them in any way and they did contact the police, which is a very good indicator they have nothing to hide. But, at this stage, they are probably the last people who saw Katerina and we need to keep that in mind at all times during the interview.'

'Yes, sir' Julia said.

Scott picked up his mobile from the cup well and switched it to silent. 'I'll do the questioning. It should be relatively straightforward – where, what etc. You do the notes, but I'll want your views on how truthful you think they are as well.'

They left the car and went into the building's small reception area, beside a large, open plan office. That room stretched back and out for 40 yards. There was a young woman sitting at a compact desk which was swamped by a large computer. The screen hid most of her body and gave the impression her head was floating on top of it. Scott caught the receptionist's attention.

'Hello – I'm Detective Inspector James. This is DC McDonald. We're here to see Richard and Sally Hood. They are expecting us.'

The young woman nodded but didn't say anything to them directly. She picked up a phone and dialled, 'Sally, the police are here to see you. OK.' She looked up at Scott, 'She'll be here in a minute to take you through.'

A few seconds later a glass door at the side of the main room opened and a young, slim lady walked through and up to them. She was wearing a dark trouser suit, white shirt and high, black shoes which clicked on the wooden floor as she approached.

'Hi, I'm Sally Hood.'

Scott shook her hand. 'Hi, I'm DI James and this is DC McDonald.'

'Pleased to meet you,' Sally replied. 'Come on through. My husband is waiting in my office.'

Sally led them through the same entrance, then along the side of the room, before ushering them in to a small office halfway back where a large desk and four chairs were arranged in a semicircle across from it. A thickset man dressed in jeans, trainers and a red polo shirt, got up from one of the chairs and shook their hands as Sally introduced him as her husband, Richard.

Sally indicated the chairs. 'Tea, coffee, water?'

Scott shook his head. 'No, I'm fine, thanks.' Julia did the same, then took her notebook out from her bag.

Scott leaned forward. 'First, can I say thank you for coming forward and contacting us. This could be a great help to our enquiry.'

'No problem,' Richard Hood said. 'We want to assist in any way we can.'

Scott nodded. 'Can you tell me what happened that Friday night?'

The Hoods glanced at each other. Sally looked at her husband and inclined her head, 'Richard?'

Richard clasped his hands in front of him. 'OK, Sally runs the operation here; she's the day manager. That shift is from 9:30 am till 6:00 pm. I'm the IT support – which I do on a consultancy basis. I'm not an employee but I spend three to four days a week here – mainly troubleshooting, sometimes installing upgrades. I was here that Friday, working on some malware which was causing issues with the response time on our telephone helplines.'

'Malware?' Julia asked.

'Like a computer virus – it's a software bug designed to get into a system and spread. The effect is to slow down the speed at which our computer systems answer queries, which in turn means that the call taker can't get the information quickly enough so the whole process seizes up. Then we get a demand for money, from the creators of the malware, to restore the integrity of our IT. I suppose ransomware is another description.'

Scott knew that it wasn't likely to be relevant to the enquiry but was interested, 'Does that happen regularly?'

'Attacks occur weekly – maybe more often. Successful ones are rare, but it has happened once since I've been involved, about a year ago.'

'Did you pay up?'

'Above my grade. But my guess is yes because the system was fully restored within four hours.'

Scott sat further forward on his chair. 'OK, so on that day? The day you picked up the hitchhiker.'

'The attack wasn't getting much traction – our internal firewalls were holding up well, but I wanted to make doubly sure before I finished. So, I ran some diagnostics until I was satisfied the problem was contained and didn't leave until I had those results.'

'What time was that?'

'I would guess about 8:30 pm.'

'It was,' Sally interjected. 'I stayed on; we only brought the one car that day. I phoned my mum, who was looking after Billy, our six-year-old son, to tell her we would be late. I gave her updates as Richard fed back to me. The last was at 8:30 pm when he came in to say he was done and we could go.'

Richard continued the story, 'We normally do a convoluted series of rat runs to get onto the road to Irvine, the A736, but at that time the M8 is quiet so we drove up to the main Braehead roundabout to swing onto the motorway. She was standing about 100 yards before it, on the grass at the side, with a sign for Prestwick Airport.' He paused. 'We were very late, but I did a lot of hitching in my teens, so I pulled up.'

Scott shifted in his chair as Richard continued, 'Anyway, I stopped. She got into the back with her rucksack and said thanks. Explained that she had been there for a while. I told her we were going to Irvine which was about six miles from Prestwick and could drop her close to the town centre. She could get a bus or train to the airport from there.'

Julia took out two pictures of Katerina. 'Are you sure it was her?'

Richard and Sally both nodded. '100 percent,' Sally replied. 'You tend not to forget someone as beautiful as her.'

Richard joined in. 'It was her, definitely! And she introduced herself as Katerina, so no doubt.'

'What was she wearing?' Scott asked.

'I think a parka, dark or black and jeans and she had a blue rucksack.' Richard looked at his wife, 'Anything else?'

Sally shook her head.

'What did she talk about on the way to Irvine?' Scott said.

'A bit about herself. She was a manager in a hotel in Nairn. She said she was going to Spain to meet her boyfriend then on to a music festival, but Sally and I were both tired, so we didn't pick up on much of what she said. It was fairly quiet on the journey.'

Scott sat more upright. 'This is very helpful but anything else you can remember could be critical. Was there anything? Did she mention meeting anybody, for example?'

The Hoods looked at each other. 'Don't think so. As we were both quiet, she sort of shutdown too. She did try her phone a few times though when she first got in the car and said it had run out of charge.'

Scott tried again, 'Did she mention how she got to Glasgow?'

'No,' Richard said.

'OK, where did you drop her?'

'We live on Malcolm Gardens in Irvine. It runs off the Annick Road, which leads into the old town centre. We let her out at the junction of the roads.'

Sally raised her right hand. 'There is one more thing. She said she was hungry. I told her if she walked a couple of hundred yards down the main road towards the town, she would come to a good fish and chip shop called Mamma's. She thanked me and said she would think about it.'

'What time was that?'

'About 9:15 pm. I didn't check my watch, but the drive back would have been around 40 minutes.'

'Was that the last time you saw her?' Scott continued.

'Yes,' Richard said. 'It's about 70 yards to our house from where we dropped her. By the time we got in, it was hailing. It was really torrential. I remember feeling a bit guilty. I wondered if I should have dropped Sally at home, then gone back to get Katerina. Asked her if she wanted to come in for a bit to shelter. But by then we were in the house. Billy was still up and I wanted to see him. So, I didn't.'

Scott let out his breath. 'Thank you both. That's very helpful. It gives us a much better picture of her movements that night! If you think of anything else let us know.' Scott handed each of them his card. 'DC McDonald will transcribe this into a statement. If you could sign it, that would be appreciated. Thank you both again.'

Scott and Julia didn't speak until they had left the building and were back sitting in his car. Julia looked across at her boss, 'What do you think, sir?'

'They seemed honest, the story was straightforward and made sense. At present, I'm inclined to accept it at face value. And you?'

Julia waited for a moment before answering, 'Almost the same as you. The only part that gave me any cause for concern was when the husband questioned whether he should have gone back out and picked Kat up again. Made me wonder whether he did go out again?'

'They didn't mention that,' Scott said quickly. 'It's unlikely – his wife would have said something if he had done – wouldn't she?'

'I'm sure she would, but to be honest, sir,' she paused, 'we didn't ask specifically.'

Scott nodded. 'No, fair point, I should have covered that off. Include it in your file notes and when you send them the statement ask it as an auxiliary point.'

'I will, sir. I'll do the note tonight and circulate it. What do we do with this information?'

'Talk to the station at Irvine first thing tomorrow morning. Ask them if it's OK to allocate one of their DCs to look at the area and take their bearings from the location she was dropped at. Ask them to walk it and try and find CCTV footage of her on that street. All in all, it's a big move forwards. We have something concrete at last. Something we can pin to. We can talk through it more tomorrow and add the actions to the case log.

'OK, sir. I'll get on it.'

'There is one other thing, Julia,' Scott said, after a short pause.

'Sir?'

He hesitated then looked directly at her, 'Yes…your dress.'

Julia laughed. 'Not wearing one, Scott.' She looked down at her outfit of Cuban-heeled brown ankle boots, dark cords, a formal black shirt and a black cardigan. 'This isn't a dress. Surprised you didn't notice!'

Scott wiped his forehead. This was as awkward as he had anticipated.

'No, I mean your dress sense generally.'

154

Julia smiled and shook her head. 'So, it's the style police. I'm having to confront, is it, Scott?'

Scott paused and thought about his words and how Julia was behaving. He never insisted that his team called him sir. In fact, he had asked that they refer to him as Scott. Julia tended to switch between the two, generally sir in more formal meetings and Scott when they were out of the office. She had gone with sir earlier and was now firmly Scott – and she was sitting closer to him. Christ, where to next?

'OK, I'm not trying to be prescriptive but there's a general feeling that some of your outfits are a bit…well…short.'

Julia leaned forward, almost to the edge of the passenger seat. 'Is that what you think, Scott? That they're too short? That you can see too much of my legs? Is that upsetting?'

Scott was sweating and feeling very uncomfortable. He had to end this before it became more embarrassing. 'No, I don't look. I don't see that. But others have mentioned it. Will you think about what you wear? Dress a little more conservatively?'

Julia touched his arm and he started. She smiled. 'Don't worry, I'm not trying to seduce you – you're a married man, after all. And I'll dress down if that's what you want. But it's just for you. Because you asked me. Not the others.'

'Thanks, Julia. Sorry for raising it. I'm glad you appreciate the sensitivities. And thanks for coming to the interview. It was helpful. Safely back.'

'And you, Scott,' Julia replied as she squeezed his hand, opened the passenger door and got out.

Part 8

"The man who has a conscience suffers whilst acknowledging his wrongdoing. That is his punishment…"

Dostoyevsky

October 20th – 11:00 am

It's been three and a half weeks since I last wrote anything, but I have an opportunity to continue the story today. Arlene and the girls left for my parent's house in North Berwick earlier this morning. A half-term meetup and excursion into Edinburgh. I am driving through tomorrow to join them for our pilgrimage to the Edinburgh Playhouse to see *Wicked* but am excused until then. My alibi is that I need time to prepare my first solo programme for Sky Sports. A trailer for the new golf year, which I am recording in late January to go out mid-March. I did the work weeks ago. That script is finished. This is the one that needs all my effort.

Since my last entry, I have questioned whether I need to write any more in my journal and if keeping going is still beneficial. I have set out what happened on the night that Katerina died and the following two days. That has helped. I'm not cured, but I am finding it a bit easier to cope. I am a little less scared about being caught and I seem to be more engaged with Arlene and the girls. I'm less distant, less self-absorbed and Arlene has commented about that change. I certainly don't spend as much time trying to pretend the death didn't happen and constructing elaborate make-believe worlds where I behaved differently. Which, in itself, is good. So, I think I will keep going, to see if I can maintain that improvement.

I feel that I have emptied out some of the destructive waste I am carrying, and that has allowed me to cope better with my family life. Not normally, not fully – but more than I expected. I feel I am part of my family once more – and that was why I made the decision to hide the mess I created. To save the family unit, to keep us together. Setting down what I did – outlining the whole episode in words – has crystallised my feelings about the choice I made that Friday night and has shown me, starkly, what I have to do now. It has driven home the stupidity of how I have been behaving. What was the point in covering up the death to protect my family life, if I am going to lose it anyway because I can't deal with the emotional aftermath? That seems harsh when I look at it in writing, but it is the brutal reality. I need to follow through with this "therapy" – not decline any further and let my family slip away. So, I will continue writing the next part of my story in the hope that it will keep me sane, keep me tough enough to reunite properly with Arlene and my girls.

I need to document the four weeks after the death and how I felt during that time. The whole period was hellish. Sunday was the most difficult day but I've already described that so I will concentrate on the following month, the fortnight before our holiday to the Algarve at the start of August and our two-week stay in Portugal. The first 14 days were terrible and looking back now, probably the worst in terms of not being able to sleep, being convinced that police cars were going to turn up at the house and that I would be arrested in front of Anna and Cathy. I spent virtually all that time avoiding going out to the grass grave to poke it, turn it over. I worried obsessively that Katerina wasn't buried deeply enough and that her body would become exposed and be seen by my girls. Days and nights, I exhausted myself fretting that I had missed something obvious in my clean-up – convinced myself that one mistake would emerge to identify me as the person responsible for Kat's death.

My behaviour was completely off-kilter during that period. I have always been quiet and a bit reserved, but I pulled into myself even more and became monosyllabic in my exchanges. The change in me was commented on by both my assistants, who, in turn, became worried about the continuing financial crisis at the club and their own positions. They thought I knew about changes that would affect them and that I was keeping them in the dark. I used that as my excuse for being so withdrawn. I told them I was concerned, but about my own position, not theirs, and that they were safe from being made redundant. I used a variation of that explanation at home, but less successfully. I had worked through and discussed our financial situation with Arlene for over a year and she knew exactly how we stood. She was back at Carrick Glen Hospital part-time and was aware that my Sky contract would keep us going in the short term, even if my income from Gailes ended. So I added a twist to the simple money worry refrain – which was that I wanted to have my name linked to Irvine Gailes for my foray on the Senior Tour, and if I was sacked, that wouldn't be possible. Arlene was savvy enough to know that even if Gailes stopped paying me, they would still want me to be associated with them. It was free exposure for both parties, and as

I am now on Sky, which is a huge boost to my visibility, my excuse didn't really hold together. But instead of poking at my alibi until it fell apart, Arlene let it go.

I tried to bury myself in additional practice sessions in preparation for going back on the tour. That helped and was partially successful in blanketing my fear – at least while I was on the range. That was the only place where I could stop thinking about being caught. But as soon as I finished hitting balls, the worry swamped me again. I was plagued with multiple waves of guilt and fear of discovery. I told myself that every day that passed increased my chances of getting away with the killing, but I didn't really believe it. I had a terrible need to know what was happening to the body. To understand how decomposition would be affecting Katerina's corpse, tucked under the grass.

I thought about what I could do to find out, other than lifting the lid on her coffin and examining the remains. I didn't want to take that risk or face that trauma. I couldn't use my own iPad or the kids to read up on the subject. There are almost weekly reports of trials in the papers and on TV which feature evidence of suspects using computers to look up data on the crimes for which they are being prosecuted. But still I had to know, so I went to Glasgow and found a slightly rundown Internet café on Great Western Road where I could use a laptop to do the research at a cost of £1 for 15 minutes. Two hours of sifting through a number of specialist sites confirmed that, by chance, I had done the right thing – the right thing when it came to body decomposition. In ideal circumstances, i.e. above ground and open to the air in moist, warm conditions, a body will decompose in about two weeks, broken down by internal bacteria. It takes about a fortnight for most of the skin to disappear and for the noxious gases to be expelled. Fourteen days for putrification to do its work. It was nearly two weeks since I had buried the body. So, I couldn't try to move it, even if I wanted to. The mess and smell would be incredible. I read through the stages twice. In the early part – up to 12 hours after death – rigor mortis occurs and cell death starts. In the next phase – initial decomposition – putrification sets in and the body begins to smell and bloat because of the gases which form inside it. The liquids in the body start to ooze out. Then comes skeletonization, when most of the body tissue has rotted and been eaten by insects. Once bones are completely dry, they begin to decay, but that is a very long process. It takes years, unless acted on by other factors. When I finished my research, I knew that I had to leave Katerina where I had buried her for the time being. The state of her body dictated that, as did the fact that the kids were off school on their summer holidays and at home most of the time. I could perhaps take the skeleton away later in the year, when the body had been reduced to clean bones.

The other nagging preoccupation that I was able to research in the café was Katerina's request, bordering on insistence, that I choke her during sex. There is a name for it – "erotic asphyxiation". Apparently restricting oxygen to the brain heightens sexual arousal and orgasm. Did knowing that make me feel better? No – because in every way asking a golf professional to compress one's throat is a bad idea. My hands are very strong. I am used to applying pressure through them – but not during sex. So, I felt doubly guilty and had to force myself to believe that I was closer to getting away with the death. As the body disintegrated, so did my chances of getting caught. Decay was my ally. That was my mantra on the return trip to the golf course.

So somehow, we got through – or more accurately, I got through – the last two weeks of July, until the start of our family holiday in Quinta do Lago, Portugal; staying at a villa owned by Brian Young. A house he has had for over a decade and one we have been lucky enough to use three times in the past 10 years. At no cost, apart from giving the occasional golf clinic at one of Crammond Holdings' golf days – Brian's main business and the one I worked in all those years ago.

Using the house didn't feel that strange in August. It does now. Now that I know Brian is in the frame for Katerina's disappearance. If I had been aware of that then, I couldn't have gone to the villa – which would have led to more problems – trying to explain the change of plans to Arlene and the girls. Anna and Cathy love Quinta and the house – a six-bedroom villa, with a pool and a cinema room, situated in a quiet cul-de-sac alongside San Lorenzo Golf Course. Brian is also a member of the Four Seasons Country Club, which we can use as well and where the girls play tennis and go to discos.

The first time we went to Quinta, about seven years ago, Arlene and I not only enjoyed tanning and totally relaxing but acted like we were back in the early years of our relationship. We couldn't manage that this visit. Or I couldn't. And I struggled to find my sex drive at all during the fortnight we were in Portugal. Which is when Arlene came to appreciate that the problem, I couldn't share with her was something major. I used tiredness as an excuse for my lack of interest in making love at the start of our holiday, but that felt lame, even to me after a few days. I had to endure some half-meant jokes, "Are you seeing someone else out here?" through to, "I should have packed the blue dress," and finishing with "Am I too fat now? Don't you fancy me anymore?".

All the times I couldn't perform, I tried to reassure her. I told her there was no one else. That I still loved her. That she was beautiful and sexy. But without the physical evidence to back that up, she didn't believe me. I wanted to make love. It would have been great to wash away the horror and guilt in a lather of lovemaking, but I couldn't manage it. I tried – which made the whole situation worse. Arlene started to back away midway through the holiday. Not spitefully, but I knew that she was hurt by my lack of desire. We kept it from the girls and we didn't fall out. We just moved slightly apart. I should have realised then that I needed to act to prevent the situation getting worse, but I was still overwhelmed with remorse and the terror of discovery. I had hoped that being at a distance from the house and the body in Symington would lend some sort of perspective, but it didn't. I still found it hard to sleep and spent more and more time on my own, thinking incessantly about the death. Worrying about what was happening back in Scotland, whether the police were involved yet, and if so, where was the trail taking them?

It was Arlene who salvaged the final part of the holiday and stopped it from spiralling downwards and out of control. On the fourth last night, when we hadn't made love again – I was too exhausted – she held me really tightly and kissed me softly. Then drew my face back so she could see my eyes before she spoke. Her words are imprinted, 'I love you. I have from the first moment I saw you at Loch Lomond. We have a fantastic family and a great life. But I know something is wrong. I don't know what, but knowing you as well as I do, I suspect that it's something you want to shield me from. This void is very difficult for me, but we will cope. You only need to tell me when you're ready. And I promise we'll get through it. No matter what. We'll get through it.'

She cried when she finished, very softly. That was my opportunity – my chance to confess what I had done.

I nearly did. I was a breath away from sobbing, telling her everything, letting her share my misery. I chose to lie instead. I told her I was having a mid-life crisis. I wasn't sure what I wanted to do but I would come out the other side soon. She and the kids would see me through. I knew she didn't believe me 100 percent, but she held me again and cradled my head on her chest. And I felt desire again. Not enough to make love. But enough to know it could come back. After that it was easier. Arlene organised things so that I had less time on my own on our final days. She kept me fully occupied with the girls; a day out driving to Monchique up in the mountains, lunch at Gigi's – our favourite fish restaurant, and evening trips to beach restaurants further along the coast towards Vale do Lobo. On the last full day, we took a cycle trip out along the salt flats in the nature reserve which borders the estate to Isla de Faro and the airport. All of this designed to keep me from falling into myself and becoming more detached. It worked. The kids loved the holiday, Arlene and I reached a temporary understanding and I remained sane.

I hoped my upwards trajectory would continue and I would be better on our return from Portugal, but I was deluding myself. It had been a break, a diversion but not a cure and any temporary improvement disappeared almost as soon as we lifted off from Faro Airport. I was flying home to a decomposing body in my garden and was still no closer to dealing with it emotionally. I tried to gee myself up with the thought that there had been no interest – as far as I could tell – in Katerina's disappearance. There had been no questions locally and nothing I could see in the media about what had happened. All was quiet.

But that didn't help me move on – I still had the same nightmares and I continued to have the same worries. My temporary recovery faded and I actually got worse, torturing myself with the thought that I looked more guilty as time passed and that if Katerina's body was found at any time, nobody would believe that it had been an accident. So, I became even more solitary, more withdrawn. The only times I managed to act normally was when I was with my kids – with them and only them, I managed to keep some sort of perspective – and when I practised golf, which I did more and more – almost becoming a recluse on the practice area. My excuse for that was my impending return to tour golf, and my publicly stated desire to get my former game back. That part of my life was accepted by my staff and by Arlene. Between those twin areas of normality, I was just able to keep functioning. But I knew that it couldn't last. I felt that I was running on nervous energy and waiting for it to trigger a more serious decline.

My introspection was punctured by three events which scared me even more and compounded my sense of dread. I will detail them individually, but the cumulative effect was to add further weight to my sense of impending doom.

The first was a phone call from Brian Young on the morning of September 15th, asking to meet me – which I did in the Radisson Blu Hotel in Glasgow the next day. He didn't tell me what he wanted – just that it was very important, and he would explain when he saw me. That meeting put me back in play – playing for my life. I was back on the course. On the last hole. On the tee. With my drive, looking like it was going out of bounds.

Brian was unusually nervous when we sat down at the front bar and ordered. It took him a few minutes to settle once we had our drinks. Then he suddenly blurted out that he was a suspect in the disappearance of his son Martin's girlfriend, Katerina Wysklow, and that the police wanted to interview him. That was a shock in itself. And doubly so, as I had been considering telling Brian what I had done – I had almost built up to convincing myself that he was the one person I could confess to – and now he was telling me that the police thought he was involved in the disappearance. I had to discipline myself not to react. He explained that the police were interested in him because of phone exchanges between Katerina and him on the day she disappeared. He knew that because his son, Martin, had questioned why he had made contact with Kat at the weekend. Brian had been forced to make something up – had lied to his son and told Martin the calls and texts were about Kat's business. But then he turned to me, sighed and put his hands on the table. I can remember his words.

'But it's a bit more than that. Katerina was very friendly towards me from the first time we met her at the hotel in Nairn. She flirted with me as well as Martin that night. I was flattered. She is an incredibly beautiful woman.' I remember his stopping for a while at that point and biting his lip before he continued, 'I know she slept with Martin that night. He didn't tell me. I didn't ask. I didn't have to. It was obvious. After her shift, she joined us for a drink. Which became two, then three. I went to the toilet and when I came back, I could see they had arranged something. Martin said he was tired and was going up to bed. Which, as you know, isn't him. He's always the last man standing. Katerina stayed for a few minutes. To make it look less obvious, I guess. We were the only ones left in the lounge bar. She sat across from me. Which gave me full view of her body; particularly her legs which were on display – really on display. She asked me about myself, what I did. My businesses and was I married. Then gave me a kiss on the cheek when she rose to go. Lingered over it. Let her body rest against mine. Then she smiled and said, "Sweet dreams, I have something I think you'll be interested in".'

He shifted in his chair and hunched his shoulders before he continued, 'That would have been that, but Martin asked her down to spend a few days with us. He was coming back from Sondrio for a weekend to see the family and wanted to include Katerina. Kevin was down from St Andrews. So, it was all of us.

Martin asked if I would pick Kat up from Waverley, then collect him from the airport. I agreed and met her at the station. She was wearing the shortest denim skirt I've ever seen, a cropped leather jacket and a pure white T-shirt – no bra. I couldn't take my eyes off her. She was unreal. We were early for Martin's flight, so she suggested we go for a drink. I took her to Norton House. You might not know it. It's a hotel and conference centre, on the A8, just past the airport on the way out of town. She sat very close to me in the bar. I felt conspicuous, but sort of proud at the same time. The staff were watching us the whole time we were there, and she was behaving as if she was with me. We just had one drink. We chatted about her idea of buying and running a small hotel. I said it sounded sensible. When we came out and got into the car, she shifted round in her seat and smiled at me. Then she took my hand before I had time to start the car, put it between her legs and moved it up over her thighs. Told me to think about her and what she wanted to do to me for the rest of the day. Then she touched me. I couldn't believe it – or that I let her. Told me she was pleased that I was hard for her. And that I would get my reward.'

Brian stopped at that point, wiped his forehead and finished his lager. 'She wasn't lying. The next day, Jean took Martin and Kevin to Haddington to see their gran. Katerina said she was tired. Asked if they minded if she had a quick nap while they were away. I said I had some work I had to do and went into my study. She called down to me as soon as they left. Told me to come upstairs – I went. She was lying naked on top of the bed. That was the start.'

Brian ran his fingers through his hair when he finished his confession and held his head. I was speechless. Then he said that he had an alibi for the first part of the night she disappeared but not for later – or didn't, unless he could tell the police that he had spent the final part of the evening with me! He begged me to back him up – corroborate his story and to tell the police that we had been drinking together. We could work out a place and a time together – choose one that would stand up. Brian pulled on every connection he had with me and finished by saying that I would save his marriage if I agreed. And his relationship with Martin. Then he reminded me how he had given birth to my golf career. That I wouldn't be where I am now without him.

I have read articles about people who claim to have had an "out of body" experience. The feeling that they are looking down at themselves – and I have been sceptical – until that lunchtime. When it happened to me. I saw myself from a totally different perspective – as if I were in a movie – and I saw that night

166

again – like a series of still photos being slowly flicked through, running in parallel to what happened between myself and Katerina but from another angle.

In a normal situation, Brian would have picked up on how strangely I behaved – but I'm sure he put my displacement down to his story – and the request he was making. When I came to, I said I would think about helping him but I had to clear my head and think it through first. I also asked him why he had told me about his relationship with Katerina and asked me to lie for him. He said that he didn't know if the police would be able to recover his and Katerina's texts from either of their mobile phone providers. If the police could recover the actual texts, then their affair would be exposed, and he would be the prime suspect in her disappearance. He was almost in tears as he told me again that he wasn't responsible, but he couldn't prove his innocence. To get me to assist, he said he felt he needed to tell me the full story.

I promised to think about it and said it might be difficult to concoct an explanation which would stand up to scrutiny, as I had been at home with my family that night. Which was when he shifted the ground from beneath me – again. He said I must be mistaken – I must have forgotten that was the evening Arlene's mum had been rushed to hospital – Arlene had told him about what had happened on the night of the Pro-Am event. I had been on my own – which, together with our friendship was why he had thought I could provide the perfect alibi. I was speechless and couldn't move – I was completely thrown by what had happened. Brian must have interpreted my inaction as deep thought because he told me I had time to think it over – the police had asked to see him the following week, but he was away on a three-week cruise so they had agreed to delay the interview until he came back.

The second incident happened at home and involved an episode of *Crimewatch*, ironically one of the last ones before the BBC decided to axe the programme. Arlene rarely misses it. She is an avid reader of crime novels and sees *Crimewatch* as a real-life illustration of what she has picked up from the fictional world. We were watching the end of *Reporting Scotland*, waiting for the weather when a trailer for that night's show came on. I was barely paying attention. Watching TV is good for me as I can pretend to be involved, when actually I am miles away. The items featuring on that evening's programme were highlighted one by one. And then, out of nowhere, she was there. A picture of Katerina filled the screen and then segued into the local press campaign to find her, a campaign which I had missed because we were in Portugal. My assumption that nothing was happening was wrong, completely wrong. Luckily, I was lying back on the settee, almost horizontal, when that section of the show came on. I didn't react. If I had been sitting up, there is no doubt I would have started or at least responded in some way, and that would have caused Arlene to notice. I held myself down physically and mentally as the presenter went through a short preview about Katerina's disappearance and that the last sighting of her had been narrowed down to Irvine in Ayrshire. Arlene and the girls latched on to that. They were excited and said we needed to watch the whole programme to find out more. So, I was committed to a two-hour wait, wondering what would be revealed and then sitting through what turned out to be a full 10-minute section on Katerina. With pictures of her. Very attractive photos used as a backdrop to the narrative which detailed her movements on Friday July 11th, from leaving the hotel where she worked in the morning, to being dropped off in Irvine at about 9:30 pm. She hadn't been seen since. The slot finished with a final picture of her and asked anyone who had seen her that day, or since, to get in touch with Police Scotland. As soon as the image disappeared, Arlene pointed out that the 11th was the night she had driven through to her mum's, the night before my golf event. She didn't ask me if I had seen the missing girl – why would she? And I am sure she didn't link me to it in any way, but it was the first definite confirmation that a search was in place for Katerina and that the trail was now much closer. I tried to take some positives from the appeal as I lay watching the rest of the show. I can remember listing them in my head.

1. I hadn't been approached directly by the police. Which meant they didn't have a trace on her phone to the house. If Irvine was as close as they had to a final location, then I was still OK.

2. I couldn't recall anyone seeing me pick her up. No other pedestrians, anyway. I was sure of that, given the weather. But had a couple of cars passed me when I was stopped? I was sure that one car had blown its horn to get me to move. Or was I? Was I creating a false memory of an incident through guilt? But even if someone came forwards, I was driving Arlene's car that night, not mine, so any sighting would be a stage removed from me.

3. All the areas Katerina had touched had been cleaned – time and again. The bins had been emptied weeks ago – Arlene hadn't noticed anything untoward – apart from the bobbles on the blue dress – and she had taken it for dry cleaning since. There was no trace of Katerina in the car or the house. I was sure of that. The only evidence was under the grass mound.

4. I knew from my meeting with Brian that the police effort seemed to be concentrated on him. As long as I didn't do anything stupid – like agree to construct an alibi for him – I would stay a peripheral character in the investigation.

I forced myself to take account of those points and managed to stay calm for the next weeks, until the third event hit me. Just two days ago, I was working in the shop when Cathy rang me. It was the third day of the girls' half-term break. I can recall our conversation word for word.

'Dad, I'm really excited!'

'Why?'

'We've decided what to do for Guy Fawkes.'

'What's that, love?'

'Mum's agreed we can have a bonfire party at the house. I'll invite all my pals from school and so will Anna. And Mum says we can ask their parents as well and do food and fireworks.'

I still didn't see what was coming. 'That sounds fun. I'll talk to Mum about it tonight.'

'It'll be great, Dad. We've started already. I've got the perfect spot. The grass mound on the golf course. We can use that as the base. Build on top of it. We put some wood there this afternoon so there's a good lot done already. We took some of the old rubbish out of the garage and dumped it. We can add to it this weekend when we come back from Granddad's and start to make a Guy.'

'Great.' It was all I could say. I killed the call to give myself time to think and ignored the first call back from Arlene's mobile. I took the second and willed myself to be steady.

'What happened there?' Arlene asked.

'I don't know. It's not a great signal in the shop sometimes but I've moved outside now. It seems fine.'

'Yes – I can hear you clearly. I'm pleased with the Guy Fawkes idea. The girls are really excited. They spent a couple of hours cleaning out the garage and erecting the start of a tower on the grass. You can help on Sunday when we all get back. Make it more stable. Build it up.'

There was nothing I could do. I couldn't say no. I had no reason to object. Plus taking away the wood and rubbish was probably more likely to reveal what lay below than leaving it. So, I enthused, or tried to, 'I'm really pleased. We can work on it when I get back tonight. It'll be great.'

The girls go to Wellington School in Ayr, and have since primary 5, so it was almost exclusively their friends from there that they invited, plus parents. Arlene also asked her mum, and her brother John and his two boys. So about 40 people in all – 40 potential observers of the gradual revelation of the body. I had waking nightmares about how that would happen. A kid spotting something first. Pulling their parents arm. "Look, Dad! Dad, look at the bottom. Looks like a skeleton."

I seemed to have only three options. Cancel the whole thing. But with what excuse? Try and move the body before the event. When? How? This weekend was an option – today in fact. How much of the body was left? Was it even moveable? My research suggested that might be realistic, but only if all the flesh and body fluids had disappeared – otherwise it would be impossible.

Or I could leave the body alone and take the chance it wouldn't be seen during the bonfire. I have experience at setting the grass on fire. In fact, five years' worth of past burnings to base my guess on. Each October/November, I set the grass mound alight at the end of the main cutting season. Apparently, that was what gave the girls the idea. The amount of detritus that remains depends on how dry the grass is. But from memory, even if it isn't that damp, the mound never burns out fully. Instead, it smoulders for days afterwards. Usually I have to spread it out on the second and third day to get the maximum burn. So, it is likely that some grass cover would remain or that the heat of the fire will burn the bones – turn them to ash and save me that way. I didn't think that was likely, but I would check.

In the end, my indecision was final. I couldn't face taking the risk of moving the body, and every day that passed, more and more wood was piled on the mound. We built it up and the girls made a Guy with Arlene's help. I have never been a fatalist; I've always believed we shape our own outcomes but for once I got into that frame of mind. Perhaps this was karma. I had covered up the initial crime, only for my family to see it revealed later in the worst possible circumstances. I went into the night in that very strange mood.

My next test – perhaps the ultimate one – will be on bonfire night.

Part 9

"An honest man's the noblest work of God."

Robert Burns

Chapter 10

August 27th

Scott left the table to check his phone before his team regrouped to score boards 17–24. He had one new text from Jim Turner, confirming that he and Alan Johnston had arranged to meet for a meal at Opium at eight o'clock and asking if Scott would be able to join them. He smiled as he read it. They were desperate to quiz him about his visit to the crime campus that morning and pump him for his thoughts on whether he would take up the invitation to transfer there. Scott texted back, "Thanks I will, subject to Mary being OK", and dumped the mobile back in his suit jacket.

He walked over to the table his teammates were sitting at, put down his scoresheet and slid onto the spare chair. 'Seventeen – plus 110 – minus 120 – flat.'

They went through each hand quickly – most were fine, apart from board 22, but when they did the tally for those hands and adjusted it for the first 16, they were 14 International Match Points (IMPs) behind with eight boards left to play. That was a hurdle but not an insurmountable one – a bit like being one down with 20 minutes to go in a football match. A deficit that could be wiped out in one hand. But they couldn't afford another bad board. If they went the equivalent of two down, the match was lost.

Scott, like so many other bridge players he knew, had become hooked on the game at university. He loved its complexities – the intellectual challenge each hand comprised and the fact that a hand took, on average, only seven minutes to bid and play. Then it was on to a new hand – a fresh set of problems with no time for boredom to set in.

He continued playing after he and Mary came back from Malawi and joined bridge clubs in Hamilton and Glasgow. He normally played on a Monday night at the Glasgow Bridge Centre with his long-term partner, Chai Patel. Chai was the only son of the two other members of their team, Manny and Surinder Patel. The family was Ugandan Asian. Manny and Surinder had come to the UK as a young married couple, in the first wave of expulsions in 1972, and had built up a chain of convenience stores, which they had sold to Morrisons when Manny reached 65. They retired after the six-month handover and spent their spare time playing bridge and nagging Chai to get married and give them grandchildren.

Manny and Surinder were very good players – they had both represented Scotland at senior level – but they were a volatile combination and never far from a heated debate about how a hand could have been played or defended better. Scott and Chai, a lecturer in computing science at Strathclyde University, were the complete opposite; calm, logical, rather than emotional and precise, scientific bidders. They rarely fell out when playing together.

Scott smiled at Chai as they sat down as North/South for the final set of eight boards and watched Chai's parents shuffle into the East/West seats at a table on the other side of the room. Surinder was audibly complaining about how her husband's signalling on board 22 had allowed their opponents to make a game that should have been defeated, the main reason Scott's team were 11 IMPs behind.

Scott and Chai played the first seven hands of the last set fairly quickly. They were relatively straightforward, either low-level part scores or easily bid games. Scott knew they needed at least one "swingy" board to redress the balance and estimated that they might have picked up a few IMPs, but nothing like enough to pull back the full deficit. He took out the South cards on board 32, sorted them in suits, then paused. It was a more interesting hand. He held eight spades to the J 10 9 – a singleton King of Hearts, Ace and the 5 of Diamonds and two small Clubs. Scott was thinking through how best to bid his hand when West passed, and Chai did as well. His right-hand opponent took out the one Diamond card from his bidding box and laid it on the table. Scott breathed out quietly. That made things a bit easier. There was only one sensible bid he could make. He put the stop card in front of him, then put the four Spade card beside it. West, his left-hand opponent, sat back in his chair, folded his cards into one and spent a full minute considering what to do after Scott put the stop card back in the box. Finally, he picked out the red double card and dropped it on the table. It was Chai's turn to bid but he didn't do so immediately. Instead, he checked and rechecked his cards. It was more than two minutes before he bid, and his selection was a surprise to Scott – redouble. East passed quickly. Scott took his time and did a sense check on the auction. Chai's bid couldn't be a rescue attempt, showing a hand with no Spades. If Chai had a complete misfit, he would have bid four no trump, telling Scott he was void in Spades and asking him to choose between the unbid suits, Hearts and Clubs. No, Chai's bid was to play. Chai thought that they could make four Spades, 10 tricks. Scott passed when he was sure he had interpreted Chai's bid correctly, as did West. Scott couldn't remember the last time he had played in a redoubled contract in a team match. And they were vulnerable, which meant that each trick was worth four times the normal amount. There was no doubt the whole match would turn on this hand. Could Scott take ten tricks, make four Spades redoubled, which would score 1080 points against 620 for a plain vanilla four spade contract. Scott checked his scorecard. The difference of 460 points would be worth 10 IMPs in the scoring system, which converted normal points into International Match Points. Scott breathed deeply and focused as he waited for West to lead.

It was only a few seconds before West put down the King of Diamonds. Chai laid out his hand. Ace, Queen of Spades, four Hearts to the Ace, two small Diamonds and five small Clubs.

Scott, as convention dictated, said, 'Thank you partner,' and had to work to keep the joy out of his voice. What a great bid by Chai. He had valued his three key cards, the two aces and the Queen of Spades, perfectly. There were only four potential losers between the hands. The King of Spades, one Diamond and two Clubs. And he could get rid of the losing Diamond. If Scott took the first trick with the Ace of Diamonds, cashed his singleton King of Hearts, went over to dummy with the Ace of Spades and threw the losing Diamond on the Ace of Hearts he would make his contract. Losing only the King of Spades and two Clubs. Ten tricks! But, but, there was the possibility of taking eleven. The play was the same for the first two tricks – Ace of Diamonds, King of Hearts, but if West had the King of Spades with one other, Scott could lead up to dummy, and if West didn't put up the King, he could finesse the Queen of Spades. Then play the Ace of Spades dropping the King. The Ace of Hearts would follow on the next round and he could throw away the small Diamond in his hand. He would lose only two Club tricks and make eleven one over his contract. A redoubled over trick was worth 400 points. Should he risk it? If the finesse lost – because the King of Spades was with East, the opponents would cash a Diamond trick before he could get rid of his loser, then take their two Club tricks. He would be one down. Which would be 400 points to his opponents. So, if the finesse worked it was worth 1480 points. If it lost, they would drop 400. An 1880 swing. 18 IMPs – what should he do? Would West have doubled without the King of Spades in his hand? That was unlikely Scott thought at this stage of the game. West would expect Scott to have the Ace of Spades, because of his leap to the four level, and therefore assume his King was a sure trick. Scott reconstructed the likely West and East hands one more time then played the King of Hearts to which both his opponents followed. He put a small Spade in front of him. West followed with the 6.

'Queen, please,' Scott instructed Chai quietly and semi-closed his eyes. East played the 5 of Spades. Scott couldn't help exhaling loudly.

'Ace of Spades, Ace of Hearts discarding a Diamond, losing two Clubs for plus one,' he said.

Chai smiled broadly at him as West apologised to his teammate. 'Sorry partner – not the best double of all time!'

The others had been finished for some time and Scott and Chai walked over and sat down at their table. It was etiquette to score the hands in sequence. The first seven boards were flattish as Scott had expected but their team had gained three IMPs to be eight behind.

'Minus 620,' Manny said dejectedly and shook his head.

Scott let Chai give the good news. 'Plus 1480 so that's plus 860 which is 13 IMPs – I make that a win by two.' Chai's face lit up with a huge grin.

Manny and Surinder both said 'What?' at the same time.

'Yes,' Chai confirmed. 'They doubled Scott's four Spades. I redoubled and Scott took the finesse – some pair, eh?'

Normally, the captain of the losing team came over immediately the scoring was done to offer congratulations. But that didn't happen. It was obvious, given the slender margin between the sides that their opponents were going through each board again to ensure no mistakes had been made in the computations. But after almost five minutes, the full team headed to Scott's table to confirm the narrowest of victories, shake hands and wish them luck in the next round. Scott was beaming as he accepted their congratulations. As captain, he offered to take his team for a celebratory drink – knowing they would decline politely – Manny and Surinder didn't drink alcohol and Chai was on a short leash with his fiancée. Instead, they shook hands in a suitably British fashion and picked up the computer printouts of the hands. They would analyse them over the next 24 hours, then email each other with thoughts on how their bidding and play could have been improved. That feedback was a vital ingredient to their success as a team.

Scott was parked on Titwood Road and was back in his car two minutes after he said goodbye to his team. He dialled Mary's mobile as soon as he was settled in the driver's seat. She picked up on the third ring, 'Hi, love, how did it go?'

'We won – by two IMPs – a 13 IMP swing to turn the match round on the last board.'

'Great, well done, you must be chuffed.'

'I am. It was so good; I've got the computer printout sheet for the hands – I can take you through it when I get back.'

He heard her laugh. 'Fab – I can hardly wait!'

Scott had tried to get Mary interested in bridge in their last year at university, and to be fair, she had been carried along by his enthusiasm. She learned the basics of the game and even played with Scott on occasions. Mary enjoyed the competitive elements of the card side but wasn't as enthused with the social interaction. This had come to a head when she agreed to partner Scott in a mixed pairs event being held in the Glasgow Bridge Centre. The location was bleak and even more depressing on a wet Sunday. But not as dispiriting as the sight of the other contestants. Scott remembered her pulling him to the side of the room and whispering, 'For God's sake, Scott, it's like Star Wars Bars in here.' When Scott had protested that it wasn't that bad, she had followed up with, 'Yes, it is. I assume the buses for Lourdes are parked round the back!'

He smiled as he recalled the look on her face that day.

'OK, fair dos. Just the last board then!' He heard her laugh again. 'I had another text from Jim Turner asking if I still wanted to join Alan Johnston and him for dinner tonight at Opium.'

'Opium is lovely. Sounds interesting as well. What are they after?'

'There'll be two main things on the agenda – a debrief on the crime campus meeting today, plus discussion of the latest developments on Katerina's disappearance. Do you mind?'

'Of course not. When is it set for?'

'The table's booked for 8 pm.'

'Enjoy it. There's a *Vera* on Encore, I'll watch that – see how a proper detective conducts an investigation!'

Scott laughed. 'Very funny. Give Donald a kiss – tell him I'll see him in the morning. Love you. See you later.'

'Bye, love.'

Scott had been to Opium once – for a celebration dinner laid on by Mary's publishers after the launch of her second book at Finnieston Docks. From memory, it was on the junction of Hope Street and West Regent Street. He Googled it on his mobile and confirmed its location, about 15 minutes from Shawlands Cross, if the traffic was light. He made good time into the centre of town but had to park at the bottom of Wellington Street, so it was ten past eight before he got to the restaurant.

Jim and Alan spotted him as he entered and waved him over to their four-seat table at the window, looking out on the bottom end of West Regent Street. Scott shook hands and sat down next to Alan Johnston. Alan and Jim had exotically coloured drinks in front of them.

'Perfect timing, Scott,' Jim Turner said, and handed him a menu. 'We were just about to order.'

Scott grinned and pointed to their cocktails. 'I see you've managed to sort out the drinks, though!'

'Now, now,' Alan responded. 'We got here a bit early and were forced to have a libation, then another. Nothing wrong with a man ordering a cocktail, is there, Jim?'

'Not at all, especially as they don't serve Tennent's Lager here.'

Scott laughed again and scanned the menu, 'Give me a minute and I'll be ready to order.'

Alan nodded, 'Good, we're Hank. How did it go today?'

'We won,' Scott said. 'On the last board, pulled the match back on the final hand.'

Alan moved his head to the right and closed his left eye in pantomime fashion. Jim intervened, 'No Scott, not your bridge match, how did you get on at the campus? How was Kinnie?'

Scott put his hand on his forehead. 'Sorry, I'm still fixated with what happened in the bridge match. But let's order first. You're both starving. I'll tell you after we've done that.'

Scott composed his thoughts about the crime campus in Gartcosh as they ordered their starters and mains, plus another round of drinks for his dinner companions and an alcohol-free lager for himself. He had phoned Mary as soon as he finished his tour and given her his first impressions of the job he was being offered, so he had a template to work from for his discussions with Turner and

Johnston. He was aware of them looking at him, waiting for his thoughts. He put his hands palms down on the table and patted it three times.

'OK, initial verdict about Gartcosh. It's a very impressive building and a first-class setup internally. No expense spared. Computers, meeting rooms, infrastructure – they all looked top notch, state of the art, but I guess they would be as it's only two-years old. I got the royal tour. On balance, I would say that it's a better working environment than Hamilton Nick!'

Turner laughed, 'Hardly a fair test, but I have to agree.'

'Who did you see?' Johnston asked.

'Three people before I met Kinnie. John Massie, a DCI who's just been put in charge of the Cyber Crime Unit. I spent most time with him, getting his view of what the job would entail and meeting some of the IT team working with him, all of whom are civilians. Then I saw Bill Livingston, DS, he's the link to the Proceeds of Crime Forensic Unit. Finally, I spent time with John Templeton, he's HMRC and the liaison between them and our organised crime team. It was interesting – no – it was fascinating, even if it was a whirlwind blast through.'

Johnston interrupted, 'John Massie is a good guy, but I'd never have thought of him as a cybercrime specialist.'

Scott nodded. 'He sort of admitted as much on the walk – said he could really do with help.'

'So, did you meet Kinnie?' Turner asked, then took a long swig of his fresh cocktail.

'I did – spent the last half hour with him, on my own. He had a slightly different take on what the job would involve. He described it as a pulling together of the three areas I saw. I would use all that information to be the liaison on the introduction of Unexplained Wealth Orders. I would co-ordinate our work and build the case for the request to the government to grant the order – I'd be the conduit between Police Scotland and the Scottish Government legal team and civil servants.'

'That sounds like a big job,' Turner offered. 'And I can see why they want you – bright young graduate – Police Scotland 2.0.'

'Not as big as Kinnie's ego,' Johnston added, 'or his office, from what I've heard.' Turner spluttered into his drink. Johnston waited until he had wiped his face before continuing, 'So, what did you think of him, and the job?'

'He was very forceful, very adamant that the crime campus was the future of policing and that I had the chance to be in from the start and be a part of that. A consequence of which would be "rapid career advancement" – to use his words.'

'Aye, that's Kinnie's schtick! Promise the world...'

Scott paused, 'Would it be fair to say neither of you have much time for him?'

'Very fair,' Johnston admitted. 'In fact, if they hung us for being fans of Alan Kinnie, they would have hung innocent men.'

Turner burst out laughing. 'True. We won't go into it now, but both of us have form for being crossed by him. As has half of Strathclyde. It's no exaggeration to say that Kinnie isn't a team player.' He turned and signalled to the waitress for two more cocktails. Then he leaned forward, 'In his first morning in his new job, he came into his room and found a plaque on his desk. It said, "The Buck Starts Here".'

Scott grinned, but he was keen to move the debate away from himself and onto Kat's disappearance. 'Very funny, sir – I'll think about what they want me to do over the next week. Kinnie said he would like a quick response, even though he doesn't have a budget for taking me on and expanding the unit until the new year – so I wouldn't start till then.' He looked directly at Turner. 'And then talk it through with you, sir.'

Turner nodded. 'OK – but you should also talk to Alan – get his views on what's on offer in Glasgow in MIT.'

'I will – if you don't mind, sir?' he added to Johnston.

'No, of course not. It's important you have as level a playing field as possible on which to make your choice.'

'Thank you, sir,' Scott paused. 'Talking of what else might be available, can I ask you where you see my case now?'

Johnston put down his drink and rolled his neck. 'Happy to do that. The first thing to say is that the work your DC did to link the videos, the notes section of the iPad – and then tie that up with the hotel register and the likely sources of the bank deposits – was first class, really good. As was finding the satchel – and the link to Brian Young.'

'It was,' Scott agreed. 'Julia's extremely capable – she'll make a great DS.'

Turner and Johnston nodded and finished their drinks. Johnston held his up to the waitress again and looked at Scott, who shook his head. Johnston indicated two more and turned back to Scott.

'I'd better get this out before I'm totally wazzed.' He closed his eyes for a few seconds. 'Christ, these are strong – lovely – but strong. Anyway, you know the first rule in cases like this?'

Scott nodded. 'Concentrate on family and friends – 90 percent of cases involving harm to an individual are down to friends and family.'

'And if that produces no leads?'

'Don't know, sir. Then look at other options?'

'No – go back to the same group and look harder! And if that comes up dry?'

'Is it time then to look at other possibilities?'

'No! It's time to look at them again,' Johnston laughed. 'OK, I'm exaggerating to make the point.'

'I understand, sir.'

'Good…' Johnston shook his head a few times and then refocused on Scott. 'So, you're seeing the dad when?'

'I'm seeing Martin on Saturday at the Hearts game – I'm planning to tell him about the second phone and the contacts on the day Kat disappeared – get his reaction and see how that plays back into the family before I ask to see his dad. Unless you think I shouldn't?'

Johnston closed his eyes for a few seconds. 'No, you should do that, throw some stones in the burn and watch the ripples – see where they spread out to. We need to step up our efforts on this and his dad has a lot of explaining to do. The problem we have is that although we've got some interesting possibilities and leads from her iPad and bank statements – we still have no sightings after Irvine – no trace, no CCTV pictures, no car details – nothing. We need a break with some hard evidence. It's all circumstantial just now. The two best paths are your interview with Brian Young and the TV exposure. Hopefully get a response, and *Crimewatch* will give us something more concrete.' Johnston stopped and leaned across the table to prod Turner.

'There is one thing I don't understand, Jim.'

'What's that?' Turner said.

'Why it's you that's doing *Crimewatch* and not Scott here – who's younger, more intelligent, speaks well and is much better looking than you?'

Turner pretended to be hurt but couldn't prevent a laugh breaking out.

'Of course he is. He's golden bollocks. His career is guaranteed, especially if he chooses Gartcosh. But I want one more step up the ladder. One more promotion. This is very newsworthy now – I want to be seen.' He sat back when he finished and tried to wink at Scott – but the amount he had drunk interfered and it came across as a half stare/half leer.

Johnston burst out laughing. 'At least you're honest Jim. I don't think Scott's upset.'

Both his senior officers examined him. Scott could tell they were now well on. 'I'm not, sir. I'm happy you're fronting it – good luck.'

'And you,' Johnston mumbled. 'We're all looking forward to your interview and follow-up.'

Chapter 11
September 3rd

The sun started to break through what was a dull morning as the train pulled into Haymarket Station. Scott checked his watch again. Quarter past one – and he had arranged to meet Martin in the Tynecastle Arms at 1:30 pm. He had plenty of time to walk down Dalry Road and then cross to Gorgie and the ground. The Tynecastle Arms was situated on the junction of McLean Street, less than 25 yards from the stadium. It was where Scott and Martin always met when Motherwell played Hearts away. The pub was mobbed when Scott got there, with a crowd of fans drinking outside and a queue at the front door. Everyone else was in Hearts' colours, either wearing a maroon replica shirt or a Jambo scarf or both. Scott's tartan Motherwell scarf, the new one with the claret and amber checks, was safely stowed in his jacket pocket and he patted it down one last time as he pushed through the door.

The pub was as rammed, as he had anticipated, and it was a real feat of bodysurfing to make progress towards the bar. As he slalomed round an extremely fat fan, wearing a top four sizes too small, he spotted Martin at the bar. Scott took a breath, then stretched out as far as he could with his right arm and was just able to touch Martin on the back.

Martin manoeuvred round and laughed when he saw Scott.

'Great – what do you want?' he shouted.

'Pint of Tennent's.'

Martin nodded and squeezed back to the bar as Scott pressed closer to him.

It took Martin a bit of time to get the order and pay. By that time, Scott had managed to insert himself into a tiny gap between Martin and a large, white-haired man standing beside him.

'Cosy,' Scott said, as he accepted his pint.

'Yeah – quick one, then we'll shoot the craw.'

'Where to?' Scott asked.

'Sorry, didn't tell you but we have tickets for the Directors' Box.'

'What?'

'Yes, Dad had them for the game and gave them to me.'

'OK – bit different from our normal seats, then?'

Martin picked up his pint of lager and drank half of it in one long swallow. He motioned to Scott with his glass. 'Get it down you.'

Scott followed suit and sank most of his drink in two gulps. Martin laughed, then did the same. They forced their way out of the maul round the bar and left through the side entrance.

Martin shook himself when they emerged into the daylight then hugged Scott. 'Just like old times – really great to be going to a game with you again.'

'It is – and in the Directors' Box.'

They walked across the forefront to the stand. Martin went through the main door and up to the reception desk with Scott following close behind him. The woman at the desk looked up.

'Can I help you?'

'Brian and Martin Young – you have tickets for us?'

The woman bent her head and scanned a typed list of names. 'Yes, I do. Welcome – here are your passes. Do you know the way to the Directors' Boardroom?'

'No.'

'OK – it's a bit confusing because the stand is not fully finished yet – but up the stairs on your right, and it's to the left on the first floor.'

'Thanks,' Martin said, as he took the passes in their lanyards and slipped one over his head. Scott nodded his thanks and walked beside Martin up the stairs and along a corridor which looked barely finished to a large open door which fronted the boardroom.

A security guard wearing a Hearts tie held out his hand, 'Welcome to Tynecastle, gentlemen. Go away in and get some food and a drink.'

They walked into a long, large room which looked out onto the front entrance to the stand. There was a bar to their left and they gravitated to it. It was still only 1:50 pm and the room was almost empty. They ordered two lagers and took them over to seats beneath the full windows.

'Bit quieter than the Tynny!' Martin said.

They were having their first sip when a short, middle-aged woman came into the room and looked around it.

'That's Ann Budge,' Martin whispered.

'Do you know her?'

'Met her once with my dad – he knows her well – let's introduce ourselves.'

They walked over to her. 'Hello Ann, I'm Martin Young, Brian Young's son. I met you with my dad in the old stand. This is my pal, Scott James.'

Ann smiled and shook their hands. 'How's your dad? He's some man. Give him my best.'

Martin returned the smile. 'I will. Congratulations on the new stand.'

Ann shook her head. 'Thanks, but it's late, not finished yet, and over budget, so not quite what I wanted.'

A fresh influx of people appeared and moved towards them.

'We'll let you go,' Martin said. 'You'll have a lot of entertaining to do – keep up the good work.'

Martin moved Scott to the end of the room. 'What is it you wanted to discuss about Katerina and my dad?'

Scott looked round the room – there was nobody near them. 'OK, bit of a bizarre setting but probably better now than later in the pub. We have some more information about the calls and texts Kat got on the Friday she disappeared.'

'And that involves my dad?'

'Yes, there were calls to and from her phone, and three texts, all involving a phone registered to a company owned by your dad's business.'

Martin took a step to the side and shook his head. 'Are you sure?' He's not mentioned he had any contact with her. If it had been him, he would have said, wouldn't he? He knows what this whole thing is doing to me.'

Scott put his right hand on Martin's arm. 'I haven't asked your dad about it yet.'

'So, it might not be him?'

Scott paused. 'Might not, but it's much more likely it is. It's a Crammond Holdings' phone and GPS locates it at your mum and dad's house and at your dad's business premises at Melville Street most of the time, so balance of probability.'

Martin reached into his suit jacket. 'I'll phone him now – find out what the fuck's going on.'

'No, don't, please not now, not when you're upset. Officially, I shouldn't really have told you. I should have contacted your dad first, only told you after, but I thought you deserved to know first. I wanted you to get the chance to talk to your dad about it before I do.'

Martin hesitated then to put his phone back into his pocket. 'OK. Thanks for doing that. I'm seeing him tomorrow with Mum for lunch. I'll find a time to see him one to one and ask him. I'll let you know what he says.'

'Good – that's much better. Face to face is the right way to do it.' Scott smiled and touched his pal's arm. 'Come on, enough angst about family and work. Let's get into some proper worry. Football worry. Another couple of beers, then we can go up to our seats, get the atmosphere.'

Part 10

**"The flames you keep touching when you're young,
you keep on touching when you're older."**

Will Walton

November 7th – 10:30 am

I am writing this in the shop. One of my assistants is away at a PGA training weekend and the other is out on the course. The shop is quiet, as I thought it would be given the weather. I brought my journal on the chance I could set out the next part of my story. I need to get down what happened on Bonfire Night – it's very important – maybe it's the end of my purgatory.

We eventually invited around 50 people to the event which was trailed to begin at eight o'clock. Arlene was in charge of drinks and food on the night: mulled wine or beer for the adults, soft drinks for the kids with hot dogs, spicy chicken wings and vegetable pakora. I busied myself with last-minute checks on the fireworks I had bought and making sure the demarcation rope round the bonfire was firmly in place – 15 paces away from the outer limit of the grass mound. Kat's body was in the middle of the pyre, so there was no point trying to place the spectators at any particular angle. When everyone was fed and had a drink, I led them out through the paddock to the bonfire using glow lights to trace a path. Then I ushered Anna and Cathy in beside me at the bonfire and gave them each a taper, which I lit in turn. They went to opposite sides of the stack and set fire to the paper we had inserted that afternoon. Both areas took first time and the flames spread quickly on what was a dry, cold night. The fire was soon sneaking up the sides of the pile and the smaller pieces of cardboard and wood caught right away. My attention was solely on the grass base, compacted and about 4 ft high, as I wondered how well and how quickly it would catch fire. It did catch, as I stared, and very slowly, as I hoped.

When the top half of the bonfire was fully alight, I shepherded the girls back under the ropes whilst I stayed ringside. The Guy caught fire to general applause and even at that stage, the bottom layer of grass was only smouldering, rather than blazing. I remember thinking, *I am going to get away with this again*. And worse – telling myself it was a sign that I didn't deserve to be found out.

After about 15 minutes, when the main part of the bonfire started to reduce, I moved under the ropes to announce the fireworks display, which I had staked out well to one side of the mound. The firework combination we had chosen had cost a lot of money, but we had decided that if we were doing a firework show, it had to be good. And it was – in spite of my less than total coordination over the timing of the different parts because I kept glancing over to the bonfire. The display ended spectacularly with a batch of six powerful rockets which burst spectacularly against the backdrop of the landfall down to the sea and Arran. I bowed, again to applause, and the girls ran in to hug and kiss me. I kissed them back and looked over their heads at the fire as I did. Most of the wood had been burned but the grass was still largely intact, although burning more fiercely now. I suggested going back to the house for more food and drinks and most of the crowd took the hint and followed Arlene and the girls in.

A few stragglers stayed to warm their hands at the fire and a couple of parents ducked under the rope to get closer. I couldn't see any trace of Katerina's body which was at ground level, still with a blanket of grass above it, albeit a thinner coating. It was a cover which had reduced by at least half and I wasn't sure if the remaining part would hold, or for how long. I hung back, talking to the four adults who were gazing at the declining bonfire. I was desperate to get them to leave but didn't want to shunt them away too obviously, so I waited for a few moments before offering the drinks option again. Three of them were persuaded, but one woman stayed on, telling me she loved to look at the embers of dying fires. She grabbed her shoulders as she spoke and hugged herself to emphasise her point. The coffin lid of grass was getting thinner by the minute and I was worried that one of the heavier logs that were only partly burnt would force a path through the remaining blanket, land on Katerina and expose her remains. I felt suddenly paralysed and unable to think what more I could do, when I was rescued by her partner, who came back out from the house to get her. She tried to persuade him to stay, said it was romantic by the fire but he told her that their six-year-old daughter was playing up and that he couldn't settle her. Parenting won. I followed them inside, knowing that nobody would come out again as the fire died and it got darker. I would return early in the morning before anyone else in the family was awake to see what the latest turn in my drama had produced.

I've taken more than two hours to write this, mainly because I've spent most of that time reliving how I felt two nights ago – remembering the sensation of hoping/believing that I had moved even further from being discovered – starting to actually accept that my ordeal might be coming to an end.

Part 11

**"There are crimes of passion and crimes of logic.
The boundary between them is not clearly defined."**

Albert Camus

Chapter 12

September 21ˢᵗ

The response to the *Crimewatch* reconstruction had been patchier than Scott had hoped. When the usual body of crank calls was eliminated, there remained only one which seemed genuinely worth following up. Tina Bridges, a part-time chef at The Ship Inn on Irvine's harbourside had called to say that she might have seen Katerina on the night of her disappearance. After an initial telephone chat with her, Scott set up an interview at lunchtime in the pub on the Tuesday after the TV screening. He took Julia with him and also offered the local station in Irvine the option to send a representative – an invitation they declined on the grounds that they were very busy and the case was too advanced already for their input to be valuable. Scott was disappointed with their reaction but decided to delay his response to it until he had interviewed Mrs Bridges and could then talk to the local DI face to face.

Scott spent the one-hour drive to Irvine chatting about the case with Julia and discussing her upcoming sergeant exam. They got to The Ship Inn at 11:45 am and introduced themselves to the owner and Tina Bridges – a thickset woman with dyed blonde hair, who looked to be in her mid-fifties.

After spending thirty minutes getting background and going through her story, Scott had no doubt that Tina had seen a hitchhiker being picked up at the Annick roundabout on July 11ᵗʰ, and that the hitchhiker fitted Katerina's description exactly. Julia concurred with that view, so they went through what happened again with their new witness to confirm every aspect of what she had seen. Tina only worked on Friday and Saturday nights and her shift finished at 9:00 pm, fifteen minutes after the kitchen shut for orders. She always tidied up before she left, so it was generally about 9:15 pm when she set off home to Dreghorn village, a few miles away. Her normal route skirted round Irvine town, but that night she had made a detour. She estimated that she got to the Annick roundabout from the Gailes side of Irvine at around 9:30 pm. It had just started to rain very heavily, which was why she remembered the scene when she saw the *Crimewatch* reconstruction. She had noticed a car stopped on the Irvine side of the Annick roundabout and someone standing beside it. As she slowed down to pass it, she saw what looked like a hitchhiker get into the car. She recalled how she thought it was nice for the driver to help, especially in the horrendous weather and had tagged the pedestrian as a hitchhiker because they were carrying a sign.

For Scott and Julia, this was a key point in confirming it was Katerina that Mrs Bridges had seen – and tied neatly to the time Katerina was dropped in Irvine by the Hoods about 200 yards from the roundabout. Julia pushed Mrs Bridges hard on the date. Tina was adamant – she didn't go that way home ordinarily, but her husband had been at a pre-Orange Walk dinner at the Hallmark Hotel in Irvine and she was picking him up that night. He had been very drunk and hadn't wanted to leave when she got there. They had fought in front of his pals. So, she was certain about the date – July 11th.

The sighting was a major step forward, even though Tina couldn't say with 100 percent certainty that it was a girl being picked up, even after a series of promptings and being shown a number of photos of Katerina. What she could testify to be a parka-clad individual, a hitchhiker who was tall and wearing jeans, but very little on the car which had stopped to pick her up. No make or registration number. Mrs Bridges explained that the torrential rain had made it difficult to see anything at all. Tina could confirm that the car was medium-sized and dark in colour. So, SUVs, large estate cars and light-coloured vehicles could be eliminated, but nothing else. After trying two more times to see if Tina could be more definite, Scott shut down the interview and thanked her for coming forwards and being so helpful. He gave her his card and asked her to call him directly if anything else came to mind.

Scott had asked Tina to trace out the route she had taken that night on the Google map on his iPad. Once they had thanked the landlord for allowing them to use the premises, he and Julia walked out to Scott's car which was parked about 50 yards away on Harbour Road.

'Would you like me to drive, sir, and you can navigate?' Julia asked as Scott opened the doors with his remote.

'Probably a good idea.'

Julia slid into the driver's seat and accepted the key from him – she spent 30 seconds adjusting the position of the seat and the mirrors before she started the engine.

'Do they really call me MSDM at the station?' Scott asked.

'Afraid so, sir,' Julia replied, trying but failing not to smile.

'Mirror, Signal, Don't Manoeuvre,' Scott intoned. 'Very cruel.'

'That's the police for you, sir – we're an unkind shower of bastards.'

Scott nodded, then directed his DC along the route Tina had used that night. It took them just under eight minutes to get to the Annick roundabout.

'Go left first,' Scott instructed. 'Up to Malcolm Gardens, where the Hoods dropped Katerina off.'

Julia did as instructed and pulled in, opposite the entrance to the road.

'OK – she was dropped here,' Scott continued. 'Did she go into town? Did she get fish and chips? Or did she move back towards the roundabout? Let's get out.'

Julia put on the warning lights and they crossed the main road when the traffic allowed.

'No CCTV here that I can see,' Scott said, after looking around for a minute. 'Let's walk into town first – see if we can find anything – there must be cameras at some point on this road. Not that we'd know that from the exertions of our colleagues at Irvine Nick!'

They strolled towards the old town centre, passing a series of businesses, then the massive new Portal leisure centre before coming to a rundown row of shops which housed Mamma's Fish and Chips. It was open for the lunchtime trade and had an old CCTV camera mounted on the outside.

Scott stopped and looked up at it for a few seconds. 'Let's check if anyone saw her – and whether the CCTV is functional,' he said, walking into the shop and up to the counter. There was no one else in the premises.

'Is the manager in?' he asked, pulling out his warrant card. 'DI James and DC McDonald. We'd like to chat to him.'

The young lad standing at the till shook his head. 'No, sorry, pal – just me and Ally,' he indicated to a heavy woman, who was emptying chips into the fryer. 'The manager – well, the owner, only comes in at night – at the busy times.'

'OK,' Scott replied. 'I wonder if you can help us. We're looking into the disappearance of a young Polish woman who was last seen less than half a mile from your shop. She had been recommended to eat here.' Scott took out a picture of Katerina and handed it to him. 'The night of July 11th. A Friday. It would have been about 9:30 pm. Do you remember seeing her? There was a reconstruction of the last sighting of her on *Crimewatch* last Thursday night.'

The server waved over his co-worker. 'Police – looking for this girl – she might have been in on the night before the walk – July 11th.' They both looked closely at the image, then shook their heads.

'Sorry, I don't recall her,' he said, 'but it doesn't mean she wasn't in.'

'Yes, it does,' the woman retorted and smiled. 'She's gorgeous. He would have tried to chat her up if she had come in. Wouldn't you, Ryan?'

Ryan reddened and turned on her. 'Shut the fuck up – you know nothing about what I'm like.'

Scott intervened. 'OK, steady the Buffs. Ryan, were you working that night?'

Ryan hesitated. 'I expect so – I work every day except Sunday – so yes.'

'Thank you,' Scott said. 'And you don't remember seeing her. Do you know if the CCTV in here and outside works?'

Ryan nodded. 'It does now – it's old but it's just been serviced. It's been broken for weeks.'

'Was it operational during that weekend – July 11th or 12th?'

'Don't know – you'll have to ask Harvey.'

'Harvey?'

'The owner – my uncle – Harvey Spencer.'

'Thank you – we will. When's best? Do you have a number for him?'

Ryan turned towards the back shelf and opened a cupboard. He handed a card to Scott. 'That's his mobile – I'll tell him to expect a call.'

They thanked the staff and walked back to the car on the other side of the road, checking again for CCTV cameras as they went. There was a bus stop just before the roundabout – Tina Bridges hadn't mentioned seeing a bus – but it was worth following up in the next batch of press releases. Had anyone on a bus seen something? Scott noted the numbers of the bus routes serviced by the stop.

It took five minutes to drive to Irvine Police Station, situated on Kilwinning Road on the north side of the town. DI John Williamson had said he would be available any time after one o'clock and it was nearly 1:30 pm. Scott introduced himself and Julia to the PC on the desk and got the early stages of a scowl for his trouble. It was more than 15 minutes before Williamson appeared. He was mid-forties, Scott guessed, and running to fat. No, Scott thought – that race was over

– and fat had won. Williamson was unsmiling and barely raised his hand to shake Scott's.

'DI Williamson,' Scott said, and decided to be pleasant. 'Pleased to meet you. DI Scott James and DC Julia McDonald. Thanks for sparing the time to see us.'

Williamson barely acknowledged Julia as he showed them into a small interview room behind the front desk. He sat down first. 'I can't spare long – we're very busy – what is it you want? Exactly?'

Scott took a breath – he wasn't going to rise to the fly. Dealing with coppers like Williamson was part of his ongoing education. And no offer of tea or coffee. He wasn't going to ask – but Julia did. She turned directly to Williamson. 'Any chance of a tea, sir? We're gasping.'

Scott watched Williamson weigh up whether he could refuse. He could tell that he wanted to, but discretion won out. 'OK,' he grunted and opened the door to bellow, 'Three teas – strong,' into the squad room.

As he did, Julia looked at Scott and then down to her right hand, which was under the table and shielded from Williamson's line of sight. She formed it into a universal comment. Scott had no problem with his junior officer mocking a superior. He smiled as she moved her hand up and down, then he pretended to cough to strangle his laughter. He had recovered by the time Williamson resettled.

'As I said in my email a few weeks ago, we would appreciate your help in the disappearance of Katerina Wysklow – since then we've staged a *Crimewatch* reconstruction and that threw up a witness, the one I spoke to you about yesterday. We've just finished interviewing her – she is credible, so we now have a sighting of Katerina on the Annick roundabout on July 11th.' Scott paused, 'I wondered how you were getting on with gathering the CCTV for that night from 21:00 until 22:30 on Annick Road and from the businesses which front the road. We'll provide the bodies to review it for sight of Katerina – and any vehicles we can identify on that road in the same timeframe. Any luck so far?'

Williamson sat for a few minutes. 'As I said, we're very pushed at present.'

Scott tried again. 'I understand that – but do you have anything yet?'

Williamson sighed. 'Nothing, but I suppose I'll have to put someone on it now. I don't have much choice – word has come down from high that we have to support you.'

Scott bit his lip. That explained why Williamson's natural truculence had been ratcheted up by several degrees, but no matter how hard he fought, Williamson would have to provide assistance.

'That wasn't my doing – but I'm glad you're able to help – DC McDonald will liaise with you to sort out the detail.'

Williamson slurped the rest of his tea then rose to his feet. 'I can hardly wait,' he said and left the room.

Scott and Julia discussed their hostile reception on the way back to Hamilton and divided up the work streams for the next morning. After dropping Julia at the station, Scott headed home. Mary had a scan booked at Wishaw General at 4:30 pm and he made it in time to take her.

It took Scott the next day to fully update the case file with all the new information which had come in since *Crimewatch* aired and turn that into a revised state-of-the-nation report about the disappearance. Scott didn't get nervous about police politics, even though his next posting into either Glasgow MIT or the Crime Campus seemed to be causing more discussion than he felt it merited, but he did worry when he hadn't pulled all the facts of a case into a coherent whole. Mary teased him occasionally about being anal, but she was probably the only person who completely understood his need for order. He used her to help him keep control when he was involved in a complex enquiry. But the pregnancy, coupled with Donald starting school, occupied most of their home time and Mary was generally too tired to act as his sounding board as he tried to fit the parts of the disappearance together. The case had gained momentum in the past week and the *Crimewatch* sighting was a marker of that. He scrolled through the other interviews which had taken place during that time and extracted the issues he felt needed to be followed up, then put an addendum to his summary.

It now looked certain to Scott that the last sighting of Katerina was on the Annick roundabout at approximately 9:30 pm on July 11th. Her final phone GPS location was in south Paisley at 8:19 pm that night, which tied in with the statements given by the couple who had picked her up just before 8:45 pm. It was about half an hour by car from Paisley to where they dropped her off in Irvine and a short walk to the Annick roundabout from that spot. The times fitted. The reconstruction of her movements up to that moment looked logical – which left the phone calls on the day of her disappearance to be analysed to see how they slotted into the picture he was composing.

The two men she had contacted that day, apart from Brian Young, had been interviewed by the police forces in the areas in which they lived. Both had alibis for that night. The initial checks of those explanations held up and were confirmed by the location data from their telephones. One had admitted to having sex with Katerina and could be linked to one of the videos. He was divorced and not in a relationship, so had no reason to lie. He also confirmed that he had given her money – nearly £2000 in cash. He claimed it was to help her start a business and not because of any threat to expose their lovemaking to a wider audience. The other man denied having sex – although his initials tied in with the notes section of Katerina's iPad – and claimed never to have given her money. If his explanation of where he was that night hadn't been as certain – a work party confirmed by his PA and his phone records – he would have merited closer attention, but at this stage, he could be eliminated. Which left the calls to, and interview with, Brian Young as the most important leads. Scott was thinking that through again when his phone rang.

'Scott James.'

'Hi Scott, Alan – progress, I see.'

'Yes, sir. It is another step forward. My team are working on the basis that it was Katerina that Tina Bridges saw getting into the car that night. Do you agree?'

Johnston coughed, and there was a pause before he replied, 'When we first met, I counselled you against relying on gut reaction in some situations. So, let's look at the information logically. We can't be 100 percent certain it was Katerina. But what are the alternatives? Another hitchhiker was out that night at the same time and in a similar location. A location less than 200 yards from where we know Katerina was dropped by the couple from Irvine. A tall hitcher wearing a parka and carrying a sign. The balance of probabilities suggests very strongly that this is our missing person. So, what else can we do now, based on the new information?'

Scott had discussed that with Julia McDonald on the journey back to the station. 'It's annoying that we don't have a registration number or even make of car. That would have let us narrow it down. We could run a check of similar cars registered around Irvine and Troon. The A78 is the nearest main road – but it doesn't have average speed limit cameras – unlike the A77 – so we can't do an AVRN between say 9:00 pm and 10:30 pm on that road, even if we knew the car went onto the dual carriageway. There's no CCTV on the edge of Irvine on that way out of the town either. We're waiting for the videos from the shops nearer the town centre. I'm not sure what else we can do, other than run a check on Brian Young's car and see if we get lucky with a sighting later that night – we're doing that now.'

Johnston exhaled. 'Don't worry. You've thought of all the obvious things. The next best bet is to go back to the local press again. This time we can be much more specific. Concentrate on Irvine, Troon and Prestwick papers. Really ramp up the storyline about our concern. Use more pictures and the bus stop angle. See what we get – I'll organise that.'

'OK – thanks, sir. I just hope we get something from the CCTV in the town. If Irvine Nick actually gets around to doing anything, I'll keep you up to date.'

'When are you seeing Brian Young?'

Scott hesitated and took the phone from his ear for a moment.

'He's away on a joint business/holiday for three weeks – he told me that when I called him on Monday to fix the interview – it's not a setup – I checked with Martin – it's been arranged for months – part of it is going back to where Brian and Sue went on honeymoon. Should it be me, though? Is it not better if one of your team takes that meeting?'

'No – I still feel you should do the initial one – you'll get a much better read on his emotions and mental state than someone with no back history.'

'OK, I'll take it – It's set up for October 19th – two days after he's back.'

'Great – pity about the delay, but let's use it to find out as much as we can. Do you believe the information Martin gave you after he talked to his dad?'

'I do – at this stage. His dad explained about the investment in Katerina's business and that he intended to give it to Martin as a birthday present – and said that was why he hadn't said anything about the calls – but I need to push Brian really hard on that when I see him.'

'I agree – Let's see what else we can find out before Young gets back.'

Part 12

"Oh, what a tangled web we weave…"

Sir Walter Scott

November 14th – 1:00 pm

I had hoped this would be the last entry in my journal – that I could mark my final card, sign it and hand it in to the official scorer. End the process.

And that was so nearly possible – because the bonfire "worked". I was out the next morning, first thing, wearing an old pair of walking boots so that I could step into the remains of the fire. It was bright and cold – the kids and Arlene were still in bed as I got to the remnants of the Guy Fawkes celebration. The mound had been reduced but the bottom layer was still smouldering, and more importantly, still covering the remains of the body, as far as I could see. I stood and looked at it for a long time – breathing slowly and preparing myself for what I might find.

There were also some bits of thicker wood which were only partially burned. I got my fork from the side of the circle and walked up to the outer limits of what was left of the fire – I thought I could see the outline of a torso – or the bones of a torso – just beneath the top level of burned grass and a skull slightly detached from it. But then I couldn't. It was the weirdest sensation. Like reality was being switched on and off. I checked and prodded through the upper cover of charred debris. I felt as much as saw something under it, and when I pushed harder, it gave way and broke up. But it wasn't a body – it was one of the larger logs with what looked like some old sacking covering bits of it. I checked again to be sure – there were no bones that I could see. The fire had been burning or smouldering for 11 hours. I had no idea how hot it had been when it reached its maximum temperature, but I had researched how bones turn to ashes and knew that crematoria operate at about 1500° F. It was unlikely my bonfire had got anywhere near that, but I hoped the prolonged burn time might have the same effect.

I pushed the grass back from either side of the shape to explore the rest of the mound. There was nothing lying underneath the top cover that I could see. No head, ribs, pelvis or leg bones – nothing. I pressed hard on the remaining debris and grass, and it broke up fairly easily as I applied leverage with the fork. I was just about to start battering the remnants of the bonfire when I looked behind me and saw Cathy waving from the paddock gate and walking towards me. I had less than a minute to hide the bottom section – just in case there were remains I hadn't seen. I threw all the grass I could on top of that part – then piled that higher from the left and right-hand sides – I built up a grass cairn to about 3 ft tall before she reached me and gave me a cuddle. We talked about how successful the bonfire and party had been, and I explained that the grass was still hot and that she and her sister had to respect that and not poke about in it, in case they got burned. Which she agreed to. She was more interested in me and how great the party had been – not the dying remains of the fire and I was able to walk her back to the house after a few minutes.

The next couple of days were less stressful – the girls didn't show any further interest in the site, and I was able to check and reorder it each morning, mainly by arranging the remaining timber to form a semiarch over the grass tent. The weather helped – it stayed dry, so the grass continued its slow burn and I pulled together a new funeral pyre each day. It took almost a week for the fire to die out completely and it was only then that I checked systematically for bones. Most of what remained of the burial ground had reduced to ashes – the overall effect of a week's burn must have had that effect on everything – I smashed the pile with the pitchfork and broke it up into smaller pieces and looked at each of them in detail – I thought that some of the detritus might be smaller bits of bone but it was impossible for me to tell. I struggled with believing I had got away with what I had done. I felt happy, absolved and guilty all at once. And then I drove the tractor over the remains of the grass to complete the process. If there was any remaining evidence, it was imbedded in the ground – I drove over it time and again, until the remains of the bonfire were completely compacted and the ash and residue were hardly recognisable. I will build a new grass mound on the site next year and go through the same procedure. There will be less and less trace each time I do that. Any remaining evidence is much more difficult to source now and I hope will be eliminated by one more season of burning and burying.

It had been my intention to finish my journal at this point. The evidence of what I did is now unrecognisable for all practical purposes. I have written down the story and that has helped me to cope with what I did.

I had begun to feel, for the first time since July 11th, that I could put it away – put it in the past where it belongs – and get on with the next chapter of my life.

But I got a phone call yesterday from the police. They want to come and see me to discuss Brian Young and his behaviour at my golf tournament, and to talk to my assistant who played in Brian's team. The interviews are tomorrow, so I need to spend the rest of today dealing with my fear and trying to anticipate what they will ask me. I am so relieved that I didn't agree to produce an alibi for Brian that night – because that would have drawn me right into the centre of the investigation. As it is, it looks as if I am only peripherally involved and I need to make sure I keep it that way tomorrow.

Part 13

"The larger crimes are apt to be the simpler – for the bigger the crime, the more obvious, as a rule, is the motive."

Sir Arthur Conan Doyle

Chapter 13
October 22nd

Scott and Julia got to Livingston Police Station an hour before the appointed time and introduced themselves to the duty sergeant and the rest of his team. They had a look at the available interview rooms before setting up for the meeting. Brian Young arrived exactly on schedule and they escorted him to Interview Room B, the smaller of the two and the less formal. Scott poured out cups of tea as they settled themselves round the wooden table in the centre of the room.

Young sat down directly across from Scott, rubbed his cheek and took a sip of tea before he spoke, 'How much does Martin know about this? He spoke to me about it after he met you on Saturday.'

'Define "this"?' Scott replied quietly.

'"This" is Katerina having contact with me independently from him and the fact she phoned me on the day she disappeared.'

Scott leaned forwards, 'You know that I told him about the calls on Saturday. He's also aware about aspects of Katerina's social life, which we think could have a bearing on her disappearance. Potential links to other men.' Scott paused. 'I'm going to record the interview, if you don't mind. It's easier to do that, rather than take notes.'

Young looked away before answering and clasped his hands under his chin. 'OK – I don't object to you recording.'

Julia McDonald switched on the machine, inserted a disc and pressed the record button. 'This is an interview with Brian Young at 2 pm on Friday 22nd October. Present with Mr Young are DC Julia McDonald and DI Scott James. The interview is in connection with the disappearance of Katerina Wysklow. Mr Young has given his consent to the interview being recorded. Can you confirm that for the record?'

Young pulled at his right ear. 'Yes, I agree to the interview being recorded,' he said softly. 'This is very embarrassing. Especially as I know you so well, Scott. As a friend. From before your time in the police. And you have a lady detective here. That doesn't make it any easier for me either. Do I have to answer your questions? Would it be better if someone else took the interview?'

Scott shook his head. 'No, on both counts. You don't have to answer. I can't force you to give me information and you're not under caution. But if you choose not to help, I need to consider what to do next. I think it's more sensible you tell me everything you know, because the investigation won't go away. Katerina's disappearance is now being treated as suspicious and has been passed to a specialist team. I've been absorbed into that squad, as has DC McDonald. You have links to Katerina – especially on the day she vanished. So, you are part of that whole enquiry. Talk me through what happened between you. Explain the relationship. Then I can make decisions on how to progress the case. But with all the facts – not just parts of the story.'

Young got up from his chair and paced to the door and back again. He sat back down before he replied. 'OK – I've explained it to Martin, so no reason not to tell you – I'm sure he has anyway.'

Scott stayed silent.

'I did have contact with Katerina the day she disappeared,' Young continued.

'We know you did,' Scott replied. 'What we don't know is (a) What that contact was about, and (b) why you didn't mention it to Martin right away, or to be more accurate, until I let him know about the Crammond phone.'

Young bit his bottom lip. 'The explanations are linked. Kat pitched a business idea to me when she stayed at the house in May. It was interesting – a sort of Scottish/Polish twist on B&B – like a boutique concept. I quite liked it, so I agreed to put in £5000 as seed capital for a 10 percent stake. That's what the calls were about on the Friday.'

Scott leaned forward. 'So why not mention it when Martin reported her missing?'

Young hesitated. 'Two reasons. Firstly, I didn't see that it was relevant – it had nothing to do with her disappearance.'

'The second?'

'That relates to Martin – I've been trying to get him to join the business since he graduated – you know that – so far unsuccessfully. This was another attempt.

It's his 30th in a month. I was going to give him the shares as a birthday present, see if that would tempt him into my world. I wanted to keep that a secret.'

Scott looked across at Julia and saw her frown. 'OK, let's accept that at present. It doesn't explain some entries we've found on Kat's iPad.'

'What entries?'

'In the notes section – it has what looks like a TripAdvisor review of a number of men.'

'Men?'

'Yes – we can decipher who they might be from the initials and the dates.'

'Explain.'

'Well, MY, for example is entered on April 23rd, one day after you and Martin left Sunny Bay. That's Martin. He and the rest are rated out of five on "SP" and "W" – we're guessing that's "sexual prowess" and "wealth".'

'That's a lot of guessing.'

'No, it's just balance of probability and you, or BY, is entered in her notes on May 23rd – the day after Kat's visit to your home. You score 3/5 for SP and 5/5 for W.'

Young closed his eyes for a second and sat back.

Scott looked at Julia before he continued. 'So, did you sleep with her?'

'No, I didn't.'

'Did you give her money?' Scott asked.

'Yes. But not for sleeping with me.'

'Are you sure?' Scott replied.

'I gave her money. As I said, she wanted to open a hotel or B&B with her mum. I said I would help. I would be an investor…'

Scott leaned forward. 'So, I'll ask you again, were you sleeping with her and paying money for that?'

Young shook his head. 'No, I wasn't paying money to get sex. I was helping her by putting capital into her business!'

Scott consulted his notes. 'Was that a company, Home From Home?'

'Yes, I put in £5000 through Crammond Holdings and became a shareholder.'

'Did you help her again? After that weekend?'

'No! I only gave her money once.'

'OK. Let's accept that for now. But I'll need details of the money you provided and the date. So we can confirm the position.' Scott looked at his notes for a few seconds. 'Was that the extent of the contact that Friday?'

Young shook his head. 'Not entirely. We were texting. A bit about her business. A bit flirting – sexting, I think they call it. She sent me some pictures of her that day. I had told her that I would be across in Troon that weekend. Explained that I was playing in a golf tournament in Ayrshire. She said she would like to see me. We could have a night together. I said no. I didn't want to get into a relationship with her. I said she could keep the money I had invested, but I couldn't see her that way. The photos she texted me during that day were an attempt to get me to change my mind. I was on the golf course at Barassie and didn't see them till I finished our round. I tried to reach her to tell her not to come to the hotel. But I couldn't get a response. Her phone went to voicemail. I didn't leave a message. I heard nothing more from her. And I didn't see her.'

'Are you sure you didn't see her that Friday night?'

'I'm sure. I didn't see her.'

'But she knew where you were staying?'

'Yes.'

'Where was that?'

'Piersland House Hotel in Troon.'

'Were you with anyone at the hotel?'

'Yes. The rest of my team.'

'Who was that?'

'Bob Wilson and Charlie Bain – both from Edinburgh and clients of mine.'

'What happened that night? Did you spend it with them?'

'Yes – we got back to the hotel after the golf about 7 pm, I guess. I had a bath and cleared my emails then met them in the main bar at 8:30 pm – had a meal in the dining room, then went to bed.'

'Did you all go at the same time?'

'Yes, more or less.'

'I'll need details. Addresses and contact details for the other two.'

Young sat back in his seat. 'Do you really have to talk to them? The reason you want to see them will spread out from there like a contagion. It'll be all over Edinburgh in a few days. That will link me to the disappearance permanently. Can't you take my word I didn't see her that night?'

Scott leaned forward and put his right hand on Young's arm. 'Brian, I need to verify what you've told me. I hope you can understand that. Katerina was last seen in Irvine. You were staying minutes away from there, you have admitted to giving her money and to her sending you sexual texts and photos. I have to check this out and I'll need your mobile phones – both of them – and any iPads where you have backed up data – with passwords.'

Young nodded and took Scott's hand – then squeezed it. 'I did a stupid thing.'

'What?'

'I got rid of the second phone.'

Scott paused and breathed out. 'Why?'

'It's obvious, isn't it? I knew it linked me to Kat – I panicked – I'm sorry.'

'What did you do with it?'

'Immersed it in a sink full of water, then broke it up and threw it in a skip.'

'How long ago?'

'Two weeks.'

'Was it backed up?'

'No.'

Scott was irritated and couldn't help letting it show. 'That doesn't look good, Brian. Doesn't look good at all. Especially with all your contact on the day she vanished. That was really stupid.'

'I can see that. But I wasn't having an affair!' Young stopped.

Julia leaned forward, 'Why did you need a second phone, anyway? It's been operational for over four years – long before Katerina – why?'

Young shook his head, 'I think you can guess why.'

'I can,' Julia said quietly, 'but tell me anyway.'

'I've been involved before with women – a couple of times – but I wasn't with Kat.'

Scott could see that Young was close to tears – it was difficult to stay dispassionate, but he wasn't going to lie to him. Young needed to appreciate what would happen now. Scott rested his hands on the table. 'I understand how awkward it is. I'll do my best to keep this contained. I really will. But we need to follow all of this up to eliminate you from the list of people who could have seen or met her that night and I'm not certain I can do that at present.' Scott paused. 'I'll need your iPhone and pin.'

Young sighed and fished his mobile out of his jacket pocket. He took Scott's right hand again. 'OK. I can see that. But please do what you can to avoid it spilling out of control. The code is 1959, the year I was born. Are we done?'

'Yes, for now.'

Young got up, breathed deeply and moved to the door.

Scott and Julia escorted him out of the building and watched as he sat in his car for a few minutes, before driving away.

'What do you think?' Scott said, when the car had disappeared from sight.

Julia clasped her hands in front of her before she answered. 'It looks bad, very bad. He knew her, gave her money, was in Troon the night she disappeared and has destroyed the phone he used to keep in touch with her. He's in her notes section. He's admitted to having affairs before Katerina. She was trying to get to him sexually. What more do we need?'

'A bit more, I think,' Scott replied hesitantly. 'I agree that everything points to him.' He paused. 'But his explanation is plausible, and his normal phone is shown in Troon all evening. It's on until 11 pm, then back active at 7 am at the same location. And there's no communication between that phone and Kat's. So, nothing to suggest he moved from the hotel. The second mobile is switched off at 7:30 pm at the same location, so if they did meet, how did they keep in touch?'

'That's a bit thin, sir,' Julia said. 'OK – let's accept he didn't leave the hotel and he didn't know where she was later that night. But she knew where he was staying – she gets a lift or a taxi, comes to his room… He doesn't have to go and get her!'

'You're right – we'll follow up at Piersland and with his golf team. Send a transcript of the interview round all the team as soon as it's back, with our thoughts and follow-ups added.' He sighed. 'I'm probably too close to this – I don't want it to be Brian. Let's ask what the others think and see what we get from the other interviews.'

Chapter 14

November 11th

DCI Johnston placed his teacup on the table to his right and stood up. The squad room was almost full, and the chatter subsided after a few seconds.

'I think you all know who I am – but let me formally introduce two of my team.'

Johnston took three steps forward to stand beside two young officers. He pointed at one with his left hand, 'DS Bob McHugh.'

McHugh turned and looked round the room as Johnston continued.

'And his alter ego – DS Roy Sneddon.'

Sneddon half rose and lifted his right hand to acknowledge the introduction.

'I've set aside two hours for the case update – I think that will be enough time – I'm doing the intros because the enquiry is now officially badged as MIT and I'm the designated officer in charge. As you all appreciate, the work so far has been handled mainly by Hamilton and lead by DI Scott James and DC Julia McDonald – so I'll let them take us through where we are. Scott.'

Scott got up and walked to the front of the room, signalling to Julia to come with him.

'Thanks, sir. It's good to be part of a larger team. And have the extra resources to get this resolved before I go on paternity leave in January.' He laughed, 'I'll have other things on my mind then.' He paused to let the room quieten. 'One key point, which again is clear from the notes, is that the woman who has disappeared is the girlfriend of my best pal and I know his family well. That has caused me a lot of worry about whether I am conflicted. So, it's good that the investigation is being passed over. Let's run through it all and see where we should go next. Julia.'

Julia moved to his side and pointed at two whiteboards set up at the back of the room.

'You all have copies of the basic information on Katerina and it's on the boards as well. What I'd like to do is go through the timelines on the day she disappeared and then match that up to our main suspect.'

DS Sneddon raised his hand. 'I know this has come to us because the working assumption is that she has come to harm – but have we eliminated all the other possibilities?'

Julia looked to Scott, who nodded for her to answer.

'Not 100 percent. You'll know much more about cases like this than I do. And I guess it's always difficult to get complete certainty, but we have no sightings of her since July 11th – no phone use – nothing on her credit card or her bank account – and no contact with her family or friends or employer – or Martin Young, her boyfriend.'

Sneddon opened his hands. 'That's fair enough – I've only had time to skim the case notes. I just wanted to ask the question – I agree with you.'

Julia smiled at him. 'Thanks. So, back to the day Katerina vanished and her connections to people of interest to us. She left Sunny Bay for Prestwick Airport at about 10:30 am, after breakfast service. She took a rucksack with her and we believe that's all she had other than the clothes she was wearing and a sign for Prestwick Airport. We've confirmed that with the couple who gave her the first lift – Bill and Marion Curtis. She seemed perfectly normal to them on the journey – they stopped twice – at Aviemore for tea and a scone, then at Skean Bridge for a comfort break. They dropped her on the south side of Fort William at around 1:30 pm. Her phone GPS for the morning confirms that journey exactly.'

She paused to have a drink of water and looked around.

'OK – the next part of the day is more difficult for us. Despite appeals in the press, local and national, and the *Crimewatch* reconstruction, we have no sightings of her from 1:30 pm until 8:30 pm that night. All we have is her phone GPS, which shows her south of Fort William, where she was dropped off by the Curtises, until just after two o'clock. It shows her moving south down the A82 for about an hour and a half. Then locates her at Crianlarich at 3:30 pm, which is the right timescale for a 50-mile journey with no break. And it stays there until 6:00 pm, when she starts down the A85 – it traces her all the way to Braehead Shopping Centre on the west of Glasgow but the signal goes at that point – exactly 8:19 pm.'

Bob McHugh caught Julia's eye and she pointed to him, 'Bob?'

McHugh nodded and then smiled. 'Any CCTV from Fort William or Crianlarich?'

'To be honest, it isn't something we've concentrated on so far – we've had to manage our limited resources. And the fact that we have her sighted and picked up at Braehead made it less important.' She stopped. 'But I agree it's something we can consider now we have a much bigger team.' She stopped and looked round the group. 'Any other questions about the early stages of the journey – apart from phone calls and texts which DI James will cover?' There was no response.

'OK,' she continued. 'The next phase – her lift with the Hoods and them dropping her on the outskirts of Irvine at approximately 9:15 pm. Notes of the interview are included in an appendix in the case file. I hope you've all had the chance to read them.' There was a gentle murmur of yeses. 'So, what does that tell us?' She pointed to the right-hand whiteboard, which had eight green discs attached to it – each beside a number.

1. Katerina was alive and well when the Hoods picked her up near Braehead just after 8:30 pm.
2. She told them her phone had run out of charge – so we have a natural end to the GPS locations at Braehead – no one forcibly turned it off or took her phone from her.
3. She seemed normal – not nervous or stressed in any way.
4. She said she was heading for Prestwick Airport – which is consistent with everything else we know about her plans.
5. She was dropped on the Annick Road out of Irvine around 9:15 pm.
6. It started to rain very heavily just after she was dropped off.
7. The Hoods had suggested a local chip shop in the old Town Centre when she said she was hungry – that is about 600 yards from where she got out. But the staff there didn't see her.
8. We have a witness who says she saw a hitchhiker being picked up at the Annick roundabout at approximately 9:30 pm. Our working assumption is that person was Katerina. Again, notes are in the appendix, including a general description of the car.

Julia paused. 'Any questions?'

'Have we ruled out Mr Hood?' McHugh asked.

'Not completely, but it's unlikely he's involved. His wife would have mentioned if he had gone out again, I'm sure. But we'll doublecheck with her and her mother.'

DCI Johnston rose to his feet. 'That's worthwhile. As we all know, in this type of case, 90 percent of the disappearances are down to someone who knows the victim. And Hood did know her after the car journey – Bob, can you take that up?'

McHugh nodded and made an addition to his notebook.

Johnston kept standing with Julia McDonald beside him.

'Anything else on this portion?' he asked.

This time it was DS Sneddon who spoke, 'The case notes say that we have only limited CCTV from Annick Road and the start of the old Town Centre, and what we have doesn't show any images of Katerina. Is there anything else on that road we can access?'

Julia twisted her head to the side and bit her lip. 'We've left the collection of tapes to Irvine Nick,' she paused. 'But to be honest, I'm not sure they've been that enthusiastic about helping.'

Johnston laughed and shook his head. 'Let me reinterpret that – they've been fucking idle – and I am going to put a cattle prod up their arses. So that's work in progress and we might still get lucky. Any other questions?'

Johnston waited for a few seconds. 'All right. Let's bring it up to date with the last sighting and how Katerina's previous calls and texts and the interview with the prime suspect fit into that Scott.'

Johnston and McDonald sat down as Scott got to his feet again and walked over to the second whiteboard.

'Thanks. Let's concentrate on the final sighting and how that might link into her communications that day.' Scott pointed to the board. 'OK, to reiterate, we have a woman who remembers a hitchhiker being picked up at Annick roundabout at about 9:30 pm on the Friday night. Our working assumption is that the hitchhiker is Katerina. All the bits fit together – time, place, weather, clothes, sign – and the witness has a very good recall of the exact location and time.' Scott paused and shook his head.

'That's good – but frustratingly, we don't have anything else – no CCTV, no car registration or even make. All we know is medium-sized and dark, and to compound it, there's no ANPR on any of the nearby roads. Not until the A79 and the approach to the airport, so it's a bit of a dead end in that respect because there is no evidence of Katerina from the CCTV at Prestwick Airport.' Scott walked back to his chair and stood beside it.

'So, let's look at the runners and riders in our suspects' race.' He put up his hand, 'And there's only one at present. The favourite is Brian Young, Martin's father. We've interviewed him once – the transcript is in the notes. He's admitted to giving Katerina money, and texting and calling her that day. And...' Scott paused for effect, 'he was staying at Piersland House – a hotel in Troon, which is less than six miles from where Katerina was last seen in Irvine. To give him the full house, he's likely the "BY" on Kat's iPad, and he has no alibi after 9:30 pm.'

Julia added, 'When he left his golf teammates and quote "went to bed for an early night".'

'So why haven't we arrested him?' Sneddon asked. 'Interviewed him under caution – examined his car for traces of Katerina?'

Scott held up his right hand. 'You're right to ask – he's odds on to be our man – but...' Scott opened out his right hand, 'One, his car is dark, but it's a BMW X5, so not really small/medium. Two, the GPS for his normal phone, the one he uses for family/friends, shows his location as Piersland House – all night and the following morning. The "special" one, the one he used to contact Katerina, was switched off at about 9:30 pm. The last contact with Katerina on that phone was a text from her at 6:30 pm so he couldn't have known where she was. But...' Scott paused, 'Young admits he destroyed that phone about six weeks ago so we can't interrogate it for further information.'

Sneddon put up his arm. 'Not conclusive, he might have prearranged to pick her up somewhere, gone out without his phones – especially as he wasn't getting any response from Kat's phone – and the witness might have been mistaken about the size of the car. The fact he got rid of that phone makes me doubly suspicious!'

Scott nodded. 'I agree, but I can't see how he could have known where she was in Irvine. I also don't buy a random encounter with her there. If it is him, the likeliest scenario is that she got the person who picked her up in Irvine to drop her at the hotel. We are going to pull Young in again – I won't do the interview this time. I'll observe.'

'I'll take a shot at it,' Sneddon replied quickly.

Scott laughed. 'Thanks – I don't think we'll have any shortage of volunteers. Brian Young is very likely our man.'

Julia touched his arm and he motioned for her to get up. 'OK,' she said. 'We're interviewing Young's golf teammates, the staff at Piersland House and the golf professionals at the club where he plays in the next couple of days. And we'll get CCTV from Piersland at the same time for that night. DI James and I were intending doing those meetings, unless anyone has a better suggestion?'

DCI Johnston stood up. 'That's sensible. Once that's done and we have all had a chance to consider the results, we'll have another go at Young, see how he fares second time around. Any questions? No? Thanks.'

Chapter 15

November 14th

It had taken a lot of persuasion and organising by Julia, to shoehorn the next batch of interviews into two days at the start of the week after the review by MIT. On Monday afternoon, Scott and Julia saw the other two amateur members of Brian Young's golf team at Saughton Police Station – Robert Wilson, an Edinburgh property developer and Charles Bain, the owner of a chain of pubs in the city. The information they provided in separate interviews was uniform and almost identical. They had been invited to play in the golf event about eight weeks before and had agreed with Brian that they would make a weekend of it. They were both clients of Brian's business – their pensions were looked after and run by IFAs Brian employed. They had been to pro-ams before as Brian's guests and always had an enjoyable time. The three men planned to drive over together on the Friday morning and play Barassie that afternoon, then stay in Troon at Piersland House on the night before the event. They would take part in the pro-am at Irvine Gailes the next day and then taxi back to the hotel after the formal dinner. The weekend was to be topped off by a buffet lunch on the Sunday at Gailes, followed by a round at Dundonald Links in the afternoon before they went home. They had arranged to travel to Ayrshire in Robert's Range Rover, but a week before the event, Brian said he had to go through separately. He hadn't given any particular reason for the change but mentioned a business commitment. Robert and Charles had kept to the original plan and travelled to the west coast together. Brian had met them in the clubhouse at Barassie Golf Course at about 1:30 pm on the Friday afternoon.

Neither of them had noticed anything unusual about Brian's behaviour during their round of golf on the Friday. They had gone back to Piersland House after a quick pint in the lounge at Barassie, showered, changed and met for pre-dinner drinks. That would have been at 7:15 pm, they estimated. But something out of the ordinary happened after their dinner in the hotel restaurant. Both Robert and Charles had expected to go through to the main bar and stay there for the rest of the evening and into the wee hours. But Brian, normally the party animal of the group, had pleaded tiredness almost immediately after they'd finished their desserts and sweet wine chasers, made his apologies and gone to bed. Which wasn't normal. And while they were staying in the main house, Brian had one of the separate cottages in the grounds. They confirmed Brian had made the booking for the hotel and had picked up the tab. Neither of them thought that Brian was anything other than his usual self at the golf day. He had been upbeat and encouraging to their young pro all the way through their round. And he was the same at the meal afterwards and the following day. There was nothing untoward about his behaviour that they could recall. They had played at Dundonald Links on the Sunday afternoon, had a quick cup of tea in the clubhouse, then gone back to Edinburgh in separate cars.

The only difficult part of the interviews was when Scott and Julia were asked why Robert and Charles were being questioned about Brian's movements and demeanour that weekend. Scott was diplomatic and explained that the enquiries were in connection to the disappearance of Brian's son's girlfriend and the police were just getting as much background information as they could. But he could tell that both men knew there was more to it, particularly as they seemed to have a good knowledge of the story and the fact that the last sighting of Katerina was only a few miles from where they were staying.

Scott discussed the interviews with Julia on the way back to Hamilton. They agreed that the evidence Charles and Robert had provided tied up with Brian's story, except for two important aspects – both he and Julia had formed the impression from Brian's interview that he had been with his golf companions all night. Not just until around ten o'clock. Nor had Young said that he was staying in a different part of the hotel to his friends. They agreed that they hadn't asked the questions specifically, but it was a couple of inconsistencies they needed to explore further.

Chapter 16

November 15th

The following day, Scott picked Julia up from her flat in Wishaw and drove them along the Clydeside, over Garrion Bridge, then along the A71 to Ayrshire, to the next batch of interviews in Troon and Irvine. The first was at Piersland House – the location Brian Young's team had stayed at. Jack Douglas, the owner of the business, introduced them to the staff who were on duty in the bar and restaurant that night – seven in total – but during two and a half hours of going over the evening, nobody could remember anything unusual or whether anyone had joined Brian Young in his room later that night. The lodges, which sat at the side of the main building, were self-contained, and unless a visitor came into the hotel reception, it was unlikely they would be noticed. CCTV covered the hotel entrance and reception, as well as the main car park but not the lodges. Scott recovered the tapes for the Friday night and Saturday morning, which he had asked to be provided when the meeting had been set up.

After the interviews, Scott and Julia accepted the offer of soup and a sandwich in the bar and were given a mini tour of the complex by the owner while they waited for their lunch. They left at 1:30 pm and took the bypass road to Gailes Golf Course to interview Ian White, the professional who had run the event, and his assistant, who had played in Brian's team. They had arranged that meeting for two o'clock, but there was little traffic on the A78, and Scott and Julia arrived early. The sun broke through a dull grey backdrop as they came to the end of the grand entrance to the course and parked in front of the clubhouse. It was chilly in the coastal breeze and both of them put on coats before they walked towards the entrance. The pro shop was well signposted and stood about 20 yards beyond the main door. A black Volvo xc90 with the number plate PRO 66 was parked to the side of it. They walked briskly to the shop. Scott opened the door, which pinged to announce their arrival. The shop seemed empty, but as he let Julia through, a young man appeared from the back of the premises.

'Can I help you?'

Scott nodded. 'We're looking for the pro – Ian White and his assistant, Duncan Forbes. We have a meeting with them in about 15 minutes. I'm DI James and this is DC McDonald.'

'I'm Duncan Forbes. Ian mentioned you were coming.'

Scott shook his hand, 'Pleased to meet you. Is Mr White about?'

'Yes, but he's out on the practice area just now. We were expecting you at 2 pm. Do you want me to go and get him?'

'No. Let him finish. We are a bit early. We can spend that time with you – if that's OK?'

'Fine – how can I help?'

'We're looking to get a view of Brian Young's behaviour on the day of the pro-am event. You were the pro on his team?'

Forbes smiled. 'I was. What do you want to know?'

Julia took out her notebook and leaned on the shop counter. Scott moved to stand beside her. 'Was that the first time you met Brian?'

'Yes. He takes part in the event every year. I know that he and Ian go way back to Ian's early days as a pro. Brian sponsored Ian's first year on tour. They're good friends. He always plays in the competition with one of the assistants – I joined the club last October – so it was my turn this year – I didn't know him at all, other than Ian's stories – Ian introduced me to him on the Saturday morning.'

'How is your recollection of that day?'

'Good. It was my first big tournament, so I was fired up. Really keen to play well. Brian had arranged a side bet with Ian on the team score – £100 per man. He explained he would put up the money if we lost – but I would keep it if we won. That made it even more exciting for me.'

'Did you win?'

'No! The boss had an amazing round – so did his team – we were third – but a long way back.'

'How was Mr Young that day?'

Forbes hesitated for the first time. 'I don't know what's normal for him but to me he was great – outgoing, funny and encouraging.'

'Nothing seemed to be distracting him?' Scott continued.

'No. He's not in trouble, is he? I wouldn't want to say anything that could cause a problem.'

'No don't worry. I'm just interested in your impressions of him that day. Did you sit with him at the meal?'

'Yes.'

'What did you talk about?'

'The usual – golf – what I hoped to achieve. Football – he's a big Hearts fan – just normal men's chat.'

'Thanks for that. If anything else comes to mind, then please contact us. Here's my card.'

They had just finished when Scott noticed a tall figure walking along the side of the course, carrying golf clubs and moving towards the pro shop. The man saw him and waved with his free hand. Scott smiled and waved back through the shop window. The man quickened his pace and was at the door in a few seconds. 'Inspector James?'

'Yes. Mr White? Good to meet you. Thanks for agreeing to see us. This is DC Julia McDonald. As I explained when we chatted, she's working with me on the disappearance.'

White shook hands with both of them. 'Let me put my clubs away. Where do you want to talk?' He dipped into the back of the shop without waiting for the answer and dumped the golf clubs he was carrying.

Scott opened his hands and indicated to the shop when White reappeared. 'Here or in the clubhouse. Whatever's more convenient.'

'OK. Clubhouse it is. Much more room and certainly more comfortable.' White led them over to the member's entrance, then through to the main lounge. 'Would you like tea, coffee or something to eat?'

Scott shook his head. 'Thanks, no food, we've just eaten, but a coffee would be great. Flat white. Julia?'

'And one for me as well. Thanks.'

White moved to the bar, then went around the side into the kitchen and came back a few seconds later. 'Won't be long. Now, what can I do for you?'

'You know Brian Young and his family, I believe?' Scott asked as Julia opened her notebook.

'I do. Mainly Brian. I've met his sons, in fact, I coached them when they were younger, but it's their dad I know best.' He paused as a waitress came over and deposited their drinks. 'Why? What's this about?'

Scott picked up his coffee cup. 'As we explained when we spoke on the phone, we're investigating the disappearance of a young Polish girl, Katerina Wykslow. You might have seen the publicity about it?'

White nodded. 'Yes, it's been in the local papers and on *Crimewatch,* hasn't it?'

'It has. The last sighting we have of Katerina is less than two miles from here on the Friday night she vanished, the July 11th at the Annick roundabout in Irvine. We think she was given a lift from there. But after that…nothing.'

'What can I do?'

'Katerina was linked to the Young family. She was Martin's girlfriend. She was also friendly with his father. He was across from his home in Edinburgh, staying at Piersland House on the night she went missing.' Scott put his cup down on the table.

'What?' White said quickly. 'Do you think he's involved?'

'I'm not saying that, but…we need to follow up on the connection. When did you first see Brian Young that weekend?'

'On the Saturday morning. About 9:30 am. He and his team were among the first to arrive.'

'How did he seem?'

'Normal, as far as I could tell. He apologised for cancelling on me.'

'Cancelling?' Scott interjected.

White sat back in his chair. 'Well, we usually meet up the night before the event for dinner or a drink. Sometimes his boys are involved, sometimes my wife Arlene comes along, other times it's just us. Discussing old times, how he sponsored me on the tour at the start. We had agreed to catch up on that Friday night – we hadn't sorted out where – and then Brian texted to cancel and say sorry, late on the Friday afternoon.'

'Did he say why?'

'As far as I can remember, it was because he needed to spend time with his team. They were all important clients, so he wanted to schmooze them. Said it would be boring for me and didn't want to put me through that.'

'Do you still have the text?'

White shook his head. 'No – I'm sorry. I get so many that I tend to delete as I go unless it's something, I need to keep a record of, like a new entry for my calendar.'

'And on the day of the event. Anything out of the ordinary?'

'No. As I said, he seemed normal. But I had a lot on. I couldn't spend a lot of time with any of the teams pre the tee off time.'

'And after? At the dinner?'

Young paused. 'Let me think. Brian spent time with my wife, Arlene, more than me. He was at a different table but I don't think he was anything other his usual self.'

'Thanks. That is helpful.' Scott paused. 'Just one more thing. I don't suppose you saw anything of Katerina that night on your way home?'

'No. Why do you ask?'

'We ask everyone we meet from this area. Just in case we get a break.'

'No, I didn't. My way home doesn't take me anywhere near the Annick roundabout. I go onto the slip road and then along to the A78 at the Gailes roundabout.'

'OK, sir. Is that your car over at the shop?'

'Yes, it is.'

'Interesting number plate – PRO 66

White laughed. 'Yes, bit of pride, I suppose. The only event I won on the tour was the Portuguese Masters. I shot a 66 in the final round to win by two shots. The number plate reminds me.'

Scott nodded, 'Good story, Mr White, and thanks again for your help. We'll be in touch if anything else arises.'

They walked out of the clubhouse together. White retreated to his club shop as Scott and Julia climbed into Scott's car.

Scott pulled out of the golf course car park before he spoke.

'What do you think?'

Julia half turned in the passenger seat and crossed her legs – her tight black skirt moved up, showing a good portion of her thighs. She smiled at him. 'Well, I think if I were going to have an affair, Piersland House would be quite a cool place to consummate it. How about you?'

Scott coughed. He felt nervous. Was this an invite? A joke? Or a reference to Brian Young? It had to be the latter – surely? He picked his words carefully, 'An affair – you're asking the wrong person. I've no experience. Nor do I want any,' he added quickly.

'Oh Scott, you are sweet – so unworldly.'

He felt himself start to redden. 'And so married.'

Julia laughed and put her hands on his arm. 'I know Scott, I know. Don't worry, you're safe with me.' She brushed her fingers along the inside of his arm. 'Safe with me.'

He didn't know how to react to Julia's more intimate contact. It felt wrong to brush her hand away but the longer she kept the contact, the more he felt a reaction. Just when he was about to say something she sighed, removed her hand and put it back in her lap.

'Anyway,' she continued, 'back at the case, Young doesn't have any real alibi. No one saw him after 9:30 pm and Katerina could have gone into his chalet without anyone noticing her.'

'But how would she have known which one?'

'He texted it to her?'

'Maybe, he got there at about 7 pm, got the room details, so a window of 90 minutes or so before her phone dies.'

'And there's a text received from his phone at 7:35 pm. It fits.'

'It does. He has a lot of questions to answer.'

'And the golf pro?' Scott said. 'What did you make of him?'

'I'm not sure. All his responses were fine, I guess, but it seemed a bit pre-programmed somehow. Maybe that's just me though.'

'No, I felt the same.' He frowned. 'Gut feeling.'

'Yes. Yet, anyone else reading my notes of the interview will wonder what we found suspicious. His answers will all seem to make perfect sense.'

Scott paused at the large roundabout at the end of the Gailes slip road and took his time to join the A78. When he had managed that he looked over at Julia. 'You're right. Let me think about it overnight.'

He took the call just before he sat down for dinner with Mary and Donald.

'Hi, Julia.'

'Hi, sir. There's been a development. Thought you should know before I logged it.'

'OK – I'm intrigued – on you go.'

Julia paused. 'It was just a feeling from the interview with White. We both thought there was something not quite right. We weren't sure about him.'

'I agree – don't know why, though.'

'Well, I decided to do an ANPR on his car registration – PRO 66 – for the night of the 11th...'

'And?'

'I got hits, but not from where I expected. We have it crossing the Forth Road Bridge at 6:00 pm, then on the M9 15 minutes later. I extended the check for the next 24 hours and we have it back on the Forth Bridge on the Saturday afternoon at three o'clock, then the M8, then the M77 at about 4:30 pm.'

'So he wasn't driving his car that night or the next day?'

'No, sir. I think we should run a location check on his phone for that evening before we speak to him again. See what sort of picture that gives us of his movements.'

'You're right. Do it. Well done.'

Epilogue

The geometry taught at school is Euclidean, and in that system, parallel lines can never meet. For centuries it was widely believed that the universe ran according to those principles. But there are other equally valid geometries. One of the main differences is that in those mathematical systems, parallel lines can cross over each other.

November 23rd – 8:00 pm

I have to explain why I did this. It's important to me – I have to justify it to myself for a final time. But not like you – not by writing it out. Your committing what you did to paper is why we are in this situation. So, I'll just say it. Tell you how I felt when I found out what you had done and how I've tried to cope since then.

I discovered your manuscript two months ago. Until then I had no idea why you were acting the way you were. I believed that you were involved with someone else. I thought you had fallen for another woman and were building up the courage to tell me. Or, that you couldn't face the prospect of destroying our family and were sticking with me, even though you weren't in love with me anymore. I suppose part of that is correct, about not wanting to ruin our family life.

It's ironic that I found out because of our family. Anna, Cathy and I have been planning a surprise 50th for you for months now. We were working on a variety of themes we could incorporate into the night of the event. I had booked the clubhouse at Irvine Gailes and put together a guest list. Anna and Cathy were rehearsing their speeches. But I was missing a centrepiece, something to really showcase your life. Which is when I thought about your daybooks. I had such fond memories of you writing them every night. All those amusing stories you documented. Some of the lovely and funny things you wrote about me and our times together on the tour. So that was my idea. Extract a set of special comments and observations and get various friends to read them out, with the big finish being my rendition of the comments about me. I was going through the earlier books in order, when I noticed one that looked a bit out of place or maybe a bit less used. It was the day you got back from London. I'm not sure why, but for some reason, that book stood out and I opened it. And I read what you had done. I must have sat for hours with it in my hands – I lost track of time and where I was. I was late going to fetch the girls from school and when they phoned asking where I was, I had to tell them to go into the afterschool club until I got there. I don't remember the drive to Ayr or picking them up – it's a complete blank. I seemed to reawaken to reality when you arrived home that night – September 29th.

It took every part of my willpower not to confront you immediately, to throw the daybook at you and show you I knew. But I didn't, because I agreed with one thing you wrote. That the most important thing you had to do was protect the girls. And raising it with you right away would have damaged them. I couldn't have done that quietly or calmly at that point. I know you won't remember anything about that night now, but I made an excuse that evening. Told you Mum wasn't feeling well and I was going over to see her. Asked you to get tea for the kids. I had to get out of the house – get away from you or I would have called you out. That was the start of my deceit and my lies running in parallel with yours.

To use the same analogy you used at the start of your story, my reaction was equal and opposite to your betrayal and deceit. And as extreme. I shied away from you. I know you didn't feel like making love, but until I found your story, I was desperate to hold you, desperate for us to be a couple again. Make love again. I wanted to embrace you, tell you that no matter what was wrong, we would work at it together to make it right. But after I knew what you had done, that feeling disappeared. I didn't want to be with you. I wanted to get away from you. I didn't want you anywhere near me. So, I had to fight my disgust and not let my emotions show. Because there was one thing you did analyse correctly. You were right to cover it up to shield the girls. That bit you got absolutely right. If I had told you I knew and thrown you out, I doubt you would have coped. No – I'm certain you wouldn't have done. So, your part in the death would have come out. The whole thing would have become public. And what you did afterwards would have been for nothing, completely wasted.

And I need to tell you a couple of other things. I want to shout them at you, but I can't. The first was something that happened to me just before I found out – at the retirement dinner for John Baines, my first boss at the Royal Infirmary. It was in a private room at The Balmoral in Edinburgh on the Friday, before I found your notes. It was a lovely meal, good speeches, drink was flowing. Some of us went on to Tigerlily and then downstairs to Lulu's Nightclub for a bop. I got asked up to a slow number by one of the younger consultants. I said yes. I was drunk and feeling a bit neglected. You and I hadn't made love for two months and I had no idea why you didn't want me anymore. He was a gentleman – danced to the side of me. He seemed to find me attractive. I could feel it, physically feel it. So, for the last part of the song I moved his hips, so he was directly facing me. He was hard, very hard, and I enjoyed that sensation. But that's all that happened. No next dance. No kiss. No fumble. No broom cupboard or back to his room. Just a thanks. We didn't end up fucking – like you and your fucking Katerina. Because no matter how difficult it was between us then, I still loved you – nobody else.

The second is what really happened with the bonfire – I've read your note about it – but you've no idea. I was out when the girls decided to use the grass mound as the setting for Guy Fawkes. When I got back, they had already dragged some wood and rubbish from the outbuilding and started to build a bonfire – I suppose I could have killed the idea at that point – made some excuse – asked them to build it somewhere else – but that would have been a bit lame. We all know that you set the grass alight at that time of year.

So, when Anna phoned you, what did I expect? Not a "No" – for the same reasons I didn't dissuade them, and because you're soft with the girls. Always have been – you rarely deny them anything. But I did think you would do something – find an excuse – get us all away from the house, then extract the remains. Or tell me – ask me to help you – we would have become a modern-day Burke and Hare. I don't know how I would have reacted – I'm unsure because I already knew. Could I have double-bluffed you? Would it have brought us closer again? I don't know. What I do know, is the choice you made – to do nothing – was the worst option. It was a test – and you failed. I couldn't take the chance of the skeleton being revealed that night. I waited as long as I could but by the Wednesday before I was certain you had nothing planned – you were across at Dalmahoy, doing classes for the PGA on the Friday – the girls were at school – so I had a window from 9:30 am to 3:00 pm and I used it. I put on my oldest clothes and wellies and some surgical gloves and a mask I had taken from Carrick Glen.

I was scared, but determined, as I set about picking the bonfire apart on the side that looks across to the sea – so I had cover if anyone was watching from the neighbouring fields. That was the easiest bit – then I dug into the grass. That was really hard to move – heavy and layered – but eventually I got to the remains. I suppose a bit of me hoped nothing was there – that your story was made up – some sort of strange sexual fantasy – but it wasn't. I found a thigh bone first –

then the rest – the smell was horrible. There was a black slime beneath and alongside the skeleton – even with the mask I almost threw up. But I didn't – I had worked through what I was going to do – like you, I couldn't face moving the body – so I sectioned it up, using a spade, part by part. I put the leg bones and pelvis in an old fertiliser bag and ran over the bag with the tractor – time after time – crushing the bones, reducing them to small pieces. I emptied the first run back into the grass and spread it out as much as I could. Then I did the ribcage, arms, and head – same procedure – and scattered them as well. I took the fork and filled up the hole I had made to get at the body with the decomposing grass and placed the fertiliser bag on the top. Then I rebuilt the wooden part of the bonfire. That's why you didn't find anything the morning after the bonfire. That's why nobody saw a skeleton on Guy Fawkes Night – it was nothing to do with you – it was all to do with me.

I almost felt for you again when I got over my initial rage and tried to think more rationally. Almost felt what? Sympathy? Pride for the hell you were dealing with to protect our children? I'm not sure it was either, but I think at least I understood that part of it. Which is why we are here now. Which is why I am explaining what I did when I got over my first wave of hatred. Because from reading your journal since then – yes, I check it daily to see what you have added – I know that the police are getting closer to what really happened. I understand that they are concentrating on Brian Young, on his role in the disappearance. But I know that you aren't far from unravelling – I know that any improvement you've made isn't really permanent. I know you too well for you to hide it. And I realise that if Brian is charged, you will probably confess at that point. What I don't know is how imminent any arrest is. So, I've had to act quickly. Do something to prevent you being charged with murder. Killing you seemed the only answer to close down any interest by the police in looking more closely at your involvement. Poisoning you seemed the best way to do that. I couldn't fake a suicide. I don't have the skills and that sort of death would reflect terribly on the girls. They would never recover. They love you so much. It would scar them for life. Just like finding out you were a killer. So, an accident was what I was left with. Which is what I've managed – I think.

How could I achieve that? I used the same type of approach you did. You used golf as a way of guiding you when you chose to hide the death – I used my pharmacological background to find the perfect poison. The research I did pointed to a toxin called abrin. It's virtually unknown, with little reference to it in scientific journals. I could only find details on two cases in the USA. The poison can be extracted from the seeds of the rosary pea by crushing them carefully, which I had the time and opportunity to do in the labs at Carrick Glen Hospital on the one evening a week I work late. I sieved the powder into a small canister, wearing latex gloves and a protective mask with a filter. Abrin works on about 1000 micrograms per kilo if ingested, so I needed just under a gram for you and I was able to produce that amount in two sessions. When I say "works", I'm being coy. That's the amount which the limited information I had said was likely to result in a toxic arrest and kill you.

But as well as the agent, I needed the place and the 30th Anniversary of the opening of San Lorenzo was perfect. Out of the UK and in an area where the diagnostic capability of the local hospital would be limited, as it's primarily a holiday destination. I supported you attending and staying at the Dona Filipa for the three-day event. I made sure we were booked into Sandbanks Restaurant in the Vale do Lobo complex that first night when I saw that cataplana was on the menu. I slipped the powder into the Bloody Mary I made you before we went out – with extra Worcestershire sauce and Tabasco. I also guided you to ordering the cataplana – only available for two – a Portuguese fish stew with local clams and mussels, squid and monkfish. I needed a prop and I chose bad seafood. A perfect explanation for your sudden illness. You tucked in, but I only had one spoonful before I said I needed to go to the toilet – I told you to eat up and not wait for me. When I came back, you had finished half the pan and left the rest for me. I waited a minute longer, then told you I had been sick in the sink and that I wasn't sure about the taste of the stew. You were going to eat a bit more, then stopped – I made sure we mentioned it to the waiter and asked for it to be taken off our bill. I caused quite a kerfuffle. But it was all acting to shift the blame to a suspect dish and to ensure I had a reason why I wasn't affected – "only one mouthful then I threw up".

I wasn't sure how quickly abrin would act but the symptoms appeared early the next morning, and by the time you met your amateur partners and started the practice round, it was obvious you were suffering. You were unsteady on your feet and looked weak, but you made a huge effort on the par 5 first and managed to knock it onto the green in two. You collapsed as we walked uphill to the green. Your last conscious act was to play a golf hole really well – a fitting epitaph, Ian.

We took you back to the clubhouse in my buggy and phoned for an ambulance, which took nearly 30 minutes. That rushed you to this hospital,

Gambelas, in Faro, with me in the back, holding your hand, as you slipped in and out of consciousness.

You've been here for three days now – the tests they have done show extreme tissue damage to all your organs – which is continuing and irreversible. They have said it looks like a massive reaction to some sort of toxin. The doctors are blaming the seafood and hygiene inspectors have been sent to Sandbanks. But it's too late for you. You won't be moved now. No flight back to the UK – the trip would be fatal. They are ready to switch off the ventilator as soon as the family all agree. You've been on it since you were admitted, and your condition is deteriorating – there's no hope.

I am listening as I tell you what I did – really listening to myself. And I sound cold – I sound calculating. It's coming out, as if completely preordained – but it wasn't. I'm not sure I would have been able to go through with it, but for the call you took from the police, just as we got to the hotel. You tried to play it down – told me it was just a routine follow-up, but that they wanted to see you again. They hadn't realised you were out of the country and asked for an interview on the Monday we were due back just to clear up a few issues. That was the tipping point. That's what gave me the impetus I needed. I knew I had to act or it would all unravel when we got back. It still might. But at least I will now have the chance to hear their concerns in a different role – playing the grieving widow.

The girls are outside with your mum and dad. And my mum. I told them I needed a final word on my own before they come in and we say goodbye to you as a family. Cathy and Anna will miss you. More than miss – they will be bereft. But they will cope. As will I. I will miss the man I fell in love with, the man I married, the father of my children. But that man died on July 11th. You're not him. You're not my Ian. So, I'm saying goodbye in absentia. I'm not going to kiss you. And nobody will see that I don't. But I will cry. Cry for everything you destroyed that night. Cry for the life we had and the future we could have had. Cry for the grandkids you'll never see.

Goodbye